I0741324

The Box Has Twelve Sides

Thirteen Curious Tales
to Delight and Disturb

M. K. Bagwell

ISBN 10: 1546601562
ISBN 13: 9781546601562

DEDICATION

On a Halloween long past, Ray Bradbury, Richard Matheson, Dean Koontz and Stephen King walked into a bar...

A WORD UP FRONT…

I know some of you may find parts of what you are about to read disconcerting but, hopefully, mostly entertaining. All of us have places into which we don't want to go willingly. Writers tap into these locations and reveal them to others. It's what we do.

I want to emphasize that I have not personally experienced everything about which I have written. Some things have been borrowed from my life, yes, but most are genuine creations. As personal acquaintances of mine, if you attempt to read yourself into these pages, you are tilting at windmills.

That being said, I am still the same friend, father, husband, relative and person that I have always been. Please don't have second thoughts when entrusting yourselves or your loved ones to my care.

Bottom line: These are merely stories. Just leave them at that.

CONTENTS

PROLOGUE: THE FIRST SIDE

I LIVE ON THE streets, but I don't come from them.

Once, I was like you. At home, warm in front of the fire, with children and a loving wife by my side, pets pawing at the door to be let in from the cold. The cold which I now endure regularly.

Once, I lived life instead of avoiding it.

If in reading this you feel a twinge of concern, a pang of remorse, a twitch of embarrassment at my situation as opposed to yours, hats off. You're human. You *feel.*

◉

The toughest things I've had to get used to are the looks I get when people finally recognize me.

I ran into an old pal of mine who used to play basketball with me at the Y on Thursday nights. I was loitering at the Hardees fast food joint downtown, sneaking packs of ketchup to mix with hot water to make tomato soup. You never know what you'll try until all the options are gone.

His first reaction, before he realized he knew this bum sitting at the table next to him, was of disgust. I'd seen it before. How could someone let themselves go, get into that type of condition? What has to happen to a person for them to sink to those depths, to run out of hope and dreams and desire? He glanced my way and immediately averted his eyes.

Then… something made him take another look. Maybe it was recognition. Most likely it was just plain curiosity. We homeless do tend to be the urban sideshow for the well-to-do masses.

He caught my eye and turned away even quicker than before. But this time I saw a recollection in his eye.

"Hello, James," I said, casually. "How's your life?"

You've got to realize what a shock it was to this guy's system. In a matter of seconds, his empathy toward me went from abhorrence to pity to recollection and remembrance. He probably hadn't had that kind of emotional swing in weeks. To say it overloaded his system was an understatement.

"Kevin? Kevin Brigman?" He was barely able to breathe the words, to exhale them from his throat. "Jesus. What...?" His breath finally exhausted.

"What happened to me? Is that what you're wondering?" I asked.

"No, no. I just... You took me by surprise. I didn't expect to run into somebody I knew downtown... down *here*. I don't usually..." Again, his words trailed off into nothing.

"Hey, Jimmy. It's all right. Trust me." I tried to flash him a smile, but that only succeeded in maiming his already wounded psyche. You see, I've lost most of my teeth since I've been on the streets. The dental plan out here ain't all it's cracked up to be.

"Damn, Kev. Where've you been? The last I heard, after the separation, was that you moved into Donny Jackson's garage apartment on the other side of town...?" Still, his eyes betrayed the raw emotions running through his core. It was all he could do to sit there and not bolt for the door.

"Yeah, well, things went south, that's for sure." By this point, we both just wanted the conversation to be over as soon as possible. It was useless for both parties to drag it out. "Jim, that life is gone. I'm not the same guy I was back then. Let's just leave it at that, OK?"

"OK, Kevin. Whatever you say, man," Jim said. He started to get up and then sat back down. "You need some..."

"Money? Not a chance. Not from you. Not from anybody." Tears were starting to sting my eyes. I didn't want this conversation, the first I'd had with anybody who knew me from *before*, to end like this, with me breaking down, crying like a baby.

"OK. It's OK, Kev. I'm just trying to help." Jim reached out and gave my shoulder a squeeze. "Just trying to make things a little better."

"Then just leave, Jim. And for God's sake, please don't tell anybody you ran into me, OK?"

"Sure, Kevin. No prob." He patted my shoulder again and then my chest the way we did back when we'd take some of the suckers at the Y on the basketball court, a hundred years ago.

And he was gone.

I put my head down and silently sobbed in the world's loneliest fast food joint.

The Hardees manager came by a few minutes later and escorted me out.

The place I call home is just like any other southern town bordering the Smoky Mountains. Its name is not important. You could throw a dart and hit a handful of identical places throughout western North Carolina, eastern Tennessee and southern Virginia. It's the type of town which attracts tourists in the fall to see the leaves change. The winters get the northern folk because it's a helluva lot milder than what they're used to. The spring and summers bring the Floridians up from the oppressive gulf coast heat.

It's a big enough city to attract some name acts to the community civic center, but it's still relatively small so people don't feel the big city rush and hectic pace. Life here is pretty decent for the people who don't live on the streets.

But… I do.

There are two shelters that we street folk frequent when the weather gets too cold or the food runs out. Over on Lexington there's the Salvation Army which is more or less run like its namesake. On the other side of town, near one of the malls, is the Miracle Day Shelter. Both are usually full during the winter and fairly empty all other times. I tend to go to either of these places only when I'm starved half out of my mind or in need of medical attention.

Life on the streets is everything you've heard or read about, multiplied many times over. I've had my head bashed in more times than I care to remember. Usually, it's by transients, people on their way through who don't have to reside in this, for all intents and purposes, community that we live in.

Trust me, if I didn't have to live like this, I wouldn't.

◎

If you're reading this, I apologize. I've had this old composition book for about two years now, but never really had anything important enough to record for posterity. Until now.

Forgive my handwriting, forgive my ramblings.

I am an educated man. Four-plus years of college, a job for ten years in a manufacturing facility, been married, had kids, a couple of pets. The American dream.

None of that means shit on the streets. I might as well had been born out here and reared by the hookers and pimps.

You may be able to overlook the incoherent writings on these pages, the constant changes from pen to pencil, the in-complete pages. I'd like to tell you that the water stains smeared on some of the ink in places was all rainfall from the times the impulse to write overcame the need for shelter. But I can't.

They'd taste salty, if you had the inclination. The saltiness of tears.

◎

I left Hardees after talking to Jim and walked towards the center of town. It was a fairly pleasant fall night with just a tinge of the impending winter in the air. It was the sort of night I used to say, in my former life, made you feel alive. Nowadays, any night I was able to take a breath made *me* feel alive.

I pulled the army coat which I'd worn for a couple of years tighter around my shoulders. In doing so, I heard a crinkling in the breast pocket. I reached in and pulled out a twenty-dollar bill. Jim must have palmed it there when he was patting me in the chest.

Hot tears hit my eyes. Again. It seemed that I was easily moved to tears these days.

I kept walking; head down, tears littering the sidewalk, trailing behind me like breadcrumbs.

I looked at the twenty gripped tightly in my hand. *The bastard.* He'd given me enough money to live on for the few weeks. I could never repay him, no matter what the situation.

I stopped and stared again at the money. What could possess someone to do such a thing, to give so easily and so blindly? We hadn't seen each other for at least five years. And when our paths do cross, he gives without even thinking twice, do so in such a secretive way as to allay any type of thanks or gratitude. He slipped it into my coat pocket without a second thought, just assuming I would find it.

I stood there on the streets of my hometown, a city that had turned its back on me, crying. Crying at the thoughtfulness and kindness a long-lost friend had bestowed upon me. Me, a once-human carcass who no longer had a real life.

And that's when someone hit me in the back of the head and I lost consciousness.

I guess they did it just to remind me that I really don't matter in the grand scheme of things. They probably did it to keep me humble, to make sure this kind act by a lost friend didn't serve to give me hope, to provide a glimmer of a way out of this hell-hole.

And, of course, they did it to take the twenty.

◉

By the time I came to, it was raining. Which was just as well; I hadn't bathed in over two weeks. I had no idea how long I'd been unconscious.

The bastards took my coat, too. And my shoes.

The sad thing was that I probably knew who did this. I had most likely sat beside them at the soup kitchen, or my cot had perhaps butted up to theirs at the local shelter. Those of us on the streets live by a different set of rules. All of us are desperate: not knowing where the next meal will come from, wondering if there will be a shelter to go to and hoping to just have clothes against the weather. Heck, most of us don't even know if we'll make it through each evening. But some of us still hang on to enough humanity to be kind to each other.

Some of us, but not all.

It had to have been early morning by that time. The rain had chilled the air and it was a lot less comfortable than it had been just a while before. I needed a place to get warm and dry.

I stumbled toward the middle of town, in the direction of the central square where a monument and fountain had been erected for some historical figure who founded this godforsaken place. I knew the city had been working on the fountain earlier in the day. I was hoping there would be a bulldozer or something left behind that I could wedge open and crawl inside. There wasn't.

Instead, the pool was empty, drained so they could work on the return feed and nozzle. There were a couple of big sawhorses protecting an area of the sidewalk where they had been doing some digging, presumably to get at the underground pipes. The hole they'd dug was about a four foot square. Just big enough for a homeless guy to crawl into and die.

And that's just what I intended to do.

As I dropped down into the hole, my bare feet made a hollow sound, like I had jumped onto a wooden chest, not the muddied bottom of a dirt hole. Squatting down, I started clawing at the dirt under my feet. By this time, my hands were cold and I was shaking with the onset of hypothermia.

After only a few inches, my dirty fingernails hit what felt like wood. I managed to clear the dirt off what appeared to be an old door. I knocked and it answered with a hollow sound. Thinking there was the possibility of a room underneath and out of the elements, I worked my way around the edges until I found a hinge and a clasp. I tugged hard and it opened. Stale air rushed past my face from inside.

Desperate to just get out of the rain and cold, I didn't give a second thought to what could've been down there. I was hurting and freezing and all I wanted was to get dry and warm.

Grabbing my backpack, I slid through the wooden door, dropping a few feet onto concrete steps. Reaching out to the sides with my arms, I felt brick walls on each side of me. Pulling the door closed behind me, I was greeted with absolute blackness.

I fished around in my backpack until I found the Ziplock baggie where I kept a box of matches to keep them dry. I struck one against the wall next to me. The flame blinded me for a few seconds, but when my vision cleared I saw a large room in front of me.

To my left were low benches against a brick wall. One of them was still standing, but the other two I could see had collapsed legs and sat directly on the floor. Straight ahead the feeble light faded into total darkness, the room stretching beyond my sight and the flame. On the right I could make out what appeared to be glass windows with more blackness behind them. Above each were faded signs which read 'Tickets' hand-lettered in old-style calligraphy.

The flame gave me a jolt as it reached my numb fingertips.

From my backpack, I found the old composition book I was keeping to write down notes, directions or anything I came across which could help me survive on the streets. So far, it was empty.

I grabbed a handful of pages, ripping them out. Lighting another match, I touched it to the end of the makeshift paper torch. The larger flame lit up the room much better and descended the steps into the room.

Still cautious, and not really believing my luck, I began gathering pieces of wood from one of the broken benches. Having practice with starting fires from a lot less, I managed to get a decent blaze going in minutes.

◉

Around the turn of the century, when this city was still in its relative infancy, the main source of transportation in the downtown area was that of electric trolley. Some of the tracks were left behind, ensconced in the few remaining cobblestone streets. A couple of the trolleys have even been salvaged and are used as part of the public bus system. The quaintness is almost sickening, but it does contribute to the historical charm of the city.

In the center of town is a square from where the trolleys used to begin their routes. The fountain and a shallow pool have, for the most part, been turned into a bathing hole for the town's overlooked residents. The street people. Us.

At the head of the pool is an obelisk which was erected to honor one of the region's revered pioneers who helped settle the area in the early 1800's. It is the same shape as the Washington Monument, only about a tenth its size and made of rough-hewn stone. To some, it's a monument; to others, an eyesore.

Early on there were facilities for the public to use when waiting on the trolleys. At the turn of the century it was safe to go down the few stairs to where the public restrooms were dug into the earth, without fear of today's common sins.

When the pool and monument were erected, these public amenities were sealed, ending that type of commonplace decadence. It was quite a ceremony from what I understand. The barbarianism of using public restrooms was at an end. Civilization was upon us.

I'd heard this tale among those of us who live on the streets. It's rumored that some of the street people have managed to find their way into the sealed off rooms and actually live down there, just a few feet below the everyday world.

I always thought it was a myth and doubted the existence of these rooms which had been sealed off. I thought it was a fairytale, something out of a Neil Gaiman novel.

I was wrong.

Once the small fire was burning, and I had gotten dried and warm, I decided to explore my new home. Finally my shoeless feet had thawed and it wasn't painful to walk. *Oh, yes,* I thought. *I'll be living down here for a while. This can be my palace, my mountain retreat, my beach house.* I always had an active imagination, even in the worst of times.

It looked like the depot windows across the room had been boarded up for years. Cobwebs and dried shells of insects littered the countertop. Behind each glass were sheets of plywood to keep the frames from falling in on themselves. *Eventually another source of firewood,* I thought.

I thought it strange I hadn't seen a single live insect or rat or anything since I'd been down here. There were plenty of empty husks and dried up shells, but no pests or bugs like I would have thought. I dismissed the thought as just being a by-product of the cold winter evening.

Parts of the ticket window frames extended down to an iron grated pass-through, allowing merchants to exchange money for tickets when this trolley depot was alive. The metal was ornate, and I wondered how much it would bring at the local salvage yard. There was a time when I would have paused to marvel at the intricacies of the iron work. But that life had passed, like this room, lost and forgotten.

So far I had explored three sides of the old depot, leaving only the blackness opposite the stairs and the trap door. I shuddered at what might lie in wait: a feral cat, trapped bats... Even a hungry raccoon would likely send me screaming from this place.

That imagination of mine could work both ways.

I picked up a burning bench leg from the fire, tapered to a point on the other end, and turned toward the dark part of the room. Holding the makeshift torch in front of me, like some knight brandishing a sword, I tentatively left the comfort of the firelight.

Blackness enveloped me. The feeble light from the flame I

was holding illuminated maybe three feet in front of me. Beyond that, for all I knew it dropped off into a gaping pit. Still, I walked forward, knowing I really didn't have much to lose even if it was the edge of a precipice I was skirting.

I began to smell something unpleasant, an odor I hadn't noticed while by the fire on the other side of the room, miles away now, it seemed. To say it was decay or something festering is not the right way to describe it. The odor was earthier, more that of nature and minerals instead of rotting flesh.

Pressing ahead, I finally reached the far wall, brick like the others, unremarkable. I could go left or right; either way provided the same amount of uncertainty about what I would find.

I chose to go right. My mother used to say, when I was a kid and we frequented weekend markets, *Go right and you'll never go wrong.* The premise was that you would eventually circle around back to where you started, catching everything along the way. I never had the heart to tell her it worked just as well going to the left.

Keeping to the wall with my ever weakening torch, I came upon a wooden door covered with peeling paint. The knob was the old brass kind, maybe worth something if I could pry it loose.

I tried the knob but it was frozen tight, no doubt corroded beyond repair. I shook it but it held fast, unyielding. I was able to make out the edges of the door, the hinges and the inch or so gap at the bottom of the door.

A gap where a soft green light shone through.

I stopped, a chill coming back over me as if I had never gotten warm from the fire. *A light.* It was very faint and very weak, but it was there nonetheless. I wasn't imagining it.

Several things went through my mind at that point. *Could someone else be in there?* That was the most unpleasant thought. The very idea I would have to either fight someone for my new-found turf, or God forbid share it with them, did not sit well with me. I deserved this place as much as any other person.

"Hey," I said, banging the palm of my hand against the

door. "Who's in there?" Although barely a whisper, my raspy voice reverberated against the crumbling walls.

I listened for a response, for the shuffling of clothes, for the sound of movement.

Nothing.

By now my source of light had diminished, the ember slowly cooling and keeping the light only for itself. But I could still see, my surroundings faintly lit by the light coming from underneath the door.

Well, if nobody is in there, I thought, *then what's the light coming from?* There had obviously been no one down here in years, maybe even decades. The uninterrupted dust on the floor was proof of that.

Mostly by the green light, I was able to make out faint writing on a sign attached to the door: JANITOR. *So this was a broom closet*, I thought. There was probably little of use in there, but the faint light coming from within, more than anything, was reason enough to get that door open.

I turned back toward the little campfire across the room. Just looking in that direction gave me a sense of warmth this side of the room had vacuumed out. I debated returning to its warmth and investigating the other side of the door in the morning. Whatever was inside the small room could probably wait. But I couldn't.

I shoved the sharp end of the wooden stick into the door jamb near the knob. As it slid between the door and the frame, I pushed harder and was rewarded with a sharp cracking sound. The wooden door had sat static for so long, dry rot had made it weak at the area where the knob and lock combined to keep it closed.

The door creaked open slowly. I pushed forward and followed the light into the darkness of the janitor's closet.

As expected, there was nothing of value in there: a bucket with one side rusted out, a headless mop with only the pole of a body remaining, and a hanger or two still on the rod against the wall. There were shelves along the wall as well, but their only inventory was dust and bug shells. A couple of cardboard boxes lay in the corner, mostly coming apart from time and mildew.

But no green light.

Disappointed and relieved at the same time, I realized I was night-blind from the flame I was brandishing. The only way to acclimate my eyes to the pitch blackness was to leave the torch outside the closet and close the door, blocking my vision from it and the campfire.

The hair on the back of my neck stood at attention as I placed the torch on the cement floor outside the closet door and pulled it shut, closing myself into the small space. I could feel panic trying its best to set in. Just because I couldn't see didn't mean I wasn't aware of the tightness of the room. I imagined insects and God knew what other creepy-crawlies there might be; ready to drive out the unwelcome intruder. Just the thought made me itch.

Putting my back to the door, I slid down, sitting on the floor and looking toward the back of the closet at nothing but blackness. I wondered how long I would have to wait before dark adaption allowed my eyes to acclimate to the dark. There was no such thing as time, it seemed. I had no sense, sitting there in the inky stillness that minutes or even hours might pass. There was only the absence of light, the realm of shadows. Sitting there I couldn't even tell if I had my eyes open or not.

It was so devoid of light that I didn't know I had fallen asleep until I woke up.

◉

I started awake.

I knew I was awake because I could make out shapes in the closet. I saw the shelves and the decrepit old bucket with its skeletal mop pole sticking out of it. I saw the paint peeling from the walls and where it had shed on the floor. I saw the boxes laying in ruin in the corner. Everything was tinged in a soft, almost shadowy green.

Then I saw the source of the light.

One of the boxes was mostly intact. Along the sides it was split open in a place or two, but for the most part there was still enough structure to hold its contents. Through the openings, green light was seeping, almost like fluid, covering everything in the closet with a soft luminosity.

Blinking, I couldn't trust what my eyes were telling me. I reached across, just barely more than an arm's length, and slid the box to me. The soft glow persisted, didn't waiver or dim when I moved it from its resting place.

The cardboard container which was its outer shell practically disintegrated, revealing another box within. Aside from the glow, it had no markings, designs or even texture. It was smooth, unremarkable and roughly the size of a shoebox. There was no lid; it was all one piece, cut and hinged in such a way as to fold upon itself and form a container.

The light coming from the box was persistent. It was mesmerizing, haunting, with a strange beauty. It felt warm and somehow familiar.

The green glow harkened back to my childhood.

When I was ten or twelve, my parents decided to build our new house and get us out of the apartment we were living in. The land we were to build on was just behind our apartment building, so I would walk over every so often and check out the progress.

On the property was a small shack, not much larger than an outhouse. It was pretty much empty, no doubt an abandoned storage shed. But inside, on one of the top shelves, I found an old AMT plastic model kit of Frankenstein's monster. I immediately grabbed it and took it home, not thinking it could have been someone's property. I rationalized my actions, telling myself that the shack would be torn down soon and its contents discarded. If anything, I was saving it.

Once home, I opened the box to reveal the unassembled model within. The clear bag containing the model pieces on their runners hadn't been opened. But the remarkable part, especially for a kid like me with an overactive imagination and no friends with which to share, was the material from which the model was molded.

The cover of the box told me what I already knew: it was Glow-In-The-Dark plastic. The letters were purposely capitalized and there was a small copyright symbol just following. *That was so cool,* I thought.

I was so amped up that I bugged dad until he took me to the hardware store to get some model cement. I stayed up most of the night putting it together, smelling the acrid odor from the glue, getting some of it on my fingers like a second skin, but not minding a bit. When I was done, I sat the model under my reading light for a full ten minutes so it could get a good dose of light.

When ready, I did the 'big reveal.' Turning my back to the model, I switched off the reading light and closed my eyes. After a moment or two, making sure I had gotten used to the dark and looking in the direction of the bedside table where the model was sitting, I opened them.

A beautiful, soft green glow greeted my eyes, emanating from Frankenstein's monster. I was in a trance, gazing with wonder at this simple plastic model I had put together. The glow brought out details in the plastic I had previously not seen. Flaws, captured air bubbles and varying wall thicknesses just added to the beauty. The green glow of the plastic illuminated the table top and everything on it, casting shadows.

It was the same green glow coming from the box in the closet of the abandoned depot I had found under the city streets.

◉

My head snapped up. I was disoriented for a moment. *What had just happened?* That memory was so vivid it seemed like I had actually been there. It was something I hadn't thought about in years, and yet every detail stood out. It felt like something more than just a memory. It was like I had *been* there and was rudely snatched back.

It seemed I could still smell the chemical odor of the model cement, could still feel the tightness of excess glue on my fingers. *Weird.*

I turned my attention back to the box and lifted it from the outer, mildewed cardboard. It was surprisingly light. I told myself it probably was empty and therefore of no value. Something in my head answered: *Not so fast.*

I tucked it under one arm and slid back up the door, reaching behind me to turn the knob and get out of there. The door opened and I stepped out. The makeshift torch was completely cold. Looking across the room at the fire I had started earlier, I saw that it was down to just glowing embers.

How long had I been in there?

I walked across the old abandoned depot, stirring up dust along the way, the box under one arm.

Reaching what was left of the fire, I gently put the box on the floor near the lone bench which was still intact. Within minutes, I had the coals burning again. Whatever chill had been in the fire's absence was soon gone.

Holding the box again, I sat with it in my lap and leaned against the wall. There was only one seam in its otherwise perfect construction. I held it to my ear and shook it. The empty sound of nothing was deafening.

The green luminescence was still there, albeit not as dramatic in the firelight. I put one dirty fingernail under the seam and began to slowly lift it up. I stopped as I saw something on the end of one of my fingers. Examining it closer, I couldn't place what it was. It had a stiff texture to it, almost rubbery, adhering to my finger like a... like a *second skin.* Bringing the finger to my nose, I took a sniff, already knowing what I would smell.

Plastic model cement. On my finger. There was no doubt.

Remembering to breathe, I looked again at the seam that appeared to be the only opening into the box. Slowly, I started to open the lid. What was I expecting? Bats to fly out? A poisonous gas? Or, worse yet, nothing?

With a quick breath, I pulled the lid open.

The box was empty.

All that drama for an empty box? Sure it glowed, but this is the twenty-first century. Things are made today that were only dreamed about in the past. This was likely just some kid's toy box which had once contained Legos or something similar long ago. The janitor probably brought it here to store oily rags. Some residue had obviously gotten on my fingers and was freaking me out, tapping into that overactive imagination I thought I'd long outgrown. There was nothing special about the box, I concluded.

Inspecting the underside of the lid for a hint of its origin, I could swear the glow seemed brighter. Not only brighter, but of a slightly different hue as well. It had taken on a slight amber tone where the green had been. Looking closer, I saw movement in that color, shapes forming, clouds churning, objects moving…

Life.

Activity.

What was happening?

Was I seeing things?

Was it the dust or something in the air down here causing me to hallucinate?

I shut my eyes tightly, but the new color persisted, even with my closed eyelids. Now I was hearing sounds as well coming from the box. Faint, but definite. I couldn't discern exactly what I was hearing. Nevertheless, I heard… *things.*

Now I could smell a hint of newly mown grass in the stale air, another of my comforting childhood memories. A slight warm breeze blew across my forehead, enough so that I felt my hair wave with it. I suddenly had a taste of peaches in my mouth. It was so real that it triggered hunger pangs in my gut.

All five senses now fully engaged, I turned my attention back to the box and stared in wonder at the world it was creating before me...

PROLOGUE: THE FIRST SIDE

JUST ONE OF THOSE DAYS

CHARLIE COOK WOKE UP late because the alarm didn't go off.

Perfect, he thought, *a great way to start the day, especially after the way last night ended.* He'd wound up having his dead battery jumped off at the local Walmart after he stopped there on his way home. But that was last night, and this was a whole new day.

Reaching over to hit the snooze, he knocked the alarm clock off the bedside table, spilling batteries and plastic pieces all over the floor. He'd have to clean that mess up later. Right now his priority was to get ready for work ASAP.

Charlie felt down beside the bed with his feet for his slippers, but found only one. The other must have gotten pushed underneath. *Damn,* he thought. *Have to get down on my knees and fish it out.* He knelt down, reached under the bed and something popped in his back. Nothing major but one of those things which reminded him that he needed to get into better shape.

Halfway into his shower the hot water went out. Painfully, Charlie had to wash and rinse his hair in the ice cold shower stream. *Well, at least I'm awake now.*

He cut himself twice while shaving and, when he went to get toilet paper to dab it with, he found an empty roll. He retrieved another roll from under the sink and pinched his finger as the cabinet door closed.

He dropped his toothbrush onto the floor which made him dig out a new, unopened one. As he was dispensing toothpaste, the back of the tube split and Crest shot out onto the mirror.

Good Lord. Hope the day gets better.

Finishing up in the bathroom, Charlie went to the kitchen, turned on the coffee maker and put some bread in the toaster. Sitting at the table, he put his shoes on and promptly broke a shoelace as he was tying the first one. *Really?*

Going back to the bedroom closet, he saw the only other pair of decent shoes was brown, not really matching the slacks he was wearing. Charlie hated not matching, but right now he didn't give a rip. He had to get to work and he was already going to be late.

Grabbing his cup from the coffeemaker and the toast from the toaster, Charlie headed out. Just as the door was closing, he realized the keys were hanging on the hook just inside He managed to snatch them but rapped his knuckles in the process. *Ouch.*

◎

As he turned the key to start his car, Charlie thought back to the night before and his (hopefully formerly) dead battery, wondering if he would be stranded in his driveway. The engine turned over without a hitch.

Hey, things are looking up.

After pulling out of the driveway, Charlie took the first bite of his toast and found it was burnt on the opposite side which he hadn't noticed. Sipping on his coffee to wash away the taste, he was met with a mouthful of coffee grounds. The filter must have folded over on itself, allowing grounds into the cup, making the coffee weak and depositing extra particles he wasn't expecting. Choking down burnt toast with chewy coffee was not his idea of the perfect breakfast, but it was all he had. He continued his commute to work.

The route was mostly highway, but one part of his morning ride involved a stretch of road cutting through part of town strewn with traffic lights. If you timed it just right, you never had to sit and wait on signals to change. This morning, of course, he hit it just the opposite and got caught by every single light on that road.

Making him even later.

◎

Pulling into the parking lot at his workplace, Charlie found absolutely no parking spots anywhere near the employee entrance. The only options were at the very back of the lot, about a quarter mile away from the door. There were two spaces left and he went ahead and took the farthest one away. *What the hell*, he thought. *May as well get my exercise.*

Charlie had walked about halfway from his car to the entrance when it started raining. *Great*, he thought. *And my umbrella is in the car.* He considered turning around and going back to get it, but decided he was already about as wet as he was going to get. So he trudged on.

When he got to the entrance, just as he walked under the overhang to the door, the rain stopped and the sun came out almost immediately. There was nobody else in the parking lot at this relatively late morning hour, so he was the only person to get wet from the rain.

When he badged in, Charlie was met with a rude beep and an angry red LED which told him his badge wasn't working. The readout informed Charlie that his badge was Currently Not Recognized and that he needed to See His Supervisor Immediately. Fortunately a couple of people were walking by at that moment and he was able to flag them down to let him in. Despite the rules and their nasty looks, they let him in with them anyway. He thanked them profusely.

He was relieved just to make it to his cubicle, all things considered. The way the day was shaping up, he'd take the small victories. He took a moment to catch his breath and booted up his computer.

Charlie stuck his briefcase under his desk and turned back to the computer monitor. A bright royal blue screen shone back. The Blue Screen of Death. *Unreal.*

He grabbed the phone and called the IT department. Once connected, he was advised to log a Trouble Ticket online. He tried for another five minutes to explain to the operator (at a desk somewhere outsourced in India no doubt) that he would not be able to open a Ticket because he couldn't get on his computer in the first place. *Oh, nevermind.*

Hanging up, from his briefcase he fished out the backup laptop that all software design engineers had just in case something like this happened. It booted up without incident, thank God.

Needing a decent cup of coffee, Charlie made his way to the break room only to find an empty pot. He threw out the old packet, put in a new one and hit the start button. Nothing happened. As he was trying to figure out what was wrong, one of his coworkers, an arrogant prick from HR, walked in and calmly informed him that the pot was unplugged.

"Thanks," he muttered and a few minutes later finally had a cup of coffee that he could drink without getting grounds stuck in his teeth. Of course it was scalding hot and burnt the hell out of his tongue, but after what he'd been through already this morning, he didn't mind too much.

◉

The usual Monday morning departmental meeting to Staff was at ten o'clock sharp. After fighting with his computer all morning, Charlie was hard pressed to get his portion of the software presentation done in time. But he did, as always.

He was the last one into the conference room, just ahead of the Marketing Director. The only chair left, other than the one at the end of the table where the Director sat, was wedged between two of the largest ladies in the department. He managed to squeeze between the two jelly rolls and sat down. And down. And down.

There was one chair in this conference room that everybody avoided, and he got it. Its pneumatic cylinder had gone out months before, and as a result, the poor occupant ended up practically sitting on the floor, bringing the table to chin level. It was the midget chair.

After a brief introduction, repeated over and over from different meetings, the Director said, "Allright. Charlie, you're up."

Struggling to his feet from ground level, an unbalanced

Charlie practically sat in the lap of one of the large ladies next to him. Apologizing, he grabbed his laptop and walked around to the front of the conference table where the projector input was and pulled down the screen on the wall. It promptly snapped back up into its case. Charlie grabbed it again, pulled it down, and it snapped back like a spring. After the third unsuccessful attempt, one of the IT geeks came over, pulled it down. Of course it stayed down this time.

As chuckles grew from the peanut gallery, Charlie quickly plugged his laptop into the projector input. Instead of his PowerPoint presentation appearing on the screen, up popped the website he was on over the weekend. It was a job headhunter's site, one he had been looking at, just to see what was out there.

As quickly as he could, he hit Ctrl-Alt-Delete to get the site off the screen, but not before the Director and everyone else in the room had seen where he'd been surfing. *At least it wasn't a porn site*, he thought optimistically. He glanced at the Director only to find him writing a note in his planner, no doubt to discuss with Charlie's boss sometime later.

Composing himself, Charlie called up his presentation and flew through it as fast as he could to avoid any other unforeseen disasters. The rushed presentation was failure enough and was certainly not one of Charlie's best. He was known for killer graphics and well composed presentations. Not this time.

◉

Dragging back to his cube, Charlie had an hour before lunch. He thought fleetingly about working through to make up for being late this morning, but quickly shelved the idea. He was on the boss' shit-list as it was and trying to make up lost time would just backfire on him, he was sure.

He plugged his notebook back into the docking station and it locked up, freezing on his E-mail homepage. It sometimes did that when coming back from using the laptop remotely. He'd have to reboot and sign back in.

Just as he was getting back to the latest project he was working on, the phone rang. It was an outside line because it wasn't showing the number, only ID Unavailable. For a moment, he considered letting it just go to voice mail. With the day he'd had so far, all he needed was another bump in the road.

"Programming. Charlie Cook."

"About time you answered your damn phone," a female voice greeted him from the other end. Not just *any* female voice. It was his girlfriend, Susie. And she sounded pissed.

"Hey, baby," he said, forcing a smile that the phone couldn't deliver.

"Don't 'Hey baby' me. Did you not get my message?"

"What message?" Charlie immediately winced. *Not* the right thing to say to an upset girlfriend.

"You should be saying *'Which* message'. I've left you *five* on your shitty cellphone starting last night about ten. *Thanks* for calling me back. Where the *hell* have you been anyway?" Her voice kept getting shriller and shriller as the conversation went on.

Damn, he thought. He'd shut the hood on his cellphone after his dead battery was jumped off last night. A nice spider web pattern had been put in the gorilla glass. Evidently 'gorilla' was a relative term when it came to slamming things down on delicate electronic devices.

"Susie," he began in his most girlfriend-soothing voice. "I broke my cellphone last night and haven't been able to get any calls. It's busted."

"Well, couldn't you have at least texted me?" *Oh Lord*, he thought. How to respond rationally to that? Maybe silence was the more prudent route at this point.

Susie went on. "This is just so typical of you. There's not an ounce of consideration for others in your shitty little world. I've had it, Charlie. I'm 29 years old and I don't need this shit in my life right now."

She also tended to swear more when she was upset. Unfortunately, or fortunately, depending on your point of view, her curse word vocabulary wasn't all that broad.

"Babe, I was gonna call you when—"

"Don't bother. And don't call be babe or baby or sugar or honey or anymore of your shitty pet names. You've lost that privilege. In fact, just don't call me at all. Shithead!"

Click.

And just like that, Charlie Cook's girlfriend broke up with him over the phone at work on a Monday morning from hell. He'd hardly gotten a word in edgewise.

He slowly hung up the phone in stunned silence, settled back into his chair and stared blankly at his computer screen. After a moment, he shook his head and went back to work on the new program he was writing.

When lunch finally rolled around, Charlie was more than ready. He'd had to reboot his computer three times already this morning. Luckily, he didn't lose any major data each time he had to fire it back up. *I have to get out of here*, he thought.

Leaving through the employee entrance, Charlie started the lengthy walk to his car in the back of the employee parking lot. He had completely forgotten about the rain earlier and, as soon as he stepped out of the covered walkway, it opened up again in a torrent. Cursing at himself for leaving his umbrella in the car, even after he had thought about getting it this morning, he hurried along.

By the time he got to his car, Charlie was drenched again, soaking the driver's seat in the process of getting in. He was understandably cautious when he started his car, expecting the same dead battery from last night. Fortunately it started right up, just like it had that morning.

He ventured out to the DQ just down the street. He figured he was pretty safe in merely getting a combo meal, sitting in the parking lot and eating.

After ordering and pulling up to the drive thru window, he

pulled out his debit card to pay.

"Won't go through," the rotund female cashier said. "Bad card."

"Try it again, please if you don't mind." Charlie was being as nice as he could.

Rolling her eyes, the cashier halfheartedly ran the card again. "Nope. Bad card," she repeated. "And the line is backing up behind you. D'ya have another form of payment?" She said this in a dull, flat voice which told Charlie that this most likely happened several times a day.

Opening the center console, he realized he'd left his money clip in his briefcase at work. "No, I guess I don't."

"Line's backing up, mister." *This gal really loved to repeat herself*, Charlie thought. "If you can't pay, you're gonna hafta move on." Consciously or not, she said this in her most condescending voice.

Biting his tongue, Charlie shifted his car into gear and rolled away without lunch. *Oh, well*, Charlie thought. *I guess it'll be crackers and a soda from the vending machine.*

◉

He was able to move up two whole rows when he got back to work. *Wow. The day is looking up*, Charlie thought sarcastically.

He decided to sit in his car for a bit and just relax. He'd gotten in the habit of listening to talk radio during lunch, but not the usual conservative fare. He'd found a station which talked about unusual things like contrails and urban legends.

Today, they featured a researcher discussing an article recently published in the Journal of Experimental Psychology. It proposed that bad luck could be reversed by engaging in a 'ritual' to undo the bad karma.

Charlie's ears perked up. If anyone was having the proverbial unlucky day, it was him. He was willing to try anything.

The researcher went on in a slight British accent. "In scientific studies, participants were told to think of something that would tempt fate, like walking under a ladder or breaking a mirror. Once the thought was securely in their mind, they were then told to make a physical movement, like throwing salt over their shoulder or rubbing a piece of wood. By doing this, they proposed, the person would be diverting the negative energy away from themselves. Of course, this is all just conjecture."

Can't hurt, Charlie thought to himself.

Since there was no salt handy, and there was a split rail fence along the walkway back into the plant, Charlie opted for the wood option.

Grabbing his umbrella this time, Charlie got out of the car, fully expecting it to start raining again. *Nope*, he thought as he looked up, *nothing but blue skies. Of course. I have my umbrella this time*. With no worries about getting rained on again, Charlie strode confidently to the end of the fence and rubbed his hand along one of the rails.

"What the–," Charlie exclaimed after he felt a sharp pain in the palm of his hand. Looking down, he saw a three inch-long splinter poking out of his palm. Blood had already started weeping from where it had pierced him.

"Sonofabitch," he said, pulling the splinter out, thereby allowing the wound bleed even more.

As he put his palm to his mouth, he thought fleetingly about writing a nice letter to the Journal of Experimental Psychology about their bullshit theories.

Right about then, it began to rain.

◉

His badge failed to work again and he was forced to lay in wait so he could shirttail an unsuspecting coworker and get back into the building. *I feel like a stalker*, Charlie thought.

The First Aid room was on the way back to his desk and he stopped to get something for his hand. Looking through all the drawers and cabinets, he could find no hydrogen peroxide, no triple-antibiotic, not even some mercurochrome. The only thing he found that would serve the same purpose was a cabinet full of rubbing alcohol. *Of all the things* not *to use, there's a shitload of alcohol*, Charlie thought. It was either that, or risk infection.

Gritting his teeth, Charlie poured alcohol over some cotton swabs and forced himself to push it onto the cut. Pain exploded from his hand all the way to the top of his head and he did his best to not scream out some curse word his newly *ex*-girlfriend would have been proud to use on one of her rants.

He assessed the wound. All in all, just a minor cut, but right in the area of the hand you always used, that you always hit something against. *Just bad enough to be a pain in the ass is all*, Charlie thought.

When the pain-induced tears cleared and the bleeding finally stopped, he was able to find a Band-Aid and put it on, albeit one-handed.

◎

After stopping by his desk to get his money clip and to put his umbrella in his briefcase, Charlie walked down the hall to the break room. He fished a couple of dollars from the clip, fed them into the drink machine and punched the Mountain Dew button. A Pepsi promptly fell into the receptacle.

Stifling a laugh, he was almost expecting that to happen. And it's a Pepsi, the soft drink he most hated. *Wonderful.*

He was going to use the seventy-five cents change for a pack of crackers from the snack machine when he realized he hadn't heard the rattling of coins as change was given. "It kept the damn change," he said to an empty room. "Why am I not surprised?"

Retrieving another dollar bill from his pocket, Charlie turned his attention to the snack machine. In went the dollar and he pushed the proper button combination for peanut butter crackers. The corkscrew mechanism rotated out to make the pack of crackers fall to the bottom. Instead of falling, they got stuck between the Plexiglas and a honey bun partially poking out from the row below.

Coins rattled in the return slot. *At least I got change this time.* He reached inside to get the forty-five cents and retrieved only two nickels.

Unreal. He put his shoulder against the machine and shoved, trying to dislodge the pack of crackers. Nothing doing. He shoved again, harder this time. The light inside the machine blinked out and the buttons went dark. Evidently he had caused the machine to tilt out.

Pressing his head against the Plexiglas, Charlie decided retreat would be the best option rather than explain to somebody how he'd managed to break the snack machine.

Taking the nasty Pepsi to his cubical, he plopped into his chair and unscrewed the top. Compressed foamy soda spewed out from the top and managed to soak his shirt, the legal pad he had on his desk, his pen holder and his keyboard before he could get the cap back on.

This is getting almost comical, he thought as he started wiping up the sticky mess.

◉

Sipping on the Pepsi, Charlie turned his attention back to the program he was writing. *At least I have control over this part of the day,* he thought. In addition to (usually) good graphics and (usually) top-notch presentations, Charlie was one of the company's premiere software programmers. Because of this, his plate was always full when it came to his workload.

After about twenty minutes of total immersion in his work, the phone rang. The display read X200, Gordon. *Crap,* Charlie said to himself. *The boss.* He picked up the handset.

"Hey, Geoff. What's up?" He had come up through the ranks with Geoff Gordon, his current boss. Charlie had always joked with Geoff about how he shared the same name as the NASCAR driver, but spelled it wrong just to be different. He'd always felt he could be somewhat informal with him. But in the back of his mind, at least for today, he doubted he still had that privilege.

"Cook," Gordon said. *Damn. Last name. Not a good way for a conversation to start.*

"Cook," he repeated. "I need to see you in my office right now."

"Sure, no problem. Do I need to bring anything?"

"No. Just yourself."

Damn-damn. This can't be good, especially today.

Charlie got up from his chair and rounded the corner, completing the ten-foot walk to his boss' office. *Gordon could have just hollered for me like he usually does. Unless he's getting ready to bitch me out.*

Entering the office, he said, "What can I help you with, Geoff?"

"Close the door. Sit." Charlie did.

"This doesn't sound good," Charlie said as he slipped into one of the two chairs facing the desk.

"It's not, Charlie. I just wasted my lunch hour listening to the Director give me an earful about how my crack programmer, who has bailed us out on more than one occasion, is job-surfing on company time." *Damn. The website popup during the presentation.*

"Geoff," Charlie started. "Let me explain–"

"No, let *me* explain," Gordon interrupted, his voice tight with frustration. "I understand there are a lot of opportunities out there, especially for someone as talented as you. I know you have to keep your options open, the way the market is going these days. But, *dammit* Charlie. If you're going to look, look on your *own* time. I can't have the Director get the impression that I'm losing control of my department. Understand?"

Charlie's best bet was a sheepish shrug. It probably wouldn't do any good to explain that he was surfing in his apartment, on the weekend, away from the office. Albeit with the company laptop, but on his own time nonetheless.

"Hey, look, Charlie," he said, leaning in confidentially.

"Heck, even *I* poke around to see what's out there. And maybe even from this desk. But at least I cover my tracks, then go back and cover them again. You're smart enough to do that. That's why I can't understand how you let something like this come up on your laptop in a room full of people when giving a presentation." He sat back and sighed. "At least it wasn't porn."

Charlie inwardly cringed at the identical thought he'd had earlier.

"It won't happen again," he said putting on his most somber face.

"Not good enough," Geoff said. "The Director wants something a little more stringent, wants to set more of an example." Charlie swallowed hard. *Here it comes.*

Extracting a single sheet of paper from his top drawer, Gordon slid it across the desk to Charlie.

"This is a Formal Written Warning. You are receiving it for misuse of company property," Gordon said, obviously rehearsed. "You are on probation for six months. If, during that time, there is *any* other infraction of company rules, the consequences will be... um, elevated."

Charlie stared at the piece of paper with a weird combination of disbelief and resigned expectation. After everything that had happened today, he'd almost expected something like this.

"Sign it?" he said.

"You don't want to talk about it, dispute it, give me your side of the story?"

"No," Charlie said. "It doesn't really matter. Appearances are that I screwed up. Your boss was there and he's having you do something about it. Nothing will change the final outcome of a write up. You gotta do what you gotta do. No hard feelings."

Gordon looked at Charlie, expecting more. But there wasn't.

"People who get written up usually have a history of bad performance or behavior. You don't. That's why the Director both wanted to make an example out of you and also why the reprimand wasn't more severe. You're lucky, Charlie."

"I know," Charlie answered obediently, not feeling very lucky. Standing up he said, "Is that it?"

"Yeah, that's it," Gordon said warily. "Unless you have something for me."

Charlie thought about telling Gordon about his day so far, his bad luck since rolling out of bed this morning, from his girl-friend breaking up with him, to his marvelous lunch. *Nah,* he thought. *It would sound too much like whining.* So he let it go.

He extended his hand to shake Gordon's and immediately regretted it. Gordon squeezed Charlie's hand right on the spot where he'd gotten the splinter.

"Oh, by the way Charlie," Gordon asked. "Is there some reason you didn't badge in this morning?"

Damn, he thought. *And it continues.*

◉

Returning to his desk, Charlie was greeted with a calendar alarm reminding him of a meeting which started eight minutes ago. Whether or not his boss had made him late was irrelevant. He was late nonetheless. At least he didn't have to present anything this time. *Maybe I can stay out of trouble,* he thought wryly.

Making his way back to the same conference room he had so miserably failed in earlier, all heads turned to greet him as he opened the door and tried to sneak in. Looking around the table for an empty chair, he saw the only one left unoccupied. *Of course,* he thought, inwardly rolling his eyes.

The midget chair. Again.

◉

Managing to get through the meeting without incident, by the time he got back to his desk, Charlie only had about an hour to go in the rest of his day. *If I can just keep my head down and stay invisible until quitting time, I'll be doing good.*

Shaking his mouse to wake the computer, he was again greeted with the Blue Screen of Death. He was almost anticipating it. So for the umpteenth time today, he hit the power button to reboot.

Twenty minutes and three tries later, Charlie was finally able to get back to his program writing duties. After that, he was able to get to the end of his day relatively unscathed.

As Charlie was walking to the time clock to badge out, the guard intercepted him before he could swipe his card.

"You Charlie Cook?" he said through a mustache which appeared to had gone months without a trim. "We have a problem with your badge."

Hello Captain Obvious. Charlie was already well aware that it wouldn't let him in this morning or again when he got back from lunch. "What's wrong with it?"

"Looks like the problem is you haven't been using it," the guard said, obviously having made this speech many times before. "What, did you leave it at home or in the car? Or just decide to not badge in so you could screw with your time?"

"Um, Bubba," Charlie said, noticing the name on the guard's badge, "I tried it this morning and at lunch and it wouldn't let me in either time. I had to come in with others when they had the door open."

"That so, Mr. Cook?" Bubba said sarcastically. "I see this all the time. People think they can cheat the system by 'forgetting their badge' and coming in late or sneaking out early without their time being recorded. All the time."

"Well I can tell you, that's not the case with me. Here, watch."

Charlie moved his badge across the proximity reader and, BEEP, a soft green LED shone, indicating a successful swipe. *Of course it works*, Charlie thought. *Why wouldn't it?*

"Yep. That's what I figured," Bubba said, full of importance. "I need to get your badge number and full name. Sorry, pal, just doing my job."

Of course you are. All Charlie wanted was to get off the premises without anything else going wrong.

◉

After giving Bubba the requisite information, Charlie started the walk to his car. After a dozen or so steps, the rain started again. *You gotta be kidding me! At least I remembered my umbrella this time.* He slid it out of his briefcase and pushed the button to automatically open it.

Nothing.

He tried again, shaking it as well. This time the shaft shot out of the handle and went flying across the asphalt. In disbelief, Charlie ran after it and managed to snag it by the fabric. Unfortunately the other end was caught under a parked car's tire and, as he grabbed it, the fabric ripped off the wire frame. Whatever little protection the broken umbrella would have provided was now null and void. *Glad I remembered my umbrella,* Charlie thought cynically.

Soaked, pissed and finally getting to his car, Charlie threw his briefcase into the passenger seat of his Honda and sat down hard. *What a day. At least it's over.*

He jammed the key into the ignition and turned it.

CLICK.

He rolled his eyes in disbelief and tried again.

CLICK.

Unbelievable. The battery had survived getting jumped off last night, had turned over this morning and at lunch, and now, of all times, it's choosing to give up the ghost? Weren't batteries supposed to build up a charge over time after getting jumped? Instead, *his* battery evidently built up *just enough* charge to make it to the end of the day and leave him stranded in his workplace parking lot. *Terrific.*

Getting out into the rain and slamming the door, Charlie walked around to the front of the car to pop the hood, then realized he hadn't released the latch from inside the car. Inwardly cursing like his girlfriend, his *ex*-girlfriend, he opened the door and reached underneath the dashboard to find the lever. When he did, he pulled it forward and SNAP, it broke off in his hand, but not before mercifully releasing the hood lever.

"Shit," he said to no one because everyone else had reliable cars and was leaving for the day. Unfortunately, he was so far back at the rear of the parking lot that nobody had a reason to come this way and help.

He started walking back to the building; miles away it seemed, through the steady downpour. Just as he got to the curb, a pick-up truck came around the corner.

"Thank God," he said, relieved to have somebody who could maybe give him a jump so he could get out of here.

The door opened and out stepped Bubba the guard, coming back from making his rounds.

You gotta be kidding me.

As Bubba gave him a ride back to his car, the rain dwindled and stopped. They got out of the truck and Bubba expertly assessed the situation as a dedicated security guard would. He asked Charlie to try and start his car one more time so he could get an idea of what it was doing. *Couldn't hurt*, he thought, getting back into the car. Just as he put the key back into the ignition and began to turn it, he cringed inside because he knew exactly what was going to happen.

The car started right up.

"O-kay," said Bubba, glaring at Charlie. "Looks like your badge wasn't the only thing 'acting up' for you today."

Charlie could almost see the air quotes.

"I don't know what your deal is, Mr. Cook, but I've got a helluva lot better things to do than play whatever game you're playing. Such as writing my reports."

You mean ratting on me, Charlie said to himself. Hard to blame him though. He probably appeared to be a nut-job at this point.

Shutting the hood, he considered himself fortunate to have not closed it on his fingers. *How much bad luck can one man endure?*

Charlie's intent was to get straight home, maybe call Susie, try to patch things up, and generally just hide away in his apartment as best he could. *The day could hardly get any worse*, he said to himself, not really believing it.

Just as he finished that thought, he saw blue lights flashing in his rear view mirror. He hadn't run any stop lights or signs, he hadn't been speeding, and he hadn't made any wrong turns or illegal moves. *There's no way those lights are meant for me*, he thought, slowing down to let the patrol car pass.

The patrol car behind him slowed as well. He could've sworn the flashing blue lights got even brighter and started blinking with more urgency. It was apparent the officer was pulling him over.

Shaking his head, Charlie turned out of traffic and slowed to a stop. As he waited for the cop to approach his car, in his head he kept going over what he could possibly have done to get himself pulled. At a loss, he couldn't think of a thing.

The policeman came up and tapped on the driver's side window. Charlie saw the patches on his uniform and recognized the city logo and badge. He rolled down the window and the officer said, "License and registration, please."

"No problem," Charlie replied, already opening the glove box to retrieve his registration card. "What am I being pulled for? I don't think I did anything wrong, sir." He handed the cop his registration.

"Your taillight is out," said the officer, flatly. "Do you have your driver's license, sir?"

"Yes," said Charlie, fishing his wallet out of the center console. "I have it right here."

He opened the wallet and was greeted with a blank spot where his license should have been; the clear plastic sleeve was empty. He laughed nervously. "I have it right here," he repeated inanely.

As he started digging through the center console, he began to realize that, with the day he'd had, it was only logical that he had lost his driver's license as well. *It totally makes sense*, he thought ironically.

Checking the name on the registration card, the cop said, "Sir, I need to verify your information against your driver's license."

"Um, I can't seem to find it, officer. I had it in my wallet and now it's gone."

"I see, Mr... Cook. You do understand it's a violation to operate your vehicle without a valid license in your possession."

"Yes sir," Charlie replied, flustered. "I have a license. I just can't seem to—"

"Please turn your vehicle off, Mr. Cook. I need to call this in." The cop turned and walked back to his car.

Numb to all the events of the day, culminating with this latest fiasco, Charlie closed his eyes and waited, mind as blank as he could make it. He ruminated on Job from the bible and came to the conclusion that he didn't have *squat* on Charlie Cook.

Fifteen minutes later, the police officer returned to Charlie and gave his registration card back to him.

"I'm issuing you a citation for operating a motor vehicle without a valid driver's license in your possession." Charlie took the ticket and looked it over. A handwritten figure stared back at him: $137.

"You've got to be kidding," Charlie said, looking at the cop. "A hundred and forty dollars for not having my license on me?"

The police officer just stared at Charlie with a look that re-iterated this cop didn't kid about *anything*. "If you'll take your license with you on the appearance date, it will most likely get reduced to court costs. About sixty bucks. I've seen it before," the cop offered.

"OK. Thanks." Charlie often wondered why people thanked officers after getting a ticket. It's amazing how most people go out of their way to avoid conflict.

"Have a good evening, sir," the officer said. "Oh, and get that taillight fixed."

The Lucky Strike Bowl & Bar was on his way home, so Charlie decided to drop in for a drink. He rarely drank, and when he did, it was usually no more than a beer or two. He wasn't really a beer lover, keeping any potential drinking habit at bay. *To hell with it. I deserve a drink today of all days.*

He parked his car and turned it off before realizing that he might not get it back on and would have to be jumped off again. *The way the day has gone,* he thought, *I really don't give a rat's ass at this point.*

It started raining when Charlie got out of his car, but fortunately the door was only a few steps away. *Ha!* Charlie thought. *Not gonna get me this time!*

Walking into the bar area, away from the noise of bowling balls meeting pins, he sat down at the counter. *Good,* he thought. Nick, his favorite bartender was working this evening.

"Hiya, Nick. How's the drink business?"

"Same ol'," Nick replied his usual answer. "How's the exciting world of computer programming?"

"I'd say pretty damn weird at this point," Charlie said, wondering if he should go into explaining his inexplicably unlucky day.

"Yeah, ain't that the way life is? What'll ya have, Charlie?"

Charlie ordered a draft beer and took a spot at the end of the bar where he could see the TVs lining the wall. At the same time he was close enough to talk with Nick and the waitresses as they went back and forth through the bar door. Monday Night Football was coming on soon and the bar would get pretty full, so he wanted to have a decent seat.

Maybe if I just sit here and don't do anything, nothing else will go wrong.

Taking a swig of his beer, he finally began to relax a little bit. *It's funny how tight you can get when you have a day like I did, and not even realize it until you start chilling out.*

Finally feeling a bit calmer, Charlie grabbed his beer mug to take another drink. Just as the glass hit his lips, one of the waitresses swung the bar door upwards and hit Charlie square on the elbow, depositing half the beer down the front of his shirt.

"Oh my God!" said the girl, obviously upset. "I didn't mean to do that! I'm so sorry!" Her excitement was almost overwhelming.

Charlie said, "It's OK, I promise. The way today has gone, it's not surprising."

He grabbed a handful of napkins from the bar and tried mopping up the mess in front of him and on his shirt. The waitress handed him her towel and he tried pointlessly to wipe himself off.

Nick came over, almost laughing. *I can't blame him*, thought Charlie. *I'd probably be laughing too, especially if he knew what a crappy day I'd had.*

"It was an accident. It wasn't her fault," Charlie said, defending the girl. "I just need to get cleaned up." People near the bar noticed the ruckus and were looking Charlie's way, curiously. The last thing he needed right now was attention. "I'll soak my shirt in the bathroom sink." Charlie slid off the barstool. "Be right back. Hold my spot."

"Use mine," Nick offered.

◉

Charlie walked around to the private bathroom behind the counter. Inside he stripped down to his undershirt and rung out his polo as best he could. *This shirt will smell like beer for a long time*, he thought. It was ironic because he really didn't like the smell.

He reached for the faucet handle to wash out his shirt. As he turned the handle, it came right off in his hand, water shooting straight up from where it had been attached and soaking the mirror, wall and, of course, Charlie. *And it continues*, he thought.

Thinking quickly enough to reach underneath, he turned

off the water supply to the sink, stopping the spontaneous mini-geyser. As he rose back up, he cracked the back of his head squarely on the underside of the sink, bringing stars to his vision and tears to his eyes. Going down on one knee in the puddled water on the floor, he managed to soak his pants as well. *What the heck, why not?*

Backing up and avoiding the sink this time, he straightened and felt the pull in his back from this morning when he'd gotten his shoes from under the bed. It was a dull ache, one he was familiar with from time to time and one which his doctor extolled him to lose some extra weight about.

I must look like a disaster, he thought, staring back into the water streaked mirror. Sure enough, his hair was a mess, his shirt was soaked, his tie was askew and he could feel water dripping down his legs.

Taking some paper towels and drying the mirror, the floor and himself off as best he could, he pulled himself together and went back out to the bar.

◎

"What the hell happened to you in there?" asked Nick after taking one look at Charlie. "Geez, Charlie. You all right? Looks like you lost a fight with a water hose."

"No, it's OK," Charlie answered. "The handle came off the faucet, water sprayed everywhere, and when I turned off the supply under the sink, I hit my head and about knocked myself out. Other than that, I'm fine. No big deal."

"Wow, dude," Nick said. "Not your day, huh?"

"Nick, my man. You have no idea."

Figuring it was time to just get home and curl up in the fetal position, Charlie reached into his pocket and grabbed his money clip. *At least it's still there and I haven't been robbed. Yet.*

As he retrieved the only money he had, he was careful to not hit his hand where he'd hurt it earlier. He'd already bumped it against something a half-dozen times today, wincing at the pain each time.

Retrieving his only three one-dollar bills, he unfolded them to give to Nick. As he did, he noticed one of the bills had an unusual mark. It appeared to be some sort of Chinese symbol, handwritten in the upper left hand corner on the backside of the dollar near the denotation. He'd never seen anything like it. But then again, Charlie had never claimed to be an expert in Chinese calligraphy. He was curious what it signified. *Like it matters*, he thought wryly. He'd often seen the 'Where's George' and other types of stamps on paper money, so he didn't give it much thought. At the moment, he was just glad to have enough money to cover his drink and tip.

He'd remembered that particular dollar from last night at Walmart when the teary-eyed cashier had given him change. It caught his attention because the lady was noticeably upset. She was so distraught she had actually given him a dollar more in change than she should have, probably screwing up her reconciliation at the end of the shift. He didn't notice until later, but by then he'd had his hands full of dead battery to contend with.

"Here you go, Nick," Charlie said as he stuffed the three beer-soaked dollars into Nick's tip jar. "I better get out of here before anything else happens. I only have so many changes of clothes."

◉

Walking to his car, he thought fleetingly about preemptively going back in and lining up someone to come help jump his car. The way the day was going, getting his car started was a fifty-fifty proposition at best. It wasn't raining on him, at least for the time being. *Give it a minute*, Charlie thought, *and it'll come a downpour.*

Opening the door, a flash of plastic between the seat and the doorjamb caught his eye. Reaching down, he retrieved his driver's license, wedged in where he hadn't noticed it before. In his haste to get in and out of the car while dodging raindrops, his license must have fallen out of his wallet and wound up next to the seat. Charlie was relieved to not have to go through the hassle of getting a duplicate. *Well that's the* only *thing that's gone my way today.*

Sliding into the driver's seat, Charlie almost winced as he turned the key. His car started right up, no problem, just like it had at lunch. *Hey,* he thought, *it's the little things in life.*

As he put the car in gear, he hoped he could avoid crashing, getting another ticket or running over someone and messing up his car. *Is that so much to ask? This unlucky day has to end sometime,* he thought. Most of the evening was wasted, so if he could just get home in one piece and settle down in front of the TV without another major catastrophe, he'd be doing well.

His cell phone rang and he looked at it, surprised. He thought it was irrevocably busted when the hood slammed it last night. It hadn't worked all day until now. He glanced at the caller ID. It was Susie.

Damn.

He thought fleetingly about just letting it go to Voice Mail. *No,* he said to himself. *I'm going to have to face her at some point. She probably wants to get her things from my house.*

He hit the answer button and said, "Hey."

"Charlie," a tearful voice said. "I'm sorry."

"It's OK, baby," Charlie said, relieved. "I'm still here."

With that, Charlie pulled out of the parking lot and into traffic. He caught the light at the corner just as it was turning green and didn't have to slow down to make it through. *That's more like it,* he thought optimistically.

And for the first time that day, Charlie laughed.

◉

When midnight finally rolled around, Nick was ready to call it an evening. It had been a pretty good take at the bar and he was more than ready to get to the house. He had been on his feet all day and those dogs were barking.

The owner was generally pleased with Nick when he was on shift because Nick knew his clientele and could relate to almost all of them. Nick was middle aged, but had an older, wizened look. Years out of college, but he could have been passed off as a grad student. He had enough hippie in him so he could talk to the stoners, but the wire-rimmed glasses conveyed just a hint of sophistication and class. All in all, Nick was the typical everyman that all bar owners wanted pouring drinks.

Nick's tips were particularly large this evening, a by-product of Monday Night Football and his well-polished bartending. He fished through the tip jar and counted out his share, the bar's share and was able to reconcile the books on the first try. Nick had majored in Accounting when in college, but had never used it except when bartending.

As he separated the singles from the other bills, one of the dollars caught his eye. It still smelled of beer and remembered Charlie's unexpected barley bath. It also had an unusual oriental mark on the back near the One:

He had no idea what it meant, but as a closet artist, he liked the way it looked and decided to add that bill to his tips, replacing it with another. He would have to visit the Almighty Google and figure out a way of looking up its meaning. He kept a binder collection of unusual symbols and signs that he had come across.

Nick grabbed the cash, his backpack and closed up the bar area. He was in a bit of a hurry tonight. It was his girlfriend's last night of evening classes this semester and they had planned on some wine and a candlelit bath to celebrate. *No way I'm gonna be late for that*, Nick thought with a smile.

Walking to the back of the parking lot, Nick unlocked his truck's door and threw the backpack onto the passenger seat. He slid inside the cab just as a spattering of raindrops hit the

windshield. *Strange*, he thought. *It's not supposed to rain tonight.*
He put the key in the ignition and turned.
CLICK.
"Huh?" He was at a loss. Perplexed, he tried again.
CLICK.
No way, Nick thought. *Is this what I think it is?*
He tried again.
CLICK.
Dead battery.
Damn the luck.

INTERLUDE: THE SECOND SIDE

REALITY REPLACED THE VISION I just had, my head throbbing with a dull pain. What I had just seen, what I had just *lived*, was now a part of me. And it reminded me, tragically, of my own station in life. I was aware that I was still the same old bum; that hadn't changed.

The fire was burning just like it had been. I had no idea how long I had been in a fugue, or trance or whatever it was. It could have been minutes or hours, for all I knew. Or just a few seconds. All I knew was that it had been unlike anything I had ever experienced before. I now realized the reliving of my own childhood memory about the model kit was just the beginning.

The beginning of what? I wondered.

Daring to peer back into the box, the underside of the lid had now grown dark, devoid of any life. As if there had been life present in the first place. What I had just seen was impossible. But so was how I had gotten to this stage of my life.

Movement on the adjacent side in the box caught my eye. Something was forming there now.

I gazed into another new world...

INTERLUDE: THE SECOND SIDE

FRIENDLY VARMINT

THE SWAMP BEHIND THE shack was lit up like an Independence Day's wet dream. There were more balls of light and rocket trails than you could shake a stick at. All colors, too: reds and blues and greens and... Well, there were a few colors mixed in here and there which just didn't have a name. It was almost as if a blind oil painter had gotten a notion of what certain colors should *feel* like, and went with that, just hoping the viewer would understand what he was shooting for.

Old Man Jacks was standing on the back porch of his two room cabin, watching the way the colors lighted up the trees and swamp moss, following the few random sparks as they rode upwards on currents of air. He wasn't worried about them falling back down to earth and catching something on fire; his little plot of land was pretty much surrounded by the swampy water. There was only the one rickety bridge leading in and out from his place and, quite frankly, he didn't care whether it burnt to the ground or not.

He was perfectly happy in his solitude. At least as happy as an old widower could be. *Childless, too*, he thought. *Only it wasn't always that way.*

Another plume shot skyward, ricocheting around in the treetops. He could see the source of all the ruckus, about a hundred yards from his house, an object in the middle of the swamp, most likely sinking to the muddy bottom. The fireworks were getting steadily weaker and less frequent.

He looked at his watch. *Two-thirty in the goddamn morning*, he thought. *Well, it's not like I was asleep or anything.*

Jacks had been sitting in his armchair when the... *thing* flew right over his house. It was close enough to the ground that the doors shook and the dirty dishes rattled in the sink. But it was silent. In fact, it didn't make a sound until it hit the trees leading into the marsh, just past his house. So the disturbance he felt was only the air being pushed out of the way as the thing barely avoided turning his shack into matchsticks.

As soon as it finished making splinters from the old Cyprus trees and splashed into the swamp, Jacks switched on the end table light (yes, he'd been sitting there in the dark) and made his way to the back door. He could see the glow from the flames and sparks peeking through the cracks in the door.

Watching the dying light, Jacks figured to himself that maybe he should go take a look at whatever had just made an unwelcomed intrusion on his property. He was in no hurry. Most likely it was a meteorite or a piece of an old satellite. He fleetingly thought that it could have also been a small airplane, but quickly dismissed the notion; he lived way too far off the beaten path for that.

He pulled on his boots, picked his light jacket off the floor next to the door where he'd dropped it, and started back out. *Hold on*, he thought. *May as well take the Remington, just in case.*

Just in case of what, he did not know.

◉

It was a relatively short walk to the dwindling light in the swamp. Jacks knew where to step and where not to step. He wasn't about to take a fall into a swamp pit or step off into the black water. He didn't need a flashlight either, as the nearly full moon and years of wandering these trails were his guides. But it was a circuitous route, taking him twice as long to get there.

As he approached the source of all this consternation, it was apparent to Jacks there was something a little out of the ordinary. It took him a minute for his eyes to understand what he was looking at. *A little out of the world is more like it*, he thought.

It was definitely a ship of some sort. About a third of it was still sticking out of the swampy water at a severe angle, and it was sinking gradually. *Some say there aren't really bottoms to the old swamps of backwoods Louisiana*, Jacks thought. *Well, if there are, this thing's gonna find it. And if there aren't, it may just sink right to the other side of the world.* Jacks considered himself a philosopher of sorts, having seen enough pain and sorrow for a lifetime.

From what he could tell, the thing appeared to be about twenty feet across. It was an odd silvery color, with some translucence which caught the firelight and gave off a multitude of colors, some identifiable, some not. It was round, and within the round outer shell, he could see another ring. Flat on the ends, it gradually bulged toward the middle. On the top was a dome which must have been made from some kind of glass or plastic. He could see through that section and make out flames on the other side of the small lagoon where some dried kindling was still burning.

And he could see movement within the dome.

Squinting, he saw what appeared to be the silhouette of someone's head moving back and forth as if it were keeping time to an old Ray Charles tune. As he watched, the head lolled to one side and was still.

"Holy shit," Jacks said out loud to the empty woods. *There was somebody trapped in there!*

As if on cue, the ship rocked backwards and began sinking faster. It must have been lodged on some tree roots under the water and had worked itself free. Now with a clear shot to the bottom (*or beyond*), it picked up speed in its descent.

Already moving before he had time to think about it, Jacks started around the shore of the lagoon and over to where he could climb up onto the ship's surface. A surge of bubbles rose up around the edge of the craft as his weight made it sink even faster.

If I'm gonna do something, now's the time, he thought desperately.

He crawled along the slick surface towards the transparent dome. He could still see the outline of the occupant's head, motionless. As he reached the top, he looked at where the dome joined the rest of the ship, expecting to see a mechanism of some sort to release and open the top. Nothing. The metal of the ship blended into the transparency of the dome. There was no separation at all.

Just then, the ship pitched again, almost throwing him

overboard. Water had spilled over the top surface and was now licking at his boots.

Without thinking, Jacks raised his Remington and fired, point-blank, at the edge of the dome and where it melded in with the rest of the ship. Sparks flew. Pieces of the dome splintered and cracked away, leaving a hole about the size of his fist. *More than enough*, he thought. A glowing gas was coming out of the hole he'd just made.

Sticking the butt end of the rifle into the hole, he cocked it to one side, wedging it in securely. With a grunt, he gave it a sharp pull and the glass, or whatever it was, started chipping away, piece by piece. Within seconds he had carved out a hole large enough for him to squeeze through.

I gotta be crazy, Jacks thought. *It's probably some dickhead millionaire out joy-riding in his fancy build-your-own and would be as ungrateful as was everybody else.* However, one thought kept going through his mind: the company policy of the plant from where he'd retired.

Do the right thing.

It was short. It was simple. And it was easy to remember.

Most of the gas had already seeped out through the gap he made. Steeling himself, Jacks squeezed into the opening. Inside lights from instruments were giving off flashing reddish light. He looked around for the lone occupant. Then he found... *it*.

Strapped into the single seat in the cramped quarters was a small, frail figure. He couldn't quite discern its color because of the flashing light and the shear darkness from whatever firelight was able to get through the dome. Its bald head was sagged over to one side, its face away from him. *Well, whatever it is, I can't just let it sink with its ship*, he thought. *Do the right thing.*

The water was starting to come in through the hole he'd made and around his body, still halfway outside. Taking the knife from his belt, Jacks sliced through the straps holding the thing into its chair. Immediately it fell to one side. He grabbed it under the armpits and heaved backwards, through the opening and out of the ship.

The dome was all that was left sticking out of the water. Jacks lifted the occupant onto his shoulder and started toward the shore. His load was being buoyed up by the water and it gave Jacks the impression that it had no weight at all.

He dog-paddled himself and his rescue to safety. Reaching the bank, he lifted the small body out of the water.

There was still no weight. Or if there was, it was almost imperceptible. It was as if he were picking up a big pile of cotton candy, the kind he bought when he used to take Sarah to the County Fair. He could feel the texture of its clothing on his hands, but there was nothing pushing back.

A *sploosh* of water made a sound behind him as the rest of the ship went under. As he watched, several pockets of bubbles appeared and dissipated. The few remaining bushes that were still on fire lit the area with a faint flickering illumination. Within a few seconds, the surface of the water was as still as it had been before being violated by the object falling out of the night sky. All that remained of the ship was a faint glow coming from deep in the water's depths.

A coughing spasm suddenly gripped Jacks. His chest felt like it was being squeezed by some kind of giant vise. He couldn't take a breath between coughs. Holding himself upright on the stock of his rifle, he spat out a wet mess onto the muddy bank. Even though the failing light made it impossible to tell, he knew the color of the sputum; he'd seen it enough over the past two months. The dark glob looked black, but he knew it was red, regardless.

Turning his attention back to the being he'd rescued, the faint light wasn't enough to make a fair assessment of its condition. He'd have to take it back to the cabin to get a better look. *Not my number one choice*, he thought. *It's bad enough when regular people come around, much less this... thing from wherever.* He stopped just short of regretting having gone in after it.

Standing up, he tucked his rifle under one arm and hoisted the being over the other shoulder. Again, he couldn't get past how light the thing was. *At least it'll be easy on my back*, he thought. He started back along the path to his house.

Behind him, the faint glow slowly receded into the swamp water, as if searching for a bottom that may or may not have been there.

◉

By the time Jacks and his burden returned to his home, both he and the small creature were completely dried off from the little swim they'd taken in the swamp. As he opened the door to let himself in, his hand instinctively went to the light switch just to the left of the door. He stopped. Although he was curious to see what it was that he kept from drowning in the bog, he also assumed the light could have some adverse effect on it. He remembered seeing an old Saturday afternoon Fright Fest movie when he was a kid featuring a big plant which transformed into a huge man-eater whenever it was exposed to light.

Although his guest (the term seemed appropriate, since he'd already brought it inside his home) seemed small and frail enough, prudence, he thought, was definitely better than curiosity. The lights remained off.

Guiding his way through the cabin by the windowed moonlight, Jacks crossed the small room and gently laid the little creature on his sofa, pausing to put a throw pillow underneath its head.

Straightening up, he tried to get a better look at the thing. It was small, that was for sure, maybe four feet long stretched out. It was wearing some kind of clothing, a slick membranous material which contoured to its body. The head was definitely bald and appeared to be slightly larger than normal. The facial features were lost in the shadows. By the light of the moon alone, he wasn't able to tell what its skin color was. Everything had a washed out, monochromatic look.

He bent back down and put an ear to its chest. It was rising and falling, but barely moving at all. He heard a muffled *thump*, then silence. After a second or two, he heard another *thump*. He waited, another followed a few seconds later. *Well, if that's a heartbeat,* he thought to himself, *its pulse rate must be in the teens. Or lower.*

Together with the slight rhythmic movement of its chest, and the slow but steady heartbeat, Jacks was sure of only one thing: it was alive, at least in its own way. He grabbed the throw from the couch back and covered the small body. It seemed the decent thing to do.

As Jacks straightened up again, he was momentarily disoriented and off-balance. With all the excitement, he'd probably overdone it. He'd felt his before as an onset of a dizzy spell. The adrenaline which had dumped into his bloodstream during his heroics was wearing off and allowing his body to find itself again, in whatever condition it may be. He was suddenly exhausted.

I'm not about to go to bed, Jacks thought, making his way to the recliner. *Not with that whatever-it-is on my couch.* He sat down, only then realizing just how tired he really was. He looked at the digital clock on the TV: 3:33 am. *Maybe I can just sit for a while and keep an eye on it until dawn. Once I get a good look at it, I'll figure out what to do. The Sheriff can take it off my hands in the morning.*

Finally relaxing, Jacks kept watch in the direction of the couch, Remington across his lap.

◎

With remnants of the dream still fresh in his mind, Jacks woke with a start, a dagger of morning sunlight in his eyes.

Dammit, he scolded himself. *How the hell could I have fallen asleep with that thing—*

He jerked his head up and looked at the couch. The *empty* couch.

All remaining was the blanket he'd draped over the little creature last night. But it wasn't wadded up or discarded the way many people leave blankets. It was folded. But not in squares, not in the conventional way people fold blankets. It was folded into a complex set of diagonal creases and pyramidal shapes. It looked odd, alien, but it was definitely, consciously folded over itself several times. A work of intelligence if ever there was one.

Marvel at its housekeeping another time, he told himself. *Where is the little thing?* He swept the room with his eyes, not daring to make any sudden moves, irrationally afraid in the back of his mind that the small being had morphed into the man eating plant from the Saturday Fright Fest. A slight laugh was stifled in his throat. *I must be more tired than I thought.*

He glanced at the door and around at the windows, all closed. *Chances are it's still in the house*, he thought. *I'm not sure that's a good thing or a bad thing*, he reasoned. But if it *had* escaped, then Jacks' worries about what to do with it were gone as well.

He felt a wetness on his chin and wiped at it with the back of his hand. Partially dried blood. Again. Lately he'd been coughing up hockers in his sleep and they were all tinged with red.

Warily, he pulled himself out of the chair and started toward the sink to get a wet dishcloth to wipe his mouth. He kept looking around for the creature, not really knowing what he'd do with it if he found it.

He stopped.

The sink was empty. The night before, it was full of dishes. And the night before that. And the night before that. In fact, Jacks couldn't remember the last time he'd washed any dishes. Despite that fact, there wasn't a single dish remaining in the sink. They were all stacked neatly next to the sink on a dish towel, squeaky clean.

OK, he thought. *This has gone from weird to off the charts.*

Jacks slowly retreated from the sink as if it were something alive and dangerous, not daring to turn his back on it. Under the sink he'd hung curtains because he was too cheap to buy cabinet doors. They were an olive green and normally hung limp. Right now they weren't. At the part in the middle, the cloth was rhythmically moving in and out, as if being breathed upon. It was slight and hardly noticeable, but there nonetheless.

Not breathing himself, Jacks eased back toward the sink, his eyes never leaving the oscillating gap in the curtain. Kneeling down, he very slowly slid the top of the curtain back just enough to peer inside.

It was in there.

Evidently, it was small and agile enough to crawl under the sink and hide behind the curtain among the dish detergent and the Liquid Plumber.

And it was looking right at him.

The first things Jacks noticed were the eyes. They were large, about twice the size of a person's. And they were coal black.

As he stared, it blinked, side to side.

C'mon, Jacks, he scolded himself. *You've seen all sorts of weird shit. This is no different. Just another one of God's mistakes. And He does make some doozies.*

Very slowly, he glided the curtain even further open so he could get a good look at the small creature under his sink. It sat on its haunches, squatted down almost into a ball. The suit it wore was a metallic, golden color, with areas giving off rainbow-like colors, depending on how the light hit it. The suit appeared to cover the being's body entirely, from ankle to wrist, leaving the hands and feet bare. On its back was what looked like a darker gold-colored triangular backpack, although no seams could be seen. The color of its skin was a pale purplish-gray. Each hand had four fingers; more like two fingers and two opposing thumbs. The feet had no toes.

Jacks turned his attention back to its face. Aside from the eyes, there were very few features to speak of. The entire head, which was out of proportion to the rest of its body, was hairless, including the absence of eyebrows or lashes. There was no indication of ears. The suggestion of a triangular bump below the eyes, together with two little holes must have been the thing's nose. Below that was a small slit, looking more like a surgical incision than a mouth. Its chin was as pointed as its head was round.

hi. A voice sounded inside Jacks' mind as the creature cocked its own head slightly to one side.

Jacks blinked, unsure of what he had just heard, or thought he'd heard.

Again: *hi.* It was more of a suggested sound in his thoughts rather than an actual voice. He could only assume it was coming from the creature.

"Hey," Jacks said quietly, sounding ridiculous to his ears. "Why are you under my sink?"

feels. right. The voice was in his mind. *safe.*

"Can you come out from under there? Are you hurt?" This conversation seemed way too normal for the circumstances.

safe? It pointed one of its two fingers in the direction of the open room. *out? safe?*

It's scared, Jacks thought. *It's probably as scared of me as I am of it.*

what? 'scared'?

"Scared is what you feel when–," Jacks stopped mid-sentence, realizing that the little creature had heard what he thought. *Can you hear what I'm thinking?*

yes. can. feel. your. words.

Feel my words? That's a strange way to put it. Jacks made this last comment in his head more to himself than to the other.

what? 'strange'?

"Stop doing that," Jacks said out loud, rather sharply. "I have enough trouble watching what I say in my head without having company in there."

please. no. hurt. me. The thought in his head took on a different tone. He couldn't hear the difference, but the change was in how the thoughts made him feel. Anxious. Afraid.

"Look," Jacks said, softening his voice, "I'm not gonna hurt you. I just need to see if you're OK. And I need for you to get out from under my sink. That's no place to stay."

like. comfortable.

Jacks was already realizing the little creature knew what

some words meant, but not others. He tried to see a pattern in the words it did and didn't know, but couldn't make any sense of it. He filed that away for future use.

"I'm sure it is. From the looks of your, um… ship, I suppose you're used to smaller spaces. But it's OK. This is a small house." *Am I really trying to reason with this thing?* Jacks was beside himself and was starting to question his own sanity.

ok.

With that, the small creature unfolded itself, eased out onto the kitchen floor and stood up, its large head moving back and forth, looking around at its surroundings.

Jacks stood up as well, now towering over the little thing. It seemed even smaller than he remembered from last night; it couldn't have stood over three feet tall. Its suit really played with the light, now that it was fully exposed to the sun. Rainbow reflections scattered throughout the kitchen. To Jacks' relief, his guest didn't morph into a giant, man-eating plant. A quick, short laugh escaped his lips.

A quick, short laugh escaped the creature's mouth as well, sounding exactly like Jacks'. It jerked its head up and locked eyes with Jacks, almost as if surprised.

ha?

Jacks smiled. "Yes, 'ha'. That's a happy sound. It's called a laugh."

laugh.

Jacks was grinning now, something he hadn't done in a very long time. He could feel the creature relaxing somewhat, confident that Jacks wasn't going to hurt it. *Some sort of bond was forming,* Jacks thought. *It knows I won't hurt it and I know it won't hurt me. Small steps, I suppose.*

Jacks looked over at the sink where the clean dishes were neatly lined up. "Did you do that?" he asked. "Did you wash my dishes?"

yes. bad. smell.

Obviously, Jacks had gotten used to the odor of unwashed dishes lying in the sink for days at a time. Either that or the little thing's sense of smell was acute.

"How did you know how to do it?" he asked.

looked. into. mind.

Jacks could feel embarrassment as the thought-voice talked inside his head. The little thing had evidently looked into Jacks' thoughts while he slept and figured out the basics, including washing dishes.

wrong?

"No. It's OK," Jacks said, unsure if it really was OK. This may be the normal way of communication wherever this thing came from. He didn't want to make it feel bad, or start an interstellar war over something as mundane as it helping out an old man by washing his dishes. "It's OK."

ok.

"But how did you get up there to do it?" Jacks continued, looking down at the small creature, standing merely half Jacks' height. As he watched, the backpack started shimmering in a slightly different golden shade than it had been. The small being rose up off the floor and was at Jacks' eye-level in seconds.

"Figures," Jacks said, shaking his head. "You can fly, huh?"

take. wing.

Again, an odd way of putting things. *I guess there must be something lost in translation*, Jacks thought. The creature settled back to the floor and the backpack stopped glowing.

"Listen, I–" Jacks was interrupted by a violent coughing fit which continued for several minutes. By the time it settled down, he spat red mucus into his handkerchief. He looked down to his little guest.

It was gone.

A fluttering of the curtains hanging beneath the sink told Jacks where it had gone. His coughing had scared the little thing. *Loud noises must bother it*, he thought, inanely feeling bad about it, as if it were something he could control. He bent down and parted the curtains again. The small creature was back in its hiding place, looking up at him with those big, black eyes.

hi. The voice sounded in his mind. The creature cocked its head slightly to one side.

Jacks sighed. *This is going to take a while.*

◉

With a little coaxing, Jacks managed to lure the small being out from under the sink and into the living room. He sat down heavily in his recliner. The little creature scrambled up onto the couch and sat there across from him, barely making a dent in the cushion. The two stared at each other like a couple of friends getting ready to catch up on old news.

"Listen," Jacks started, "We are gonna have to give you a name. I have to call you something. Do you have a name?"

name?

"Yes, a name. Mine is Jacks. Jacks. Can you think 'Jacks' to me?"

jacks. The thought came in clear and focused. *jacks.*

"Good," Jacks said. "That's what I'm called when some-body wants me. It's what identifies me as me. Now, how are *you* identified?"

jacks.

Jacks shook his head. "No," he said. "That's me, not you."

me?

"Yes, you. I'm Jacks. You're–"

not? jacks?

This was getting frustrating. He'd have to try something different.

"Are there others like you? The same, but apart from your-self? Companions?" It was obviously intelligent; smart enough to pilot a ship and travel from wherever it came. Surely it could grasp the concept of individualism. "Something that makes you... well, you and only you."

only?

"Yes, only you, and no other." Maybe he was getting somewhere. "Just you."

only.

"Yes, one and apart. You are you and only you." Jacks never thought the notion of understanding mere names could be so difficult. "Only isn't a name, it's something that describes something else."

me. apart. something. else. only. only. only.

"Only? Is that what you want to be called? Only?" Maybe he wasn't getting through after all.

only. only.

"OK. That's kind've strange, but if you wanna be called 'only', then who am I to argue?" *Oh, that's right*, Jacks thought. *The name 'only' is strange... as compared to what? Some alien crashing its UFO into the swamp behind my house, and me rescuing said creature which was now sitting in my living room having a damned conversation, half out loud, half in my head, about, of all things, its name? I think I'm giving the word 'strange' a whole new definition.*

Only was looking at Jacks with a blank look, most likely the lone expression it had. But in Jacks' head, he could sense Only's confusion. It must have gotten bits and pieces of the mental sparring match Jacks just had with himself whether it wanted to or not. *Time to bring this conversation back to earth.* Jacks chuckled at the irony.

"Only," Jacks began. "Are you hurt? Did you get injured last night when your ship crashed?"

not. hurt. jacks.

Jacks smiled to himself. At least Only seemed to grasp the concept of names and called Jacks by his.

jacks? hurt?

Jacks paused for a moment. Was Only asking if Jacks was hurt or mimicking the question Jacks just posed? "No, Only. I'm not hurt. Why are you asking?"

Only pointed its odd fingers at the handkerchief poking out of Jacks' shirt pocket. The one with blood on it that Jacks had wiped from his mouth a few minutes ago.

jacks? hurt? Only repeated.

"No, Only," Jacks hesitated. He didn't know if Only could grasp the idea of terminal cancer at this early stage in their relationship. *Only the basics for now*, Jacks thought. *Too early for the heavy stuff*. "I'm OK. I just get sick sometimes."

understand.

"Only," Jacks started the conversation again. "Where are you from? Why are you here?"

from. up. here. help.

"From up?" Jacks repeated what he'd felt. "From space?"

from. other. place.

"And you're here to help? Help who? All of us? Mankind?"

what? mankind?

"What's mankind? That's us. The human race. The inhabitants of this world." *How do you describe to an alien the definition of mankind?*

others? same? apart? companions?

"Yes. That's it, in a way. But not everybody is considered to be companions to one another. Some are friends, others are enemies." It dawned on Jacks that he was ill-equipped to be an ambassador to an alien race. What if this was a First Contact situation and Jacks screwed it up for all humanity?

people.

"Yes, people." Again Jacks was relieved that Only was catching on. It took the pressure off. Changing the subject, Jacks asked, "Was that your ship that crashed into the swamp last night?"

transport. yes. only. stranded.

Jacks suddenly realized Only couldn't get back to wherever it came from. With his ship at the bottom of the swamp, it couldn't leave earth. "What are you going to do, Only?"

reach. others. same. apart.

Only needed to contact its own race of creatures to come get it. "If you call them, they can come get you. Take you home?"

what? home?

"Home is where you came from," Jacks answered. "It's the place where there are others like yourself. It's the place that makes you feel safe and comfortable. It's that place where you belong."

jacks? home? Only spread its arms open, looking around Jacks' house.

"Yes, this is Jacks' home. This is where I live."

jacks? alone? others? same? apart?

"Yes," Jacks answered hesitantly. "I live here alone. No family. Not for a long time."

now. only.

"Yes, I suppose you're right, Only. You're here now and in my home. I suppose that makes you a guest." Jacks wondered where this was going.

only. safe. only. home.

Jacks looked at his visitor, a small creature from another world, sitting on his couch, basically asking if it could make Jacks' home his own, at least for a little while.

"Yes, Only. I suppose that would be fine, at least until your friends get here to take you back."

what? friends?

"What are friends?" Again, Jacks was floundering for words to answer Only's questions. "Friends are those people that you like and they like you back. Those that help you and keep you safe. Who you can rely on when you need them."

where? jacks'? friends?

"I told you," Jacks said, this time a little short with his answer. "There hasn't been anybody but me around here for a long time. Not since... I don't need anybody. I'm better off by myself."

friends? need? jacks?

"Nobody needs Jacks either. It's better that way."

only. needs. jacks.

Jacks looked over to where the small alien was sitting. He hadn't been told he was needed by anything, by anybody, in quite some time. He didn't know how to react, so he just sat there.

jacks. needs. only.

It wasn't a question. It was a statement.

friends. need. friends.

Something in the back of his mind told Jacks that he was in way over his head.

◙

Jacks could tell by the way the sunlight was slanting through his windows that the morning was gone. The small house was getting stuffy too, likely because there had been more activity inside than there had been for a very long time. He switched on the generator so the air conditioning could cool the place down a bit.

He looked over at his new friend, asleep on the couch. No doubt it was still shaken by last nights' crash. Either that, or the sleep cycle was different for its kind. Only had fallen asleep on the couch not long after it and Jacks finished their conversation. Like he did last night, Jacks draped a light blanket over the small creature. It seemed like the right thing to do, but he really didn't know if it was hot or cold, or if it was even capable of either.

Jacks sat back down in his recliner, watched Only sleeping and tried to come up with a game plan. What the hell was he supposed to do with it? Was he supposed to treat it like a pet? Was he supposed to turn it over to the authorities and let them perform God-knows-what kind of experiments on it?

Jacks reviewed what he knew in his head: It was definitely an extraterrestrial, not some deformed kid or carnie freak show headliner. Its ship fell out of the sky and now resided at the bottom of the swamp. While he was saving its little butt, Jacks could tell the ship wasn't any kind of flying machine of this world. He knew Only wasn't a leader of its race, but rather a technician or a pilot of some kind, most likely here on an exploratory mission. He couldn't tell if Only was a he or a she, or even if there was that distinction among its species. It appeared to be uninjured from the crash. It could communicate with Jacks via telepathy. Jacks was more than a little uncomfortable with that thought, but Only had given its word that it wouldn't pry into Jacks' mind without permission.

And here was the kicker: Jacks didn't know *how* he knew, but he was certain the little alien was peaceful in such a way Jacks couldn't fathom. Just by communicating with it, Jacks felt an unparalleled sense of calmness and innocence. A strange juxtaposition in this harsh world.

As Jacks watched, the little being displayed faint twitches and muscle activity. It was dreaming. It's been said that all intelligent beings dream. Only was definitely dreaming, its eyes moving back and forth underneath the enlarged eyelids. Jacks wondered what alien dreams were like.

Suddenly Only's eyes snapped open. The black orbs were looking directly at Jacks.

visitor.

"What? What do you mean?"

visitor. here.

At that moment, Jacks heard the crunching of a car's tires on the gravel in his driveway. A car was pulling up outside. Only had sensed it and was warning Jacks.

visitor? see? only?

Jacks understood instantly. Only was concerned about being seen by another, possibly hostile human being. Someone who wouldn't understand like Jacks did. And he was right. Anybody coming into his house and seeing a three-foot tall alien sitting on Jacks' couch could definitely be a problem.

Jacks heard the car door shut and the sound of footsteps walking toward his front porch. He looked around for a place for Only to hide. "Under the sink. Back where I found you this morning. Quickly."

what? quick—?

"No time, Only. Get under there now. I don't know who is out there, but I don't think it's a good idea for them to see you." Jacks was a little panicked also by what might happen to *him* if he were found harboring an extraterrestrial.

Jacks crossed the room, took Only's frail hand and led it into the kitchen area. Only evidently got the message and scurried underneath the sink, the curtain falling back in place.

◉

A knock rattled Jacks' doorjamb.

Crossing the room to the door, Jacks glanced back at the sink. Through the part between the two curtains, he could just make out the slight reflection in one of the black eyes. Only was watching intently.

Jacks opened the door to find Deputy Sheriff Balfour raising his hand to knock again. Balfour looked through the screen door. "Hey, Jacks. How you doin'?"

"Douglas," Jacks replied. "What brings you out this way? I know you weren't just in the neighborhood."

"You gonna invite me in, or leave me out here to roast in the heat?" The younger man smiled at Jacks. Balfour was about forty with a married-man's paunch beginning to stretch his polyester uniform top.

"Sure. Sorry. Of course, c'mon in." Jacks opened the door and invited the man through. Jacks furtively looked back to the sink. There was no movement in the curtain below the sink.

"Any chance I could get a glass of water?" Balfour started toward the kitchen sink.

Jacks moved quickly - maybe a little *too* quickly - and intercepted the deputy before he could get too far. "Sure," he said. "I was just gonna offer you a drink."

"So how you doin, Jacks? I never see you in town, so I'm just assuming everything is OK out here. Do you need anything? Any meds or supplies?" Pretty much everyone in Grand Chenier knew about Jacks' condition and that always seemed to piss him off. He didn't need anybody's pity. Nobody was around when he lost Karen and Sarah. And now that he was losing his battle to cancer, he sure as hell didn't need anybody's sympathy.

It must have shown in Jacks' response to the young deputy. "I'm fine, Douglas. Always have been. What can I help you with, anyway?" His tone was sharper than he intended, but right now, he didn't really care. He handed Balfour the glass of ice water.

who? karen? sarah?

Jacks looked abruptly at the deputy. He was pretty sure Only's words were just in his thoughts, but they sounded as clear as if having been spoken from across the room. The deputy's lack of reaction told him what he suspected.

Jacks looked over at the curtain hanging beneath the sink. The part moved ever so slightly, still leaving a crack which could be seen through.

Balfour's gaze followed Jacks to the sink. "Well," he started, "Other than checking on you I was told there was a meteor or something that came down around here last night. The guys at the airport said it lighted up the sky over this way. I was wondering if you saw anything."

Jacks moved into the living room. "Come on in here, Douglas," he said, diverting the deputy's gaze from the kitchen. "Take a load off. Sorry if I was short with you. I'm a little more exhausted than usual."

Balfour moved to the couch where Only had been lying only minutes ago. He sat down, back to the kitchen. Jacks breathed a little easier.

"No problem, Mr. Jacks. I understand." Jacks laughed inwardly. *No, you don't. You couldn't possibly understand.* Balfour continued. "So, did you see anything last night?"

"Nope," Jacks responded, maybe a little too hastily. "I must've been asleep."

"I didn't tell you when they saw it, though. Maybe you were awake."

"Well… when was it?" Jacks was feeling a little trapped, although he knew it was just his imagination.

"Around two in the morning. I was thinking you were maybe awake and–"

"Nope. Like I said, I was asleep. Jesus, Douglas. At two in the morning, *everybody's* asleep." He was being a little too defensive and tried to relieve some of the building tension. "Whaddaya think? I was up doing my shopping on QVC or something? Trying to hit those George Foreman Grill specials?" He laughed and hoped it would be contagious.

Deputy Balfour joined him, although it was more reciprocal than genuine. "No, Jacks. I figgered you were asleep. Just checking, doing my job."

friend? balfour? friend?

Jacks looked toward the sink. The curtain was being pulled back, slightly, by those little alien fingers. He could see more of Only's face. If Balfour chose this moment to turn around...

"No," Jack said, louder than necessary. He stood up. "I mean, no, I didn't see anything. Sorry." *Only, stay put. Stay where you are.* Jacks was thinking this as hard as he could. *C'mon, dammit. Read my thoughts and stay under there.*

The curtains slowly drew back together and were still.

Balfour interpreted Jacks' movement as being dismissive and took the hint. It was obvious he didn't want to be here, asking a dying old man about something that he didn't care anything about. Jacks took the glass from his hand, beaded condensation dripping to the floor.

"Well," Balfour started. "I don't want to overstay—"

"No problem, Douglas," Jacks interrupted. "I'm sure you want to get back at it."

"Of course. I'll let you know what I find out about the meteor or whatever it was."

Or a ship, thought Jacks. "Sounds good, Officer."

Jacks opened the door and saw the deputy out, staying on the front porch and watching his cruiser maneuver the narrow drive. Jacks hoped he didn't act too suspiciously. No doubt the deputy would just attribute his behavior to the disease that was eating away at Jacks' pancreas.

As soon as the car was out of sight, he went back inside, locking the door behind him.

◉

The one thing Only wanted to eat was ice cubes. Jacks tried to convince it to eat something else, trying potato chips, bread, even a beer. Only just wanted ice cubes. It would sip on them delicately, like a hummingbird taking nectar from a flower.

Jacks, on the other hand, was ravenous. Which, in and of itself, was strange. He hadn't much of an appetite in months. The doctors said his hunger would slowly fade until only a meal or two a week would suffice. He would have to force himself to eat right up until the end.

After the second turkey on rye sandwich, along with two PBR's to wash them down, Jacks finally felt full. He hadn't had that sensation in so long; he couldn't remember what it was like to feel his full belly straining against his belt buckle. He supposed the events of last night, coupled with having company, albeit not human, had piqued some part of his brain and convinced his subconscious that life was suddenly worth living again.

He laughed to himself. *Great*, he thought. *I'm going crazy on top of losing the battle to the Big C.*

what? big? c?

Only was looking at Jacks as it was sucking on an ice cube, sitting in its usual place on the couch. He had given it a bowl of ice as a meal. Its black eyes blinked once, side to side.

"Cancer," replied Jacks. "It's a disease which can't be cured. It's something that gets in your body and kills you. Makes you stop living. Makes you dead." The formerly cool room felt stuffy again.

what? dead?

Jacks could've bet good money that particular question was coming. Hell, he had a hard enough time explaining concrete things like people and dirty dishes. How do you describe death to something that might not even be living, in the terrestrial sense of the word?

"It's when you cease to be." Jacks was looking for simple words to describe the difficult concept. He went on.

"On your world, do others like you come into being? Are they born?" *Or hatched for all I know.* "Was there a beginning for you?"

origin. only. was. alpha. in. beginning.

"Alpha? The beginning?" Jacks vaguely felt Only's presence in his head. He didn't say anything and allowed it this time. It was like Only was trying to convey a difficult concept to Jacks and was meeting with the same obstacles. Perhaps putting thoughts in his head was the better way to communicate this concept.

Jacks caught fleeting visions of what he assumed was Only's world, bleached out, overexposed brightness, devoid of details. Here and there he saw spots of brighter white, almost like a flashbulb. And once the flicker subsided, there would be standing in its place another one of Only's kind. *Was this the way they were born? Light upon light?*

alpha.

"OK," said Jacks, a little shaken by the vision. "So y'all come into being... somehow. You have a start, an origin. Then you must have death as well." He was assuming an awful lot. "After some time passes, do your people... go away? Cease to be? Die?"

omega.

Jacks could sense he was again on the right track. Only's mental fingers tickled Jacks' mind again. This time he saw the same stark white environment. Others of Only's kind were moving around, but there was one being standing perfectly still. Jacks wasn't sure he really wanted to see what came next.

"Only, I–" Jacks stopped mid-sentence as the vision became clearer.

In his mind's eye, Jacks watched as the still figure's face slowly raised up, looking skyward. A black spark, the opposite of the white on white flash, suddenly enveloped the small being. A fleeting look of wonder registered on its face and then the blackness blinked out of existence along with the creature. Alien life went on; the others who were milling about didn't even notice.

omega. gone. no. more.

Again reeling from what was happening in his mind, Jacks thought he understood what Only was trying to show him. All he wanted to do was establish some common ground regarding birth and death. Instead he felt like he was witness to more than he bargained for. It was like Only had confided in Jacks, let him in on a secret, allowed him to witness something almost sacred.

"I understand," said Jacks softly. "Your people experience life and death just like we do."

life. death. everywhere.

"Yes, life and death are everywhere." Jacks continued. "I will be... omega soon. I have something wrong with me which can't be fixed and I will die soon. I will become omega."

Jacks could sense Only was understanding what he was telling him. Along with that sensation, he felt sadness.

jacks? omega? alone?

"Yes, Only. I will die alone. And that's fine with me. I don't need anybody around watching me go. I'd rather it be that way than all hooked up to wires and tubes in a hospital."

Only took another ice cube from the bowl and put it to its mouth, all the while watching Jacks as if it expected him to croak at any minute.

"No, Only. I'm not gonna die on you. At least I'm not planning to. Besides, that'd be damned rude of me, dying on a guest in my house." Jacks snorted a laugh. Almost simultaneously, Only snorted the exact same laugh. It was like it and Jacks were connected in some way where external emotions were concerned.

Only gingerly placed the bowl on Jacks' coffee table. It laid its large head on the pillow and shut its eyes. *Naptime again,* thought Jacks. Almost by habit, Jacks rose and draped the blanket over the small creature

The light outside was fading and nighttime would soon fall. Out here in the swamp, it got late early.

Jacks took the time that Only was sleeping to do a few of his routine chores. He relished in the banalities of everyday life. These would be the things he would miss the most when he was gone: The mowing of his small patch of grass with the push mower, weed eating the few stragglers which sprang up from time to time, taking the trash down to the end of the driveway every Thursday morning. He didn't look forward to dying in the least, but simply because it would interrupt his routine.

He looked in on Only one last time before he got started working on his old pick-up. He'd never paid for an oil change in his life and he wasn't about to start now. Only was still asleep on the couch, its oversized eyes darting back and forth under the unusual lids. Again, thought Jacks: *Dreaming of what?*

It took about an hour to drain and change the oil. It was a job he actually looked forward to. It reminded him of the value of working with one's hands and not relying on others to do what he could do perfectly well on his own. The only time he'd ever put himself in anybody else's hands was right after he lost Sarah and Karen. Admittedly, he wasn't much use to anybody then.

◻

After cleaning up and putting everything back in its place in the small garage, Jacks walked around the porch and into the coolness of the living room. He looked over to the couch to see if Only was still sleeping. The couch was empty.

"Only?" Jacks said, not too loud. Only would be able to sense his thoughts whether he shouted or not. "Where are you?"

other. side. sit. place.

Jacks walked around the couch and saw Only sitting in the floor, back resting against the opposite side of the couch, looking at the contents of a box next to it.

Sarah's box.

"Only," Jacks said calmly. "What are you doing?"

found. curious. learn.

"That is not yours, Only." Jacks' emotions were just under the surface. He was doing his best not to get upset with the little creature. Obviously it didn't know any better. After all, it was an explorer of sorts and just doing its job. Jacks was trying to remember where he had put the box for safekeeping. Wherever it had been, Only found it.

"The things in that box are Sarah's," Jacks continued. "They are private things."

not? jacks'? things?

"No, Only. They are not my things. They were my daughter's. She's not here anymore and she doesn't need them."

where? daughter?

Oh God, he thought. *Here it comes.*

"Sarah is dead," Jacks said, very softly. "Omega. Not alive. Gone forever." As he was saying these words, he was doing his best to picture their meanings in his mind, just in case the little bugger was snooping around in there.

Only looked at Jacks with its large, black eyes.

lost?

"No, not lost. Dead and gone. Never coming back."

after? omega? found?

What the *hell* was it talking about? "No, Only. Here on this planet, when you die, that's it. There is no *after*. There is no *found*. There is just nothing."

Only shook its large head, slowly, side to side. Jacks couldn't remember it picking up that gesture.

jacks. wrong.

Jacks stood up, almost angry at the creature. Obviously its planet was quite a bit different than earth. Only's alien *omega* might not be anything like terrestrial death. It could just be a transition period, or a larval stage. It was apparent that Only had no idea what death was.

how?

Such a big word for only three little letters.

"Only, I..."

how?

Jacks had been through this a hundred times it seemed. What was once more, this time to something which was not even of this earth? He sat back down beside his otherworldly visitor.

"Twelve years ago," Jacks began," I was a pretty selfish person. I drank a lot. I didn't get along with people, coworkers, family. I hated myself. I hated life. I was a miserable human being."

earth? varmint?

Jacks smiled. It was picking up on things quickly.

"Yes. Earth varmint. And not a nice one. Not a friendly varmint like you."

Now it was Only's turn to smile. Ever so slightly, the corners of what passed for its mouth turned upward.

"Like I said, I drank a lot. I was out pretty much every night after work, leaving my wife and ten year old daughter alone waiting for me to come staggering home."

karen? sarah?

"Yes. Karen was my wife. We were married for fifteen years. And Sarah was our daughter. They were both beautiful and both deserved a better husband and father than I could ever be."

Jacks hated this part.

"One night I was out drinking and got so drunk the bartender wouldn't let me leave. He even called the sheriff to take me home. The sheriff was on a call and couldn't get away. There were no cabs available at one in the morning. So he called Karen, told her where I was and to come get my sorry ass so he could close up and go home. Karen woke Sarah up and loaded her into the car to come get me. About halfway to pick me up, a pickup truck went left of center and hit her car head on. Karen and Sarah died instantly. At least that's what I kept telling myself. The driver of the truck walked away; he was so drunk the crash didn't affect him at all." Jacks was choked up.

"You see," he managed to say. "My wife and daughter were

killed by a drunk driver on their way to pick up their drunk hus-band and father. It might as well have been me who was driving the truck that killed them."

Only looked at Jacks, then back at the contents of the box. It withdrew a stuffed Big Bird and held it up to Jacks.

"That was Sarah's favorite." Tears were rolling down his face now. "When she was a toddler she would carry it around by holding Big Bird's beak in her mouth. That way she kept both her hands free. Even then, she was a smart kid. I never was able to throw it away after she outgrew it. I put it in the box of her stuff after they died. I forgot I even had it."

Only stood up with the stuffed toy. Standing, it was just taller than Jacks was sitting. It put one of its strange hands on Jacks' shoulder and, with the other, gently placed the toy in Jacks' lap.

sarah's. keep.

Jacks stared down at the toy Big Bird, looking back at him with its buggy eyes.

"Do you like it?" Jacks asked Only.

only. likes. toy.

"Then you go ahead and keep it. I won't be needing it soon and I have a feeling, if Sarah were here, she'd be OK with you taking it. Besides, I bet your people will have a fit trying to fig-ure it out when you bring it home."

only? keep?

"Yes," Jacks said. "Only keep."

In his heart, Jacks knew Sarah would approve.

◙

By the time they finished going through the box, Only had ac-cumulated a pile of toys, trinkets and knick-knacks that Jacks said it could keep. Only seemed pleased with the stash.

Meanwhile, night had snuck up on them. Out in the swamp, away from the lights of small towns and houses, the darkness was absolute. Jacks loved the way there was no light whatsoever, making you rely on the senses God gave you. He flipped on a couple of lights in the house so he and Only could see what they were doing. Jacks made himself some dinner and filled another cup with ice for Only. It was content to suck on the frozen delicacy.

Jacks had a couple of coughing fits, but by now, Only was used to them. It waited patiently for them to pass and would get Jacks a handkerchief when he needed one. If Jacks had been feeling better, he would have been amused to watch the little being lift up by its glowing backpack, flying from the couch into the kitchen and back, almost like a loyal puppy fetching its master's slippers.

Since it was dark and the lights from an approaching car would be seen well in advance of its arrival, Jacks felt it would be safe for the two of them to sit on the porch and relax in the outdoors. He wanted to be as hospitable to his guest as he could be, but prudently. Jacks felt night was the perfect cover.

As they sat in the two rockers (Jacks had no idea why he kept an extra one), Only's eyes appeared to be bigger than ever, seemingly amazed at this alien world. Jacks' eyes had adjusted to the darkness and he could make out the small being's facial expressions. Extraterrestrial or not, Jacks could tell it was in awe of its surroundings.

"Pretty, ain't it?" Jacks said, looking up into the star-filled night sky, feeling like he should make conversation.

pretty?

"Yes," Jacks replied, realizing only too late that he'd once again opened a can of worms and would be relegated to describing the indescribable for the next thirty minutes. He just didn't have it in him right then. He was still exhausted from the previous night's efforts and a full day of entertaining his alien visitor. "Take a look in my head. It's OK this time."

Jacks began thinking about things he thought were pretty. He started with the sky in front of them, stars so plentiful they cast shadows through the trees. Then he pictured a sunset he'd once seen over the Grand Canyon. He followed that with the flowers his mom had grown along the fence when he was a boy. Suddenly his head was filled with images, cascading one upon the other: cute kittens, the American flag, his dad's strong hands lifting him up when he'd fallen off his tricycle, his dad's weak hands which Jacks held as his father passed away, waterfalls, skies so blue they shocked your eyes, the wood grain of his mother's casket, fog licking the surface of a small lake he'd seen when he was stationed in Germany during the war, Sarah's face, Karen's hair, Karen's' face, Sarah's hair, the Aurora Borealis he'd seen from an airplane years ago, the first car he'd ever owned (a '56 Corvair), seashells, a sunrise over the swamp he'd witnessed a week ago when pain had kept him all night, a bald eagle in flight, autumn leaves in endless hues of yellows and oranges from when he'd visited his brother one fall (his brother's *last* fall) in the Virginia mountains, cream mixing with coffee, the purples and whites of the Rocky Mountains touching the underbelly of heaven, the color of rust... All these images flooded his mind from different moments in his life, flashing before him like a mountain stream washing over water-worn rocks. Through it all, he could feel the light tickle of Only observing it in wonder.

pretty?

"Pretty," Jacks said. "At least my version of it. Things I think are pretty may not be so to someone else. That's just how it works in this world."

understand. agree.

Jacks smiled. If nothing else was accomplished by this otherworldly visit, Jacks' idea of what pretty was at least appreciated by his alien guest.

The reverie was short-lived as another racking cough-fit took over Jacks' lungs. This one lasted for a good ten minutes and it was another ten before he could catch his breath. By the time it was over, his kerchief was just about soaked through, looking black and glistening in the moonlight.

Man and alien grew silent again for several minutes.

go. soon. only.

It must have been Only's turn to break the silence. It looked over at Jacks, black eyes reflecting the darkness.

go. soon. only.

"You're leaving soon?" Jacks asked, voice cracking just a bit. He realized he would miss the little critter. "When?"

day. light.

"Tomorrow? You're leaving tomorrow?" Jacks was growing more uncomfortable with the idea of his newfound friend leaving. "How?"

others. same. apart. come.

"Your people are coming to get you tomorrow?" He was trying not to sound upset.

day. at. light.

"In the morning?" Once again, Jacks was saddened by the thought of being all alone. Again.

jacks. come.

There were no question marks in Jacks' head. This was a statement if he'd ever heard one.

"You want me to come with you? Up to where you're from? Back to your planet?" Jacks wasn't sure if that's what Only meant, or if that was its way of saying goodbye.

jacks. come.

"Oughta clear that with your people. I mean, taking back some plant samples and some old toys is one thing, but a whole human being - that might be a little much, dontcha think?" Jacks really wasn't sure how he thought about the situation. He wasn't sure if he should be flattered or a little worried. *Wasn't this how those alien abduction cases always went on the TV shows,* he thought.

He looked over at the small alien, child-like in the large rocking chair. It was looking up at the sky now, likely in anticipation of going home and getting away from this alien environment. Jacks envied it, he now realized. Although it was not of this earth, he knew life when he was around it and this little creature was full of it. The feeling of kindness radiated from Only like the sun, warm on Jacks' skin. Only was *good people.*

"Only," Jacks said, almost in a whisper. "I can't go with you. I'm not like you or your race. Besides, even if I made the trip, I'm going to die soon..." He unconsciously twisted the blood-stained handkerchief in his hands.

Only slowly turned its head toward Jacks and made an uncannily human gesture, putting one of its four fingers up to its mouth, effectively shushing Jacks. Behind that hand, Jacks could once again make out the slightest of smiles on the small alien mouth.

Jacks smiled back. He sure was going to miss his new friend. It was just as well he wouldn't be around for too long after it left. He hated being alone.

They both went back to looking at the night sky; one dying old man, and one creature not of this world, both content with silence and the star-tinged darkness.

Nothing much else was said all the rest of the night.

◙

Bright lights and a strong wind rudely shook Jacks from his sleep. He must have dozed off in the rocker on the porch and had bolted out of it before he even knew he was awake. By the growing morning light, he looked to the source of the commotion in his front yard.

Only's ride was here.

It was definitely a spaceship of some sort, bigger than the one Only had arrived in two nights ago. The shape was similar, though: outer and inner rings around a central spherical body. The color was hard to make out because of its highly reflective surface. It rode on a blanket of bright blue light, hovering just above the ground. Dust was kicking up all around his yard, blinding him. Suddenly, the noise and wind stopped and the ship slowly settled to the ground. A moment later, a doorway appeared on the side of the craft where there had been no apparent seams. A bright, white light shone out from it.

Jacks looked from the ship back to the house, trying to find

Only. It was nowhere to be found. When he turned his attention back to the ship, he saw three of Only's kind hovering in the doorway, silhouetted by the light from within.

Is this actually happening? Is this real? Jacks was trying to convince himself this whole experience with Only wasn't just a dying man's mind going south. He took a step off the porch and started walking toward the ship.

jacks. come.

It was Only. He'd recognize that… that *thought* anywhere. *The hell with it.* He was tired and achy and he didn't even bother turning around to speak directly at the creature. He shut his eyes and answered in his mind.

Only, I've told you I can't go. I couldn't make the trip. Besides, I have this house that I have to—

He turned back to the house and saw Only padding through the door, its arms laden with the prizes and trinkets it had collected during its visit, including the Big Bird.

Which it was carrying in its mouth.

By the beak.

Oh my God.

Jacks glanced over at the two rocking chairs on the porch and saw himself, sitting in one, chin on chest, eyes closed. He realized he was staring at his own dead body in his favorite rocking chair, asleep forever.

He looked back over to Only, the small *child*like creature, carrying her favorite toy just the way she always used to.

Sarah. My Sarah.

Jacks dropped to his knees in the dusty driveway.

My little girl has come to take me home.

As he watched through his tear-filled eyes, Only… Sarah came over to him and gently put her hand on his head. A tingling sensation radiated throughout his body.

daddy. come.

"Yes, baby," Jacks choked out. "Yes."

All this time, it was my baby girl here with me. Jacks thought back in wonder at the last two days, at how the small creature had grown on him for some unknown reason. Of how he had taken to it in the kind of way he thought he'd never be able to feel again. Of a familiarity he couldn't quite place. *God works in mysterious ways.*

Yessireebob.

Somehow he made his way to his feet without realizing it. His little girl was at his side, but at eye level now. Through Jacks' eyes, he no longer saw the outwardly appearance of the alien he had pulled from the wreckage. He was now looking past what he *saw* and gave in to what he *felt*. He looked at where the backpack had been and saw wings.

Angel wings.

Jacks took one last look back at his old ramshackle house, his earthly body peacefully sitting in the rocking chair on the porch. Vaguely, he wondered how long it would take for anybody to discover he was gone.

He turned back to the ship and realized a better description of it would be wheels... a wheel within a wheel, just like Ezekiel had described a millennia ago. The three beings were still in the doorway, hovering, supported by their angelic wings also. It was only when Jacks looked down did he realize his feet were no longer touching the ground. He probably had a set of his own by now.

Smiling, Old Man Jacks took his daughter's hand and started toward heaven.

RESPITE: THE THIRD SIDE

DAZED, NAUSEATED, NOT SURE of my surroundings, I found myself slumped against the wall, the fire still burning to my right. Vaguely, I felt a string of saliva running through my scraggly beard and onto my chest.

The box was still in my lap, its lid open, inviting.

The next side of the box started forming another image, another escape for me. As the new vision began, I thought to myself *twelve sides*.

Counting the insides and the outsides of a box, there are twelve sides.

Twelve stories.

The box has twelve sides...

THE THROW

JAMIE FOUND THE THROW at the flea market, along the back wall which butted up against what was left of the old drive-in movie screen. The flea market had been in business for about ten years now, ever since outdoor movies went the way of dinosaurs, New Coke and the pet rock. They just hadn't yet torn down the screen; it made for amusing discussion and a public conversation piece.

The throw was half-buried in a box of children's clothing and stuffed animals. Just a piece was peeking out, a flash of black and white and gray against the child's colorful garments. But it was enough to capture Jamie's attention. On that visible portion, Jamie could see an eye.

She managed to extract the blanket from the box without the space-holder noticing. The one thing Jamie didn't really care for about flea markets was attracting the attention of the sellers. They always seemed to have something for her to buy that she didn't really need. Or they would engage her in meaningless conversations which went nowhere.

She held the throw up, spread out at arm's length. *How odd*, she thought.

It was a woven blanket, about five feet in length by about four feet in width. It was fairly heavy for a coverlet, meaning it was woven from three threads of cloth instead of the usual two. This usually implied the blanket would have a wider range of colors in the pattern. Not so with this one.

Depicted on the blanket was a Victorian-looking clown. Its face was half-white, half-black from forehead to chin. It wore a gray conical hat ending in a white furry ball. Around its neck was the wide collar usually associated with clowns and mimes: ruffles upon ruffles crisscrossing back and forth, over and over. The clown was wearing what appeared to be a half-white, half-black satin jumper, the black opposing the white half of the clown's face and vice-versa on the other side. Dancing in the background were fairies, sprites, hobgoblins, elves; all things magical which floated in the minds of children. One arm was behind the clown's body, presumably holding a surprise in its hand for the viewing audience. Held in the clown's only visible hand was a single long-stemmed rose, the petals of which were the only color on the entire throw. Blood red.

But the most enrapturing feature was its face. Even split into day and night as it was, the clown's expression was one of sorrow, piercing deep into Jamie's soul. Never before had she seen a face so despondent, so alone. It was hard to say exactly which lone facial feature conveyed this emotion so strongly. Rather, it was a combination of the clown's entire disposition that gnawed at her feelings. Fittingly, and just to make the point, one single solitary tear was rolling down its left cheek.

"Perty, ain't it?" The elderly lady asked, startling Jamie out of her reverie. She was so enraptured that she hadn't even noticed the seller coming up beside her.

"It's unusual," Jamie countered, sensing she would have to endure another round of pressure buying. "What's its story?"

"Oh, no story to speak of," the old lady murmured, just loud enough to be heard. "That throw belonged to my niece years ago. She don't need it nomore."

"Really?" Jamie said, instinctively leaning in so she could hear the old woman better. "Why not?" Jamie asked before thinking. *Great,* she said to herself. *Now I'm stuck here, listening to some long-winded story about this lady's family.*

"She died when she'uz eight. Of the flu. Woulda' been, oh, ought near thirty now, I s'pose. During a snow storm up in the hollars, she got caught wi' th' flu and died. Shame, really. Doctor wuz just 'cross the pass, snowed in like everybody else."

Jamie was silent. She hadn't expected to hear something like that. She'd prepared herself for a boring tale about somebody's girl who had grown up and went away to school, or maybe an account of how the throw was given as an unappreciated gift which got discarded in an attic somewhere. No, she wasn't prepared for what she heard. And her face showed it.

"Now child, don't look like that. It's Ho-kay, really." The

old lady's voice, soft as it was, conveyed sincerity. "She'uz a sickly one, right from the start. It'uz jes' a metter o'time a'fore she woulda' been with Jesus anyhow. Lest that's what the preacher-man said when they put her in th' ground when it finally thawed. I 'member, 'cuz I'uz sittin' right there with her Maw n' Paw. I think they'uz more relieved than anything, her bein' sickly and all."

"I… I'm sorry," Jamie heard herself say in the distance. "I didn't mean…" Her voice trailed off.

"I know, child. Nobody ever means to, it jes' happens." The old woman's Appalachian drawl was soothing, more of a comfort than a language obstacle, almost hypnotizing. "You didn't know. How could you've?"

Jamie tried to compose herself. She hated when she got emotional like this. She was usually one steel-assed bitch, going up against the best and meanest in the corporate world. But lately she would catch herself teary-eyed at the end of sad movies. And recently she found herself longing for more company than her Persian cat could provide.

"How much?" she blurted, not trusting her tongue to much else.

"Oh, darlin, I cain't *sell* that blanket. It's family, ya' know." The old lady backed up a step, obviously upset with the prospect of trading a family heirloom for money. Jamie was certain she wouldn't be taking the throw home with her.

"I'll give you twenty dollars for it." Jamie heard herself getting a little desperate, but didn't know why. "It's dirty and torn. It's certainly worth twenty bucks, isn't it? I mean, it's just being used for padding in your box. You'll take it home and put it back in your basement and it'll be forgotten until you decide you need to get at that box again, right?"

"No, sweetie, no." The old lady seemed genuinely sorry she couldn't bring herself to sell the old throw. "I cain't sell it fer money. Sorry."

"That's OK," said Jamie, telling herself it wasn't really that great of a find. "Couldn't hurt to try, right?" She dropped the throw back into the box, turned away and started down the aisle towards the next booth.

"But…" Jamie heard the old lady say, "I could jes give it to you, eh? That'd be Ho-Kay, wouldn't it?"

Jamie looked back over her shoulder, not really trusting her ears. People selling at flea markets didn't just *give* things away. "What's the catch?"

"Thatcha' clean it up an' mend the holes and patch the worn spots. Thatcha' put it in a special spot in yer home where it can be seen. Thatcha' don't use it fer packin' up stuff in a dusty ol' box. And thatcha' never sell it fer nothin'." The old lady was fighting her own internal battle. Obviously, she was upset about the prospect of parting with the throw; there was definitely sentimental value involved. "Promise?"

"Promise," answered Jamie. And she meant it.

The old woman folded the throw carefully and placed it in Jamie's hands. "It's yours." She seemed relieved somehow.

"Thanks," said Jamie. "Isn't there something–"

"No, child," the old lady whispered. "It's yours now. It's done."

That's a strange way of putting it, Jamie thought.

"Thanks," Jamie said, still a little unsure. "I'll take care of it."

"You do that, sweetie, an' it'll take care of you," the old woman said with a slight smile.

Jamie turned away from the little old lady and her spot in the flea market where she was selling her meager worldly possessions. Until now, Jamie hadn't even noticed what other items the old lady was selling. Her attention had been solely on her newfound prize. But now she saw the woman's inventory.

The old country lady had neatly arranged her things, a sight uncommon in the disorderly world of flea markets. Two long tables were butted together, bookended by racks on which she had hangered clothing. Arranged on those racks were dresses and frocks and sweaters and blouses, each antique in their age, each exquisite in their beauty, each washed (by hand, no doubt) until they were bare thin. On the tables were dozens of hardback and soft cover books, neatly arranged alphabetically, authored by Lovecraft and Keats and Poe and as many others as there were titles. The old lady had lamps and globes and gazing balls and other curiosities. There were statuettes of animals, old wine bottles with macramé coverings, ornate wine glasses, ceramic ashtrays, delicate stained glass panels refracting light, doorknobs so antique they had to have been created around the turn of the century, cookie cutters and cake molds which were incredibly intricate in their design, tins and boxes with what appeared to be hand-painted vignettes on their sides and tops, lampshades featuring delicate motifs which would cast interesting shadows on nearby walls when illuminated. Commonplace mediocrities were displayed together with extraordinary wonders. Making it all the more surreal, she was sandwiched between a guy selling pirated DVDs on one side and a lady touting herbal vitamins on her other.

Jamie looked again at her throw. The teardrop appeared to sparkle on the clown's cheek.

Jamie smiled.

◎

On her way back through the flea market, throw on one arm and a small bag full of used paperbacks on her other, Jamie intended to stop and thank the old lady once more. She walked down the aisle where the old woman had been, but couldn't seem to find her spot. Between the herbalist and the counterfeiter now dwelt a large, tattooed man hawking suggestive airbrush paintings.

"How long has the sweet little lady been gone? The one who was here earlier?" Jamie asked.

"What lady?" the man answered. "I've been here all morning." He blatantly looked her up and down, head to toe. She hated when guys did that sort of shit.

"An hour ago, this little old lady gave me . . ." Jamie

stopped. *This was weird.* "Thanks."

"No, thank you!" The creep was obviously his own best audience. "Come again. And again, if you wanna!"

"Bastard," Jamie muttered as she walked away, aware of his lingering gaze on her ass.

As she thought about it more and more, there was no way the elderly woman could have taken her goods down, packed, left and this guy set his stuff up in just the hour or so she'd been walking around. At least she thought it was impossible. Improbable, perhaps, but not impossible. *Besides*, she reasoned, *the lady likely had somebody helping her.*

That still didn't explain the chill at the base of her neck or the uneasy feeling in the pit of her stomach. That still didn't explain why she was suddenly so attached to a throw she'd just found. That still didn't explain why she had a single tear lingering on her cheek.

Just like the clown's.

◉

After the flea market, Jamie had dinner with Susan, her best friend from college. It was just a coincidence that she and Jamie had ended up in Charlotte after school. Jamie was a Visual Arts Engineer for an industry-leading computer graphics company which had pioneered the animation used by Pixar and others in today's FX-heavy films. Susan worked as a receptionist for a local plastics manufacturing company. They both had the same education and qualifications. They each had different motivation.

Dinner was good. They met at a little Italian restaurant called Vincenzo's on the edge of town. They ate, they talked, they laughed. Most of all, they just needed each other's company. Nothing new.

Jamie drove home toward downtown, deliberately taking the side streets instead of the freeway. She liked smaller streets. They seemed more personal. It was dark by the time she pulled into the parking garage below her apartment building, but the area was well-lit. She felt safe, even with an armload of bags and boxes from the day's shopping excursions.

She lived in an apartment in the heart of downtown. Most of her girlfriends thought she was absolutely nuts to be living right in the middle of street gangs and homeless people. She didn't mind. She relished the thought of a woman like her living right in the center of such chaos. But she wasn't stupid, either. Her apartment was recently wired with an APT home security system. Deluxe model.

The elevator ride from the parking garage to her apartment on the fifth floor was interrupted a couple of times by a flickering overhead light and some weird noises coming from the cable box. While her apartment building wasn't the newest in town, it had been updated in the past decade, giving it a leg up on most of the other comparable mid-city residences.

She unlocked and opened the door to her studio flat. Balancing her packages with one hand, she disarmed the security system with the other. The short beeps which sounded until she was able to punch in the security code always brought Garfield running. He slinked around her calves, his long fur tickling her ankles.

"Hey, dude," Jamie said smiling. Garfield was her bud. "I trust you don't have any jealous lady friends in here waiting to pounce on me?" Again, she was kidding. Garfield had been de-nutted two years ago.

He answered with his distinctive rrrroowll. It seemed at times that he was actually trying to form words and communicate with the unfathomable human species. *God only knew why he'd want to,* Jamie mused.

Jamie flipped on the hall light and walked into the rest of her modest apartment. It had two bedrooms, one of which had been converted into an office. The good sized living room and kitchen were separated by a high bar. It looked just like any other middle-income apartment in any other big city.

She dropped the packages on the couch and practically ran

to the bathroom. Her period had started yesterday and she was feeling particularly uncomfortable. Garfield yelped as she nearly stepped on him in her haste.

She took care of business and lingered on the toilet, lost in the latest issue of *Premiere* magazine. Same old stuff: Bradgelina was off and on again; Robert Downy, Jr. was back in drug rehab; Sean Connery was making another action flick in his midseventies. Hollywood was a soap opera.

After a quick shower, she went directly from the bathroom to her bedroom and got ready for the night. Slipping on her PJ's, she glanced at herself in the mirror. *Not bad for thirty-three,* she thought. It was just a shame that nobody else thought the same thing.

She strolled back into the living room and began going through her flea market bounty, digging to the bottom of her tote. The throw the old lady had given her at the flea market, the one with the beautiful black and white Victorian clown, the one that she'd attached herself to almost immediately, was not there. She turned the bag upside-down, emptying its contents. It wasn't there.

Then, out of the corner of her eye, she saw a black and white shadow. The throw was at least ten feet from the couch, on the floor on the other side of the room, near the window. It was unfolded and configured in such a way that it looked like it had been trying to crawl away. She was reminded of the image of the magic carpet from Disney's *Aladdin,* how it had taken on human characteristics when walking and moving around. It looked like the blanket was trying to get around, to move on its own.

Shit, she thought. *What planet am I from? It's a blanket, for Christ's sake. Here I am giving it human qualities. I must have dropped it on the way in, before I threw the other bags on the couch,* she thought, upset at herself for her overactive imagination.

She didn't acknowledge, or didn't *want* to acknowledge, the fact that the wall with the window was on the opposite side of the room from where she'd entered. To get the blanket over there would have taken a conscious effort on her part.

She reached down and gathered it up, tucking it under her arm. *Tomorrow it gets washed and mended. That is if I don't have to perform an exorcism on it first.* Jamie's sarcastic thoughts were trying to bring her back to reality.

She tossed the throw in the dirty clothes barrel. For good measure, she threw three pairs of jeans on top of it. *There,* she thought, *that ought to keep it in for the night.* She smiled at her own Machiavellian wit. She turned out the apartment lights, set the alarm, and called for Garfield. Together they retired to the bedroom for the night.

Unnoticed behind Jamie on the living room floor, illuminated in the moonlight's glow through the window, was a single scarlet rose petal.

◉

The next day, Monday, started her workweek, just like it had for the past five years. Jamie managed to struggle through the motions, just like the rest of the Charlotte workforce.

Tuesday and Wednesday came and went uneventfully. The highlight of the week as a killer racquetball match at the Y with Susan and drinks afterwards at the local bar to fully counteract the effects of physical exertion.

On Thursday night, after successfully burning leftovers from the Sunday dinner with Susan and nearly setting off the smoke alarm (foiled by quick thinking - the cracking of the living room window next to the fire escape and a speedy disarming of the security system), she finally got around to doing her laundry. By then, the pile had grown substantially. She had actually forgotten about the throw until she came upon it as she was sorting clothes from the hamper.

"Wash, then mend," she said to the throw.

She vaguely considered washing it separately because of the lone red color of the rose petals against the rest of the monochrome palette. She talked herself out of it by rationalizing that the throw had likely been washed dozens of times by a country family who did not know nor care about the nuances of proper laundering. If the red was going to fade, it would have done so long ago.

Three loads later, she filled the dryer, the throw going in with the last load of the night to tumble dry with the rest.

Six o'clock came early, as always, especially on Friday mornings. Jamie stumbled from her bed, rousing Garfield as usual. After a quick trip to the bathroom, she quelled his figure eights around her feet with a can of cat food. She made her way into the laundry room - and froze.

The throw with the clown was hanging up over her dryer, strung between the auxiliary shelves and the top of the door, clothes pins securing it at the corners and in the middle.

The red rose petals were vibrant. The tear on the cheek was poignant. The clown was looking right at her, the way portrait painting stares followed the viewer.

I don't recall hanging it up, she thought. The last she remembered was her throwing it into the dryer with the rest of the blankets and towels. She stood there, stunned.

And then she realized: *Ambien.*

It wouldn't have been the first time she had done something screwy on Ambien. Obviously she had taken her nightly dose, fallen asleep, and then awakened in a stupor, taking on additional housework.

A few months back, she had ordered two pairs of Ralph Lauren pumps, a Coach purse and the Phantom of the Opera soundtrack from Amazon one night after falling asleep. Her issues with Ambien were few and far between. She'd heard about how some people had more severe side effects with this particular sleep aid. From ill-advised texting to imaginary air racing on flying mattresses, the stories ranged from mildly amusing to downright disturbing. Sex with ex-boyfriends, pets locked in closets and late-night bus rides across town were some of the more commonly reported Ambien acid-trips.

Thank God hers were not as severe. And besides, the pumps ended up being really cute, the purse matched the pumps and she'd been meaning to add Gerard Butler's movie version to her Broadway music collection. *A win-win-win in my book*, she thought at the time.

If adding to the Ambien side-effect list was the hanging up of an old antique throw to air dry was as bad as it got, then Jamie felt like she could deal with it.

She unpinned the throw, folded it and draped it across the back of her lounger in front of the TV. She couldn't wait to wrap up in it later in front of a good movie. Maybe even Phantom.

A fast breakfast, a quick change of clothes, a cup of java for the road and Jamie was on her way out the door to work. As she closed the door to lock it, Jamie never thought to glance back at the window across the living room, still slightly open from the night before.

The clown on the throw, however, was facing in that direction, ever on the lookout.

◉

Jamie knew this would be one of *those* Fridays when lunch was cancelled in favor of a New Product Launch meeting for a client on the West Coast. Then, about ten minutes before she was to pack up for the end of the day, one of the Oregon-based CGI startups called her with questions about the latest VR release. Ever helpful, Jamie elected to humor the technician on the phone and talk him down off the metaphorical ledge. Despite the hassle, Jamie felt vindicated in that her job was somewhat important, at least to the clients she helped.

It was past eight o'clock when she pulled into her garage. The concrete structure had fewer cars than normal; weekends tended to send most of the Charlotte natives out of the city. The garage seemed dimly lit and every sound echoed through the large chamber. Also, it seemed like more and more overhead lights needed replacing.

During the elevator ride, Jamie was already thinking about the nice, boring evening which lay ahead of her: a change of clothes into her most frumpy sweatpants, replacing the damned uncomfortable bra and blouse for a more relaxed oversized shirt, a glass of wine and the TV remote. Dinner would come later; she'd had it for the week.

She got off the elevator and walked the few steps to her apartment, unlocking the door and entering, not even bothering to turn on the lights. It was only after a few minutes of putting her briefcase away and calling for Garfield did she realize that she, not only didn't disarm the alarm system, but it wasn't beeping at her to do so.

The flimsy curtains billowing at the open window by the fire escape captured Jamie's attention. That thought was quickly replaced by a loud crack she fleetingly recognized as something hard popping the back of her skull.

As shards of light showered her vision, she was more concerned about where Garfield was hiding than she was about her own demise.

Darkness took over.

Jamie woke to the sound of breaking glass. She was tied up, legs free but her hands bound at the wrists to the headboard of her bed. One bedside lamp was on, dimly illuminating the rest of the room. From her bathroom another sound of shattering glass rang out. The first thing she thought was rape. But if she still had her clothes on, chances were that hadn't happened.

Yet.

Her eyes adapting to the low light, she took in the room a little more. All her dresser drawers had been pulled out completely, clothes and sweaters were thrown about in haste. The mirror on her hutch was shattered in several places, reflecting her jagged image back to her, multifaceted and scared.

"Bitch." It was an almost guttural utterance. She turned her head to see a man emerging from her bathroom, a quick-fold baton in one hand and a plastic garbage bag in the other.

He was tall and skinny, with a black Journey concert t-shirt touting the Revelation album on one side and their 2008 tour schedule on the other. The shirt itself had seen better days; Jamie thought to herself that it was probably a Goodwill purchase. The wearer didn't look old enough to have actually bought it at the concert it was advertising. He had on dirty jeans and crusted work boots, tracking mud wherever he stepped. Most of his blonde hair was stuffed up under a ball cap, one of those flat billed types which looked ridiculous to Jamie. She noted it was an Atlanta Braves hat, bright red with the stylized white 'A' on the front. Appearing to be barely past puberty, the intruder sported a wispy moustache below a particularly hawkish nose.

Jamie doubted she had seen this kid before, but it was possible. Her choice of living in the middle of downtown Charlotte put her in proximity with all kinds of people, from the homeless and derelict, to street vendors and bums. Chances are she had crossed this guy's path somewhere. Now she was paying the price for the location of her apartment.

"Rich bitch like you, livin' on your own here in the city. Lookin' like you do. I bet you make bank one way or the other, don'tcha'. It'll go a lot easier for *one* of us if you just go ahead and give it up now. It may not stop me from enjoying myself along the way, though" he said as he dropped the bag and stared.

"Damn, look at you," he said, breathing strained either from trashing her apartment or from something else, something more primal. She saw him eying her breasts, tracing down to her stomach and beyond. She pulled against the restraints, no doubt her own bras converted into effective bindings. There were no words for how helpless she felt.

"All my money is in the bank, you dumb shit," Jamie said. She was never one to back down, even in the face of improbable odds. "Welcome to the 21st century."

"Now yer talking, baby," he said coming closer, seemingly rising to the challenge. "By the time I'm through with you, you'll not only give me all yer PIN numbers, but you'll be begging for…"

Her bedroom door shuddered. The intruder stopped and looked at where the noise came from. "Who the fuck is that?" he whispered. "Who else is here, bitch?"

Jamie kept quiet. She recognized the sound of Garfield pawing at her bedroom door, demanding to be fed. She wasn't about to let on that the source was an overweight orange fur ball and not a six-six, two-fifty boyfriend. *Yeah, I wish*, she thought.

His attention now more on the door than on his captive, the young man stepped over to it as silently as he thought he could. He put his ear to the faux wood grain and listened.

The sound came again, something between a knock and a scratch. But to the untrained ear, it sounded urgent. And large.

He yanked the door open. Garfield darted in, an orange blur at full gallop, startling the man. He let out a low laugh in relief and turned his back on the door to face Jamie.

"Two pussies for the price of–" Cut off mid-sentence, the kid was jerked back through the door, legs lifted off the ground and snapped out of sight, one dirty sneaker suspended momentarily in mid-air, flung violently from his foot. The red ball cap flew off the kid's head and fell just inside the door jam, the flat bill keeping it at a forty-five degree angle against the frame.

Shocked, Jamie stared at the empty doorway, a black rectangle into the living room beyond. She couldn't see anything past where the light from the nightstand was able to shine. But, she could hear.

The kid was screaming, either in pain or terror. His voice was wet with blood or phlegm, or both. It was a high-pitched shriek which ran goosebumps down Jamie's legs. She could hear thumping and crashing and crunching sounds coming from the other room. She could make out the kid whimpering in agony, pleading under his breath, begging his attacker to please stop. Jamie's benefactor chose to not listen. Instead the sounds of torment and violence became even more frenetic. The kid's voice was cracking and gurgling. She could no longer make out distinct words, but now only heard grunts and groans and snorts and murmurs echoing off the walls. Next came scratching sounds, as if someone were trying to tear through the walls and floor, scraping and scrabbling in vain against the floorboards. Finally, after what was likely only seconds, but seemed like an eternity to Jamie, all sounds from the living room mercifully stopped.

Absolute silence. No breathing or gasping.

Nothing.

Complete and utter silence.

"Hello?" Jamie found her voice. "Who's there?"

Nothing.

"Hey, it's OK, I promise," Jamie said, a little louder this time. "Thank you for saving me. Can you please come in here and help me. I'm tied up. Please."

Still nothing. The doorway to the living room remained dark and quiet. She looked down to the bottom of the door jam and noticed the kid's Braves cap was no longer leaning against the frame. It must have gotten kicked around during the fight.

Garfield jumped up on the bed, startling Jamie who let out a quick scream. She could make out a distinct odor coming from the living room now. It was an organic metallic smell, a mixture of feces and iron.

"Help! Help me!" Jamie's voice began to get louder and bolder. Whether or not someone was in the next room was immaterial at this point. She needed help. *Now.*

As Jamie continued to shout at the top of her lungs, Garfield settled down at her side, purring loudly. The cat watched the edge of the door leading into the living room, a tuft of black and white and gray thread snagged on the frame, gently rocking back and forth until it dislodged itself.

Instead of investigating, Garfield opted for a nap.

◉

Jamie's neighbors finally heard her cries for help and called 911. About an hour after the ordeal began, police arrived and forced their way in. Before they even made it to her bedroom, she could hear them talking amongst themselves, anxiously relaying information over their radios. She couldn't make out specific words, but the tone was one of urgency. She also heard at least one person puking his guts out.

As embarrassing as it was to be found strapped to her own bed, tied up with her own bras, Jamie was grateful to be rescued. Garfield never left her side through the whole ordeal. The paramedics even put him on the gurney with her for the ambulance ride to the hospital.

As they were wheeling Jamie through the living room, the police made a definite attempt to shield her from what they had found when they arrived. A noble gesture, but ineffective. No matter how they tried, the cops couldn't screen her view of the walls and the ceiling. Blood was everywhere, as if someone had thrown blood-filled water balloons indiscriminately all around the room. It was like a party had gotten sadistically out of control.

A gap in the wall of police and paramedics allowed Jamie a glimpse of her would-be assailant. As they rolled her toward the door, she saw him lying on his stomach near her lounger. She saw one socked foot and the other mud-caked boot come into view, followed by the filthy jeans freshly soiled with shit. Finally the black Journey t-shirt which was now ripped even more, a slash of blood obscuring the Las Vegas stop date. The rest of him was covered from the shoulders up.

It took her a minute to realize she was looking at the old throw she'd gotten from the flea market, the tear on the clown's cheek now flecked with blood.

As the paramedics wheeled her out of the apartment, Jamie noticed she couldn't tell where the threads of the red rose on the throw ended and the blood which was staining it began.

Garfield settled in for the ride.

◎

Jamie was released from the hospital the next day. The kid who was robbing the place, the one who had assaulted her and would have probably raped her, was just another of Charlotte's homeless mass, lost in the societal ruin. According to his wallet he had a name, stayed at a local shelter and sometimes showed up on street corners where construction crews rallied the vagrant workforce for day laborers. He had probably been scouting her building for some time, picking out potential robbery prospects and tracking their comings and goings. She was just another random victim, chosen because of where she lived and the fact that she was a female.

As for her unknown protector, the police were less forthcoming. Someone had obviously heard her struggles and had come to her defense, stopping the would-be attacker rather violently. They did not go into detail about what had presumably happened, other than the fact that they would not let her back into her apartment for several days while it was being 'cleaned.' A detective would get in touch with her once she was back on her feet.

Jamie and Garfield stayed the week with Susan. It was a healing experience in both mind and body. Always the good friend, Susan declined to press Jamie about her experience and seemed to be just thankful for a roommate for a while. Susan made a couple of trips to Jamie's to tidy up and do laundry after the police gave the landlord permission to have her do so.

Finally her apartment had been rid of all signs of the assault and Jamie was able to move back in. Cat in tow, she started getting back to her life.

◎

Upon her return, Jamie inspected the bedroom and living room for any signs of what had happened. Whoever cleaned up the mess had done an exceptional job. In fact, new carpet had been laid and new paint covered the walls. All her furniture had been professionally reupholstered. No doubt the owners of the apartment complex were behind this. To maintain a sense of safety, they had gone to great lengths to keep their now highest profile tenant happy. Jamie was thankful; she wasn't going to raise a stink about it, even if it wasn't their fault. After all, she had been the one who had forgotten to close her window that night, allowing the assailant's entry into her apartment. The landlord didn't have anything to do with that.

Jamie appreciated Susan straightening things up. She had taken care of any dishes, refilled the refrigerator and had done Jamie's laundry, all in an effort to help her back on track.

Jamie was able to find all her dishes and clothes and towels. She restocked her shelves and placed the folded clown throw over the back of her lounger, right where it belonged.

◎

The detective showed up two days after Jamie had returned to her apartment. She was still a day or so away from returning to work and facing the inevitable questions. She'd hoped the longer she was away, the more hesitant the inquiries would be into what happened that night.

At just after eight o'clock, Jamie greeted Detective Gibbs at the door, a short, balding older man with the proverbial rumpled shirt and tie askew. She offered him water and he took it, both of them settling down in the living room. The detective sat in one of Jamie's retro sixties high armed chairs. It suited the investigator, she thought. Jamie took the throw off the back of the lounger and wrapped it around herself against the chill of the coming fall night.

"I'll get right to the point, Ms. Wilson," Gibbs began. "I've been a detective for likely longer than you've been alive. We have cases like this all the time. I've seen my share, trust me. Successful, pretty young lady living on her own, assaulted, robbed, nearly…" He struggled with being a gentleman and trying to pick the right words. "Rarely does anybody get hurt. The assailant usually does a quick smash and grab, threatens the homeowner and leaves. Only once was a lady assaulted and, in that case, by the time she was through with him, the perp was the one who wound up in the hospital."

"I understand, detective," Jamie said. "I know I'm extremely lucky." She pulled the throw tighter around her and glanced down at the clown's sad face looking back at her. Over the past couple of days, she had gotten more and more used to his expression. His left arm was ever extended, offering the bright red rose.

"Are you sure you don't have any idea who came to your rescue?" the detective asked, leaning forward slightly. "I know he saved your life and all, but the damage inflicted on the perp—"

"No, sir. I'm sorry but I never saw the person, he never said anything to me. In fact, I can't recall even hearing him enter or leave. The only things I heard were—"

"I know," he interrupted. "We don't need to put you through that again. It sounds like it was a terrifying experience."

"Yes. If it hadn't been for that person, I don't know what would have happened to me." Jamie felt herself getting choked up. She looked back down at her clown's face for comfort, his presented hand with the rose and his other arm behind him. She hadn't noticed until now that there was another spot of color peeking out from behind the clown's grey top. A pattern of red fibers, near where the clown's other hand was hidden with its secret prize.

"The thing is," Gibbs continued, "There was one part of this case that wasn't publicly released, that we've neglected to even tell you about until you had gotten over the trauma from the attack."

Jamie was listening, but was distracted by the throw. A

wrinkle in the fabric was partially obscuring the red design she'd just noticed. Tilting her head to change her viewing perspective, she slowly straightened the concealing fold. She was confused by what she was looking at, partially hidden behind the clown, the red threads looking newly sewn.

"Ms. Wilson. There was something we never found, a piece of this puzzle that remains a mystery. It was the reason why we delayed you from getting back into your apartment for so long." Gibbs wasn't sure he was getting through to her.

Jamie's eyes were intent on the object partially in view from behind her clown's back, to what he was holding in his hand, hiding from sight.

"Ms. Wilson," the detective continued, glancing around. "We never found the kid's head. It was never recovered. We had people go through this apartment from stem to stern and it never showed up."

"What are you saying?" Jamie asked, distractedly, still absorbed by the throw on her lap. "That the head is still here, in my apartment somewhere?" Slow realization was beginning to dawn on her.

"No, Ms. Wilson. In fact, I'm telling you exactly the opposite. The one place we *know* the head is *not* is in this apartment. The blanket covering the perp from the shoulders up was wrapped in such a way that we had no reason to expect the guy's head to be missing." Detective Gibbs nodded in Jamie's direction. "In fact, it was that blanket you have right there—"

Gibbs stopped mid-sentence, looking intently at the throw.

"Ms. Wilson, may I see that blanket please?" he asked.

"It's not a blanket, detective," she corrected him. "It's a throw." Jamie was speaking, but her words seemed disconnected in her mind. "An old lady at the flea market gave it to me a few weeks ago. She insisted it remain a gift and would not let me pay for it. Now I know why."

Jamie extended the throw to the investigator so he could see what she had just discovered. Gibbs leaned forward and saw what Jamie was showing him.

From behind the clown, in the hand in which it was hiding a surprise, a newly sewn bright red baseball cap could be seen, the white Atlanta Braves iconic 'A' just coming into view.

"I think we found the head," Jamie said.

THE THROW

DEATH BE DAMNED

WE MOVED INTO OUR new house two months before we found out my wife was going to die.

I'm sorry, Mr. Williams, there's nothing we can do. The doctor's words stuck in my mind like mud to shoes when coming in from the rain.

I always thought those rainy days weren't good for anything.

Not anymore.

◉

The old house on Mercer Island, just southeast of Seattle, had a history stretching back to the thirties. I had done my research well before we put in an offer, trust me. The *last* thing we needed would be to move into a place which had a bad past. While we liked to watch those ghost hunting shows on The Travel Channel and A&E, I never truly believed in those sorts of things. I didn't *exclude* the possibility, but I wasn't about to believe in something I hadn't personally seen for myself. My wife, however, didn't share my skepticism.

Judy's dad passed away about ten years ago and she swore he was still following her around, giving her comfort in times of need, helping point to good decisions on things. Several times she even claimed to have felt the bed move as if he was sitting on its edge, giving that little shake and shift. While I didn't discourage the feeling she had, I did, at times, feel a little uncomfortable whenever we fooled around, always with the feeling her dad was watching and disapproving of some guy having his way with his little girl. But I was probably just projecting the feelings I would have if the situation was reversed.

We had made a conscious decision even before we got married that we were not planning on having children. Some would disapprove, but we both felt strongly about it. Her father was her rock when he was alive, but he had endured decades of a bad marriage. Judy often said her parents should have gotten divorced before she was even born. *Would have solved a lot of problems, me included,* she would say. Because of the situation she grew up in, Judy carried that baggage with her. It had been an obstacle for her over the years, facilitating wrong turns and poor decisions. Like so many, she was a good person, but scarred by her upbringing.

My parents had busted up long ago when I was just ten. I have very few memories of my mother, just of her screaming at my dad. And I could still see my dad, reeking of booze, popping her on the side of her face.

Funny how bad memories are often more memorable than the good ones.

◎

Judy and I had dated back in high school, a whirl-wind romance which lasted about ten months before I got stupid and thought I was doing her a favor by 'letting her go.' Truth was I was afraid of even the slightest commitment. I had a pretty successful senior year on the basketball court, and I had my sights on playing in college and beyond. But after four years of being a back-up at Vanderbilt, it was apparent the talent pool was stocked with much bigger fish than myself.

Once I realized my chances at professional sports were slim to none, I friended Judy on Facebook and was able to make my way back into her life. The amount of ass-kissing was embarrassing. I didn't deserve it but only by the grace of God did I get her back. We ended up making our home in Fish Hawk, Florida, about twenty miles southeast of Tampa.

I was able to parlay my short-lived basketball career into a job with a decent sized pharmaceutical company as a sales rep. It seems like many who are in sales these days are ex-jocks. Maybe it's the confidence which comes from playing college-level sports. Many employers look specifically for former college athletes to sell their products.

My college coach was able to get me into Horizons Medical, a company which was set to rival Pfizer. Although I had no experience in marketing, with a little training and basic people skills, I was on the fast track to becoming one of their top producers.

Fast-forward a couple of years and I was hand-picked to start up a new sales office in Seattle, Washington.

◎

Investigating real estate histories is relatively easy in today's age of Bing and Google. Even from our home in Florida, I was able to see who had owned the place all the way back to when it was built.

The old house was originally constructed in the early thirties by a restaurant owner who had some property on Mercer Island. He ran a deli on the outskirts of Seattle which was essentially managed by his two sons. He and his wife lived there until 1969 when they both moved to the nursing home in the neighboring town, dying within weeks of each other, both peacefully in their sleep. Their sons rented out the house for about five years until they finally got tired of the landlord hassle and sold it to a young couple with three children. That family lived there for ten years until the husband's job required they move back east. A divorce' moved in next, making it her home for twenty years until she got married (in her seventies!) and moved to Europe with her new husband. It sat empty for the next couple of years until another family of five chose it for their own. They lived there until last year when the wife made an impulsive stock investment of $100 in an obscure oil company in the gulf shortly before their lone rig hit a pocket of oil which had the potential output rivaling that of Alaska's Prudhoe Bay. Within days, her investment paid off ten thousand fold, making her a multimillionaire literally overnight. Two weeks later, she moved her family to Indianapolis and now resides in a mansion on the shores of Lake Charlevoix.

The bottom line was there had been no fatalities, not even any major sicknesses which were tied to the house. Nobody had died there. Usually, if a house was around for as long as this, there would have been at least one death within those walls, either naturally or accidentally. It wasn't the case here. This house was as clean, supernaturally speaking, as they came.

I make this point for a reason. Like I said, my wife believed in ghosts. She believed in the supernatural, paranormal, the occult, ying and yang, hell, even good luck and bad luck. She was convinced there was some sort of an afterlife meant for everyone, whether they believed or not. She was convinced that spirits were among us all the time, whether they could be felt or not. If they were angels or the souls of people who had passed on, she couldn't say. I'm not sure she knew which, nor if it honestly mattered to her. The ultimate outcome, as far as she was concerned, was that there were things in this world which simply could not be explained.

Me? Not so much. I didn't have the faith and, I guess, an imagination active enough to trust in what she believed. We never had words about it or never even got into long discussions. It was just what it was. A thing, like her having blonde hair and me having brown hair. Both convictions were just a part of each of us and made us the people we were.

She believed. I didn't.

That's why I researched the house. To provide some comfort in knowing, at least to her, there were no spirits or lost souls lingering around. It was imperative enough to her that I suspended my beliefs, at least for a while, in order to give her some security. If it was important enough for her to believe in, it was at least as important enough for me to take seriously.

○

Our new home was essentially move-in ready when we arrived on a Tuesday morning with the biggest U-Haul we could find, packed to the brim. We were determined to make only one trip from Tampa to Washington State, so we had every bit of our meager belongings stuffed into that truck, my 4Runner in tow and Judy's Honda.

We didn't have any friends to help us unpack on Mercer Island, so we paid a local moving company. Luckily, it only took a day to get everything in the house. Of course it would probably take us another five years to unpack each and every box. Isn't it funny how we carefully pack things we can't live without, to never unpack them again, realizing only when you come across them at another move, that you still had them? That was us.

We were deliriously happy to be working our asses off, making this new-to-us house our soon-to-be home. We had been married five years and were still very much in love. Even the trials and tribulations of everyday life, the stresses of our jobs and the paying of bills never got to us. We had each other. Sometimes love *is* all that matters.

I had taken a transfer position with the company and had my pick of major cities. It came down to either Phoenix, Arizona or Seattle, Washington. We chose Seattle for no particular reason. As a result, we moved diagonally across the span of the country. We immediately decided to not live in the city and that a short commute maybe wasn't the worst thing for me. I've found having that half-hour or so to unwind after a particularly grueling day was a blessing in terms of keeping a marriage sane.

A realtor we had commissioned via the internet gave us virtual tours of several houses, but I migrated to the one on Mercer Island. Judy didn't care as long as it was a place to make our 'forever home.' The idea of living on an island was something I'd never given any thought, but it intrigued me this time around.

The new position was also a promotion. The best part was that Judy would not have to work anymore and could devote full time to her home-based bakery business. As such, my homecoming present to Judy was to prepare for a second, fully-equipped kitchen, devoted totally to her business, separated from the rest of the house. I was planning to install top-of-the-line appliances and cabinets into the unfinished part of the basement.

Only the best for my girl.

After a few days becoming acclimated to the area and figuring out where things were, both around town and in the house, we had finally settled into a routine. Judy was content to put the final touches on the house, even painting a couple of rooms by herself. I was immersed in the banalities of starting up a new sales office, screening and hiring people, setting up services and putting out feelers.

It was mid-August and hot, particularly so for the northeast. The days were long, especially for us not being used to Pacific Time. Daylight usually stretched well past seven o'clock, capturing the heat until nightfall.

◉

I came home around six one evening after the usual ten hour day. I remember it was a Tuesday because it was exactly two weeks from our first day in the house. Walking through the back door into the kitchen, I was surprised to not smell dinner being prepared. Judy was a hell of a cook and was always making something most people would think were delicacies. To her, those dishes were 'just the usual.' She could bake, she could cook. She was the ultimate foodie.

A little concerned, I looked around the corner into the living room and saw Judy lying on the sofa, blonde hair spilling over the edge of its arm. Despite the August heat, she had a blanket clutched tightly around her. That concerned me even more.

"Judy," I whispered. I never did like waking people up, even when they give me a time to wake them. "Baby, you OK?"

No response, not even movement.

I shook her shoulder, gently. "Judy," I said again, a little more urgently this time. "Are you all right?"

She stirred groggily, coming out of the haze of sleep. "Billy?" It was almost as if she didn't recognize me. "Are you OK?" she asked of me.

"Hey, I'm not the one I'm concerned about right now. Why are you asleep?" It wasn't like her at all to be napping this time of day.

"Head was killing me. I took some Percocet and a muscle-relaxer. Must've knocked me out. What time is it?" She was disoriented and confused.

"A little after six. I just got home"

"Give me a few minutes and I'll get dinner going."

"No," I said. "If you're not feeling well, I'll make something for us."

"Reservations?" At least her sense of humor was still as sharp as ever.

"You wish. No, I'll cook for us," I offered. "Whatcha want?"

"No. Seriously. Reservations," she said, looking me squarely in the eye. "I've had your cooking. I don't need salmonella on top of this headache."

"Think you're funny, don't you?"

"No. I *know* I'm funny." And she was.

I was able to reserve a table at the Melting Pot in the city, her favorite restaurant, for later that evening.

We would never go out for dinner after that night.

I called out from work the next day, telling my assistant that I'd be in after lunch. It would be her first true test of handling the office by herself and I was anxious to see how she'd do.

I was concerned enough about Judy's headache that I contacted the local doctor's office we had targeted to use. We were fortunate enough to had gotten a cancellation and they were able to work us in at eleven that morning. I let Judy sleep a while longer before waking her to get ready.

"How're you feeling?" I asked.

"Headache's still there, just not as severe. More of a dull throb, but not shooting like it was yesterday. We can probably skip the appointment today." If there was anybody in this world who didn't get headaches it was Judy Williams. In all the years we'd been together, this was the first time I'd ever known her to have a headache. And one being so bad as to make herself take pain killers had me even more concerned.

"No. We need to go in at some point anyway, so today's as good as any." She reluctantly agreed.

Since this was our first time at the practice, we went in together to meet the doctor. We chose that office because it had a good mix of male and female doctors. I was more comfortable with a male, and Judy, of course, felt more at ease with a woman doctor.

We met with Dr. Harris, an older, wizened lady and one of the founding doctors at that practice. She listened patiently to what we had to say and admitted her office was woefully under equipped to handle the kind of symptoms Judy was having. She referred us to a specialist, but it would be several days before they could get us in.

After we were finished, I asked Judy if she wanted to grab some lunch, but she declined. Her head wasn't hurting so much as she was just tired from yesterday. All she wanted to do was go home and lay down.

I dropped her off at the house just past noon and asked if I needed to stay with her. Of course she said no, gave me a quick peck on the cheek and tossed an I Love You over her shoulder as she disappeared through the front door.

I drove to the office and was soon immersed fully in my job.

I worked over that evening and got home a little after seven. Rain began about halfway home and, by the time I reached the house, it had turned into a full-fledged downpour. The rains made the twilight fade quicker than usual.

I unlocked the front door and let myself in. There wasn't a light on in the house. There was no smell of dinner long since prepared, ready to be reheated because of my tardiness. The silence was interrupted only by the rain pounding on the tin roof of the old house.

I quietly walked into the living room and saw Judy asleep on the couch. Her breathing was regular and she seemed to be deep in restful slumber. I thought about waking her, but then realized she probably needed sleep more than I needed dinner.

Moving down the hall, I opened the door to the basement. One of the first things I did when we finally got semi-settled was to fashion myself a small Man Cave down there. It really wasn't anything to brag about, but the only room that was already finished in the basement I claimed for my own.

It was small, only about a hundred square feet, with a half-bath attached. I managed to squeeze in an old entertainment center on which sat a TV (one of the old boxy kinds that weighed a ton), an antiquated stereo system which still had a functioning cassette tape player and turntable, a dilapidated Simmons recliner I'd purchased from a Goodwill across town, and a mini-fridge which had just enough room for two six-packs of beer. It wasn't much, but it was my little getaway.

Closing the hall door behind me as quietly as I could, I started down the stairs to the basement. At the bottom of the stairs was a small landing with the Man Cave to my left and the rest of the open, unfinished basement spread out to my right. The washer and dryer, along with the oil furnace and water heater were the only things in that area. We didn't even have moving boxes down there because the house was so big and our possessions so small. At the far end was a door leading to the backyard, the top half of which was glass-paned. I thought to myself that eventually I would need to replace that door with something more secure.

By habit I glanced over into the larger, unlit part of the basement, more as an afterthought than anything else.

In the far corner I saw a muted light.

I was able to make out vague details in the rest of the basement due to the rain-diffused light coming through the outside door. The color of the light from the outside was a bluish grey; the light across the way was a warm amber. The two conflicting colors could not have been coming from the same source.

Thinking this could have been a cell phone left by one of the movers, I stepped off the landing to cross the basement. Immediately I was hit by a pocket of extremely cold air which almost took my breath. It was the last thing I expected to encounter because of the unusually hot summer we were having in Washington State. For the most part, it had been polo shirts and Bermuda shorts since we arrived.

I looked around for the source of the cold air: a fan left on or the door to the outside cracked open allowing the rain-cooled air into the basement. But the air was as still as stone and the door appeared to be securely closed. There was nothing I could find to explain the frigidness.

Turning my attention back to the unknown light, I took several more steps toward it. The coldness of the air did not dissipate and, if anything, intensified. The rain pounding on the outside door was amplified in the cavernous basement which ran the length of the house.

Still several yards from the source of the light, I stopped again. I'd left my cellphone upstairs, so I didn't have the convenient flashlight app or any means of contacting someone if the light turned out to be something more problematic.

Physically shaking, I continued forward, concentrating on the light, trying to determine exactly what it was. It seemed as though I couldn't quite center in on its source; it stayed blurry no matter how I squinted my eyes or turned my head.

Then it almost *snapped* into focus.

About three feet above the concrete floor a disembodied arm from the elbow down to the fingers was suspended in mid-air. And it was holding a book.

Thank God breathing was automatic.

The coldness I had felt now paled in comparison to the literal shiver that went down my spine. *What was I looking at?* It had to have been an illusion created by the rain refracted light coming through the door, forming patterns and dancing along the wall.

I could see through it to the floor and the wavering light from outside. The amber glow seemed to intensify as if the source realized it was now being observed. As I watched, another hand appeared in the air just beyond and slowly turned a page of the book, as if the owner of these spectral hands was passing the time reading on this rainy evening.

The golden light started to fade. But there was one striking characteristic of those hands, one thing I could not shake: They were the most feminine, most delicate hands I had ever seen.

And then they were gone.

◉

"Bill?"

I could hear Judy calling from upstairs. I was still shaking from whatever it was I had just encountered. The coldness had passed and if anything, it felt warmer than usual, my forehead now brandishing beads of sweat.

"I'm in the basement, baby." I raised my voice just enough to be heard from downstairs. "I'll be right up."

I looked back toward the corner. It was as dark as the rest of the basement. There was no unusual light, no ghostly hands leafing through a book. The basement was as ordinary as it could be.

I laughed, mostly to myself. Evidently the long days and my worry about Judy had caught up with me. But I never thought my exhaustion would manifest itself as a vision.

Walking back to the landing, I thought about whether or not to tell Judy. Hearing that her husband was having hallucinations or that there was a ghost in the basement certainly would not help the situation with her head. We had enough worries without adding my overactive imagination to the mix.

I mounted the stairs, went up and into the hallway. Without thinking, I locked the door behind me, something I usually didn't do.

Judy had just woken up and seemed a little out of it again. She told me that within an hour of being dropped off, her head started hurting again, with sharp dagger-like spurts of pain. She'd taken some Tylenol and hit the couch, sleeping this whole time. Evidently the long nap helped because she claimed her head was pain-free at the moment.

She asked if cold cuts would be OK for dinner and that it would be ready in half an hour.

"Grab yourself a beer from downstairs," she said as she walked into the kitchen.

I declined, not wanting to go back down there at the moment. "I'll just have tea."

◉

The evening went well, us having dinner in the living room, watching Food Network (food porn, she called it) and cuddling like old times. Any night like this, where we were just enjoying each other's company and not doing much of anything, Judy liked to call a Date Night. I had forgotten about the incident in the basement.

Eventually the night caught up with us and we retired to the bedroom like any normal couple would. Our lives seemed blissfully perfect in that one moment and, for a while, all our cares and concerns were gone.

We truly became one, like we always did whenever we made love. Ours was a passion, a devotion we shared, unique to us alone. Sure, we both had other lovers years ago, but we'd never connected with any of them on an almost spiritual level the way we did with each other. And when we had intercourse, everything fired on all cylinders. We were so in tune with each other's bodies that we knew exactly what the other wanted, when they wanted it and how to deliver.

With me on my back and Judy straddling me, I recognized her approaching orgasm and I was pacing her body's movements with mine. Her rhythm became more urgent, her breathing more strident as she climaxed. I wasn't far behind.

And then she screamed.

Her hands flew to the top of her head and her face contorted, not in the expected pleasure, but in downright agony. What was supposed to have been the height of sexual release, the best feeling two lovers could share, had quickly turned into a nightmare.

"My head," she cried. "God, Bill... it hurts! Oh, God..."

Judy was fully crying and screaming in pain at the same time. Her hands continued to press against the top of her head. By now we had separated and my satisfaction was long forgotten. I didn't care, though. All I could think of was Judy's pain.

She fell to one side and curled into the fetal position, hands still atop her head. I felt helpless. I covered her naked body with the bed's comforter and held her, praying the pain would quickly subside. We stayed like that for at least a half an hour, Judy rolled into a ball, holding her head, with me holding and comforting her as best I could.

Eventually the pain lessened and I could feel her body finally relax. Fighting the explosion in her head had drained her completely. She was exhausted. So was I. But I was also scared.

What the hell happened? I wondered. I could only guess that, as she came, the pleasure center in her brain became so active it triggered whatever was going on in there. The fact that it manifested itself at that moment, in that situation, at her most vulnerable, was frightening. It had turned her most pleasurable experience into one of blinding pain.

Judy was fading into sleep and I did my best to reassure her. If she was still hurting in the morning, we would go to the emergency room. She agreed, but was so exhausted she would have gone along with anything. I rearranged the covers around her, and slid in myself, next to her, putting as much of my body against hers, attempting to reassure her with my presence. Eventually, I faded as well.

It was the last time Judy and I would ever make love.

The next morning Judy woke up with only a dull headache and told me it wasn't enough to warrant a visit to the ER. I insisted that it scared the crap out of me and we needed to get her checked out. She won the argument, of course, as those of you who are married can attest.

Days which followed were relatively uneventful. My office had finally settled down and things there were proceeding smoothly. I had assembled a strong team and was giving them more and more responsibility. We had just landed our first account in Seattle and things looked promising.

At home we finished unpacking our paltry belongings and began making the house into more of a home, putting our touches here and there. I say ours but I really mean Judy's. She was the one with all the style sense. I would just as soon decorate the whole house with sports posters and neon beer signs like a college dorm room. Thank God Judy had some sense about her.

Although unspoken, her headaches were never far from our thoughts. She would get one occasionally, but they weren't debilitating like those first couple. Usually some Tylenol and a thirty minute nap would take care of them. When they occurred later in the evening, she would just go on to bed earlier than usual. Eventually, 'earlier than usual' pretty much became every night.

We discussed a couple of times canceling the specialist appointment scheduled for the upcoming Monday, but I invariably nixed the idea. *Better be safe than sorry*, I told her on more than one occasion.

How ironic.

One evening, a couple of days before the appointment, Judy had gone on to bed and left me in the living room watching Sports Center. The jock in me refused to die and I couldn't get enough of all types of sports.

The lateness of the hour caught me by surprise and I ended up dozing on the couch in front of the TV. A rumble of thunder woke me up. It must have started raining while I slept.

Something from the direction of the TV caught my eye. Something I hadn't seen in years, since cable and satellite had taken over. Something out of place in this day and electronic age.

Static. Pure snowball white static filled the screen.

I half expected to see the little blonde girl from *Poltergeist* to be sitting in front of the TV, turning her head back to me, saying, "They're heeeeere."

Nowadays, when the cable goes out, TVs generally default to a black or blue screen, stating its intent to reacquire satellites. Other than being a convenient tool in horror movies, static-filled TV screens were a thing of the past.

Picking the remote from my chest where it had lain while I was napping, I started punching buttons.

Nothing. The static remained.

There was no accompanying sound, just an eerie silence and the flickering light casting shadows about the room. It seemed colder, as if a window were open letting in the rain-chilled air.

I got up and started toward the TV, intent on using the manual controls and doing it the old-fashioned way. As I approached the flat screen, the static began behaving differently, likely reacting to the electricity in the air from the storm and whatever interference I was giving off as well.

Thunder sounded from outside again. The rain started pounding harder on the roof and the sweet familiar smell wafted in through the screened windows.

Then, there was another sound. Not thunder.

My name.

"Bill." It was barely more than a whisper, but it seemed to echo in the room.

And it was coming from the TV.

"Bill." Again, more persistent.

I squatted down and looked closely at the TV, still full of snow. Only this time, there was an eye filling the screen. The static had coalesced into wavering patterns forming the image of a single eye. It was indistinct and very faint, but it was there nevertheless. It looked like one of those close-ups from a movie, where the camera starts in tightly on someone's eye, then slowly retracts, revealing the face and surroundings. Until it backs away, you don't know whose eye you are looking at. All you knew was that it was looking back at you.

And this one was looking directly at me.

The eye quivered slightly with the minute movements of life. Then it blinked, just once.

A single teardrop escaped from its corner.

"Bill." It was more of an actual voice this time, a harsh whisper, intent on getting my attention. As my name was said, the static on the screen pulsed and quivered. There was no doubt there was a connection between the image on the screen and the voice I was hearing.

And the voice was female.

As was the eye. Beautifully feminine.

"Who's here?" It was all I could muster at that point. I was in a state of shock, to say the least. I mean, after all, I was talking to my TV. "Who is it?"

"I am here." Again, back to a whisper, barely audible above the rain slapping at the windows.

A lightning slash lit up the room and the boom of thunder shook the house this time. Together with the TV freaking me out, I was suddenly aware of how full my bladder was. I considered myself lucky that I hadn't pissed my pants right there in the living room.

The TV blinked with the lightning and suddenly I was staring at Stu Scott recapping the Yankees-Sox game from earlier in the evening. The static was gone. The eye was gone. The voice was gone, replaced by the bantering between sportscasters.

It was almost as if it had never happened. But the goose bumps on my arms and the hair on the back of my neck standing at attention begged to differ.

I heard the ceiling above me creak with the sound of footsteps. The loud thunder had probably woken Judy and she was most likely coming down to see where I was since my side of the bed hadn't been rustled yet that night.

"Billy? Are you OK?" Her voice echoed down the stairs.

"Yeah, baby. I'm just coming up. Let me turn off everything down here." I looked around for the remote.

"OK. I'm going back to bed then." I could trace the sound of her soft footsteps from the upstairs hall back into the bedroom. She'd probably be back asleep before I made it up there.

I gathered my beer bottle and bag of chips from next to the couch and took them into the kitchen. I made a quick pit stop in the bathroom and returned to the living room. I warily looked over at the TV, still shaken from what happened. By now ESPN had gone to a commercial and Lou Holtz was hawking Ensure. The picture was a clear as it could be, free of static.

I found the remote on the couch and pointed it at the TV to shut it and the cable box down. Before I could press the Power button, the TV and cable switched off abruptly. Normally strange, but after what I had seen, I took it in stride. A wiring problem *had* to be the source of what happened. There was no other explanation.

Putting the remote in the caddy and switching off the lamp, I turned in the darkness and started toward the stairs.

Behind me, a woman whispered, faintly, "Goodnight."

There was no way in hell I was going to look back. I continued walking and didn't answer.

I went upstairs and crawled into bed with my wife, now snoring softly, blissfully asleep.

It was some time before I managed to join her.

Monday arrived quickly. The rest of the weekend had passed without another headache and, thank God, without another one of my hallucinations.

Her appointment was scheduled for ten o'clock and it was in the heart of Seattle. The name of the practice was the Northwest Neurological Clinic, mundane in any book. But, as is my habit, I had done the research and it was the best in Seattle. Plus, they were able to get us in quickly based on Dr. Harris' recommendation.

We filled out the usual paperwork and were soon back in the exam room. They had Judy change into the typical hospital gown (strange I thought, since the problem was with her head) and gave her warm blankets to ease the usual chill found in doctors' offices.

Within a few minutes one of the neurologists came in and introduced himself as Dr. Phillips. He was tall, lanky, most likely a weekend marathoner and fitness buff. He was as friendly as we could have possibly asked for and ran us through a series of questions, relaxing us as best he could, considering the reason for the visit.

With the questions out of the way, he personally took Judy to the back of the building for a battery of X-rays. I waited in the exam room, reading on my kindle, and within an hour Judy was back, this time with one of the nurses. She was told to dress and that Dr. Phillips would be back in a few minutes. She did, and he was. The conclusion from this visit was that he would look at the X-ray film within the next day or two and get back with us.

We left the office in high spirits, calmed by the effect the office and the neurologist had on us. It was good feeling and we both felt positive about the appointment.

I asked Judy if she wanted to go back home while I went to work, but she decided to go in with me. There was an outlet mall next door to our building and she said she'd like to do a little window shopping.

We had lunch on the way in. I went to work and Judy went shopping. Life felt normal again.

◉

The next morning, before my alarm could sound, I was awakened by Judy crying in her sleep. She was flailing around, twisting the covers, sweating profusely. Her hands were clamped to each side of her head, no doubt the source of the pain. Her head was killing her again.

As gently as I could, I shook her awake. She started crying even more loudly.

"Bill, I'm scared." Her eyes were pleading with me to make the pain stop. "It feels like someone is taking an ice pick to my head, jabbing it over and over..." Her words trailed off into her sobs.

"What do you need?" I asked, hoping she'd have some migraine medicine around. "Baby, how can I help?"

"Take my head off," she said, still crying. "At least the pain would be gone."

"No can do, baby," I said, hoping my calmness would rub off on her and she could relax. "I like your head just where it is. Works better that way."

I fetched a couple of Tylenol and we lay in bed with me holding her, the tears slowly getting out of her system. Soon she was back to sleep and I stayed with her for another hour. Eventually I got up, went downstairs and called the office, telling my assistant that I would be late again. I decided it would be better to just stay downstairs and let Judy sleep. I made a pot of coffee, grabbed the newspaper from the sidewalk, and settled in on the couch.

At exactly nine o'clock my cell phone rang. It was Dr. Phillips' nurse. He wanted Judy back in the office this morning to discuss the results of yesterday's X-rays.

"Isn't that a little quick?" I asked. "We were just there yesterday."

"I know Mr. Williams." Her voice was professional but polite. "Dr. Phillips has cleared his ten o'clock slot for you. Can you make it?"

I told her we could and hung up. An ominous feeling set in. *Why would the doctor call us back to his office, just twenty-four hours after seeing us?* I didn't like this at all.

I went back upstairs and woke Judy. Again, she seemed disoriented, obviously still in pain. I told her what the nurse had said and that we needed to get ready to go. She was lethargic enough that I had to literally help her into her clothes.

She softly cried the whole time we were getting ready.

◉

By the time we got to the doctor's office, Judy's headache was manageable. We were taken straight back to the exam room as soon as we got there. Within minutes, Dr. Phillips joined us. He sat on the low stool next to a flat screen monitor. The room seemed colder than it probably was.

"I'll get right to the point," he said, fully professional now. The sense of relaxation from yesterday had been replaced with one of tenseness and edginess.

"Yesterday's X-rays showed us something unexpected," he continued. "It's better if I just show you." He flipped on the monitor.

The display came up quickly. It was obviously the X-ray of Judy's head, taken from the side. You could make out her optical voids, the nose and the roundness of her head.

I heard Judy gasp. Evidently she had 'gotten right to the point' quicker than I had.

Dead center in the cranium, where the haziness of her brain

shown through, there was a defined ball that appeared to fill up almost a quarter of that cavity.

All the air had been sucked out of the room. It felt like I was breathing vacuum.

"I know it looks bad," said Dr. Phillips. "That's why we brought you back in as soon as we could. We need to get you to—"

"Looks bad?" someone with my voice said, in the distance. "*Looks* bad? What the hell *is* it?"

"Billy," Judy said quietly. "Let's see what the doctor has for us." She was as calm as I was upset.

Dr. Phillips continued, skirting past my interruption as if he knew it was my anxiety talking, not me. "We need to get a CAT scan on you today. I've contacted the Seattle Regional Medical Center and they are ready to take you as soon as you can get there."

"What is it, doc?" I asked again.

"We don't know which is why we need that CAT scan ASAP," Phillips answered patiently. "It could be anything from a cyst to just a group of dense blood vessels blocking the X-ray. We can't jump to any conclusion until we see exactly what's happening in Judy's head. One thing is certain," he said, "I'm pretty sure it's the source of her headaches."

I bit my tongue before a *No shit, Sherlock* came out. Thankfully Judy was keeping her composure.

"Give us directions, please doctor," she said, still calm. "We can go right now."

◎

It was cancer.

Two weeks after rushing Judy to the hospital for the first CAT scan, and the beginning of many tests, Dr. Phillips gave us the news. We had spent those two weeks at the hospital virtually every day. Judy was checked in and out several times. She was poked and prodded, samples taken, tests performed, over and over and over. And it all culminated with us sitting in Dr. Phillips' office on a cloudy afternoon, receiving the news we both suspected, but neither had verbalized.

It was cancer.

A brain tumor. Malignant.

And it was inoperable.

Dr. Phillips went over our options. Of course, to start with, there was radiation treatment to try and selectively target the cancer cells with ten to thirty doses administered over several weeks. His description of the various types of radiation went unregistered by me, and, I suspect by Judy as well. At the same time chemotherapy would be attempted, administering a combination of drugs along with the radiation treatments. Combining the two would be our best bet to beat this thing. He also mentioned some alternative therapies, such as external beam radiation and directed laser focus, which we could explore if the conventional options failed to yield results.

But… it was cancer.

I knew Judy and I knew what she was thinking. She had no intention of spending what could possibly be her last days on this earth sicker than a dog. She had always been full of life. If this was her fate, then she'd face her death with the same zeal she had lived. She would throw Life into Death's face and laugh at him.

We discussed these options with Dr. Phillips. We discussed no options with him as well. It wasn't as if Judy was giving up, but considering the potential survival rate from this type of brain tumor, it was as viable an approach as any. Dr. Phillips understood and left us alone for a few minutes to talk about things neither of us wanted to talk about.

"I love you," Judy said. "Always have, Bill. Always will."

"I love you, too, baby." I was getting choked up already, my throat constricting and tears stinging my already cried-out eyes. "We need to fight–"

"We need to be reasonable," she interrupted. "We both know that no matter what they do, whatever kind of beams they shoot into my head, whatever concoction of drugs they pump into me, it'll turn out the same in the end. I'd rather prepare for that than hide behind some false hopes."

How in the world did I deserve such a woman? Her strength and inner resolve had always astounded me. This was such an occasion. Here she was, the one with a death sentence buried deep in her skull, and *she* was consoling *me*. I felt almost ashamed and looked down, watching my tears fall to the floor.

"Here's what I want," she continued. "I'm not one to just lie down and not try. Let's give the radiation therapy a week and see if it has any effect. If it does, we continue. If not..."

She gently cupped my chin, bringing my head up, locking my eyes with hers.

"If not, then *we* face this thing *together*. It's always been Team Williams and I don't expect that to change just because one of us might not be around. Give up on me now, dipshit, and I may just come back and haunt your ass."

Bless her heart; Judy always did have a way with words.

Dr. Phillips gave us the typical talk about the advantages and disadvantages of both decisions. He personally set up the radiation appointments for us and offered to be there if we needed him.

Judy went to the therapies. I went with her to all of them. My office could run itself. After nine days another CAT scan was done to see if the radiation was affecting the tumor.

It had.

It was four millimeters larger.

The hardest decision of our lives had just become a much easier one to make. They would give Judy the strongest medicines possible to treat the pain of her headaches, but we would no longer pursue treatment. Without treatment, and a tumor of that size and still growing, Dr. Phillips gave her six weeks at best.

Judy was going to die.

◉

Neither of us had any family to speak of. We were alone in a new city with just my coworkers and a couple of friends Judy had made at the local gym.

My company was extremely understanding. They sent in a regional manager from Denver to look after the office until... well, until it was over. It would be there when I was ready to return. My staff rose to the occasion and kept doing their jobs admirably. They insisted I take all the time I needed. I continued to go into the office, if only for a few hours, a couple of times a week. Judy made sure I didn't isolate myself. It would be harder *after* if I did. Of course, I did what she told me to do. *How does a man say 'No' to his dying wife?*

She kept busy around the house, continuing to put her touches on everything. She knew that after she was gone, I'd be seeing her influence everywhere in our home. She wanted to keep it that way. The only thing we put on hold were the plans for her baking business. The tragedies of unrealized dreams are some of the worst, and most common, of all of life's unfairness.

The medicine Dr. Phillips prescribed (I can't even remember its name now) seemed to work most of the time. There were no more episodes like on the night we made love, no debilitating pain. Most of her headaches now were relatively minor but persistent. I think she was OK with that.

However, her memory started slipping, and she sometimes got dizzy when standing. Most nights she went to bed early and alone. Even those nights I joined her, in bed by nine, I waited until she was asleep, then went back downstairs to numb myself with a beer and some mindless television.

◉

One rainy evening a week later, after putting Judy to bed and retreating to my room in the basement, I sat in my recliner listening to some old vinyls I had: Elton John, The Doobies, Jim Croce. I didn't have the music very loud because I wanted to hear if Judy needed anything. We bought a baby monitor and put it in our room. I took the receiver with me wherever I went around the house. I wanted to be able to respond in case she needed anything, in case something happened.

I could hear her gentle breathing across the monitor, only interrupted by the occasional soft snore like she sometimes did. The monitor also picked up the sound of the rain pelting the windows in our room, echoing across the hardwood floor of our bedroom. I felt some comfort in hearing her sleeping noises, knowing I was still not alone.

The second beer from my mini-fridge reminded me that I had to use the bathroom. I went into the half bath off my Man Cave to do my business, leaving the door open so I could hear the monitor. I was looking in the mirror as I was washing my hands.

I saw movement. Behind me, reflected in the mirror, the door was slowly closing, taking its time. As I watched, it shut itself with a faint *snick*.

Suddenly, I was surrounded by cold air. It was like taking a plunge into an icy creek in the winter. It felt like the air had been sucked from my lungs. I was rooted in place, staring mutely in the mirror at the reflection of the shut door behind me. My focus shifted to myself in the mirror and I could see my breath in the cold air.

As I watched, one faint and translucent hand slowly came from behind my right shoulder and slid down my chest. Then, from my left side, another hand reached around my waist and across my stomach. Again the hands and arms were delicate, feminine. But firm; I could feel their pressure and could even see in the mirror my shirt wrinkling and bunching from the path they were leaving.

I looked down, expecting to see those ghostly hands on me. There were no hands. My shirt was moving around as if there were someone putting their hands on me, but there were no hands. Looking back in the mirror, they were there, lovingly and slowly moving back and forth.

I was frozen in place, both from the temperature and the sheer terror I was experiencing. Then, in the midst of all that cold, I felt a warm breath on my neck, followed by a long, lingering kiss on the side of my throat.

The hand on my stomach began moving downward toward my crotch. I could feel its touch as it teased along my lower stomach. As I watched in the mirror, it slowly began caressing me, gently massaging and tugging through my jeans. It had been so long since Judy and I had been intimate and I felt myself beginning to get an erection. A moan escaped my lips and my eyes closed in pleasure.

Then they snapped back open. *What was going on?* I turned around quickly, not sure of what I was expecting to see. There was nothing there but the door. The *open* door. *Had it opened back up on its own? Or had it ever been closed?*

I looked back into the mirror. The hands were gone. The temperature had returned to normal. And I was standing there with a chubby brought on by getting felt up by a ghost. A quick laugh escaped my lips. It would have been comical if I hadn't been so terrified.

Was I truly being haunted by a frisky female ghost? The house was clean; I made sure of that before we bought it. And there was no ancient Indian burial ground under the foundation. *No, I don't believe in ghosts, remember?* The stress of Judy's condition must have been getting to me.

I quickly splashed my face with water and walked back into my den. Through the monitor I could hear the bedroom floor creaking as Judy had gotten up, probably to use the bathroom.

I plopped down into my recliner, still in shock from this latest encounter. It was the third time something inexplicable had happened to me in this house since we moved in: The basement, the TV and just now in the bathroom.

I thought again about talking to Judy about it, mainly because she was a believer in the supernatural and I wasn't. But on top of everything else that was happening, I didn't want her to be stressed out, worrying over something which, in my mind, didn't really exist. And besides, if I went into detail about to-night's encounter, she'd think I was either going crazy or was a horny pervert. Or both.

No, I decided. Better to let her be ignorant to this part of what was going on and deal with it myself. No doubt after this was all over, I'd need to seek professional help anyway.

Sanity is fleeting, even among the sane.

It had been four weeks since Judy was diagnosed. We'd stopped the radiation treatment a week after that and was now purely on pain management. It was working, but she was steadily getting weaker as the days passed. Short term memory was spotty. She was unsteady on her feet almost all the time. There was even some slurred speech and vision issues now, mostly an inconven-ience, but persistent enough to remind us of the inevitable.

Judy slept a lot then, napping an hour or two several times through the day, then sleeping mostly through the night. Curi-ously enough, her already metaphorically tiny bladder had got-ten even smaller. Dr. Phillips told us the tumor was likely press-ing on the area of the brain which regulated bodily functions and, for some reason, had picked bladder control to mess with. She couldn't sleep through the night any more without getting up at least a couple of times to go to the bathroom.

Dr. Phillips was great. We had a standing appointment at his office every Monday morning, and he personally called a couple of times a week to check on us. At no time during all this did he try and talk us into resuming treatment. I suppose he'd seen enough of these types of cases to know when enough was enough.

Judy and I finally began talking about what I was going to do after she was gone. She dragged me into those conversations; it was the *last* thing I wanted to talk about, but obviously the most important thing *to* talk about. The house and the cars would all be paid off from the insurance money, if I wanted to stay. I didn't have anywhere else to go, I told her. *Besides*, I kept to myself, *I needed to stay close by so I could visit her grave often.*

We never brought up me moving onto any other relationship after she was gone. We both knew neither of us wanted that, but also knew neither of us truly had any say over our destinies. What was happening to Judy was a prime example. We hadn't been in control up until now; why should that change in the future?

Those were the saddest talks any couple could have, knowing one would be leaving and the other would be staying behind. Tears flowed freely until there weren't any left. We were both scared of what lay ahead: Judy into the unknown and me into a future without her.

If it was possible, we became even closer in those last few days.

◉

I came to bed with Judy on the night she died.

It was Friday evening, early, around nine thirty, but I didn't care. She wanted my company with her, to be held and rocked to sleep like a child. I obliged, kissing her gently on the cheek and telling her I'd always love her.

I made sure she was asleep and breathing normally. I considered getting up and going downstairs, but decided against it. This was where I belonged. I spooned up behind her and was soon asleep myself.

I was awakened some time later by Judy getting up to go to the bathroom. In my sleep I had rolled over and was now facing the clock on my nightstand. It was just after three in the morning.

I turned my head and could just make out Judy in the moonlight, almost angelic, padding to the bathroom, trying not to wake me. I could smell the rain through the screened windows.

"You OK, baby?" I asked.

"Shhhhh," she whispered, as if whispering would keep from waking me although I was already awake. "Just gotta go potty."

"OK. Love you," I said. We told each other that all the time, even when we'd just said it a few minutes before.

"I love you too, Bill." And she slipped silently into the bathroom.

I was asleep before she returned and never felt her get back into bed.

I woke the next morning, Saturday, around eight. I was usually an earlier riser; my idea of sleeping in was staying in bed until nine at the latest. I looked over at Judy, still snuggled up on her side, under the blankets, turned away from me.

Getting out of bed, I quietly walked around to Judy's side of the bed, intending to let her sleep as long as she wanted. I looked down at her face, as peaceful as I'd ever seen it, even with a hint of a smile. I bent down to kiss her on the cheek, slowly so as to not wake her.

Her cheek was cold. Ice cold.

I raised back up quickly and my hand instinctively went to my lips. *No. Not yet.*

"Judy," I said, urgently shaking her shoulder. "Wake up, baby. Wake up!" Tears started stinging my eyes. My breathing accelerated. My throat constricted. *Oh my God.*

Judy had died during the night, in her sleep.

I looked again at her face. She was as beautiful as ever. I now noticed the slight grayish pallor of her skin. I couldn't stop looking at her, peacefully asleep.

But I knew this was more than sleep.

◉

I phoned Dr. Phillips, the only person I knew to call. He must have known what had happened because I was calling him so early on a Saturday morning. Within twenty minutes he was at my front door, on his cell phone making arrangements for my wife. He took care of everything, including calling the undertakers and the hospital. Within an hour, an ambulance arrived, a non-urgent call.

Without me in the room, Dr. Phillips examined Judy's body. He came downstairs to tell me that it definitely looked like she passed in her sleep, most likely painlessly. From what he could ascertain, it appeared she died before midnight. I thought back to when she woke me on her way to the bathroom. I could have sworn the clock read three o'clock. Because it didn't matter in the scheme of things, I dismissed the thought.

We'd all agreed earlier, Judy, myself and the doctor, that her brain be donated to the local clinic in hopes of learning something from what killed her. She would be taken to the hospital, the procedure performed and then she would be transferred to the funeral home the next day.

I remember asking the attendants to please be gentle with her.

◉

Three days later we had Judy's funeral. She was buried in a nice, small, peaceful cemetery about two miles from our house. There were only a handful of people there: myself, Dr. Phillips, his wife, my office staff and my college coach who had helped me get the job which had eventually transferred us to Seattle. He flew in the day before. It was good to see him.

It was a short ceremony, concentrating on her life, not her death. Everyone agreed she'd been taken well before her time and that she wasn't in pain anymore. She was in a better place they said.

Dr. Phillips and his wife had stayed with me the few days leading up to her funeral, but they couldn't stay forever. They spent another hour at the house after the funeral, along with my coach. Eventually everyone had their own lives to lead and they were soon gone, leaving me to myself in the world's loneliest home.

I walked back into the living room and looked at the couch where I had made my bed since Judy died. It just didn't seem right, sleeping in our bed without her. But sooner or later, I told myself, I would have to go back up there and cope with her loss. Tonight was as good as any.

I piddled around for the rest of the evening, looking through photos, running my hands across Judy's dresses still hanging in the closet, pulling them close to smell her perfume lingering on her clothes.

It had started raining again. That, combined with the past several days of grief soon had me getting ready for sleep. Reluctantly I climbed into my side of bed, habitually being as gentle as I could so as to not shake the bed too much. Old habits.

I went to sleep with my arm stretched out onto Judy's side of the bed, touching nothing but sheet.

◉

Later that night, still half asleep, I could feel the bed slightly shift like it did when Judy would come back to bed after a 'potty break' as she used to call it. I was out of it, groggy and obviously more asleep than awake; I must have been dreaming. I could almost feel Judy's arms wrapping around me, cuddling up to my back, comforting both her and me with that feeling only two lovers know, bodies pressed against each other's. I could feel her lips on the back of my neck, her breath soft and warm...

This was no dream.

I shot out of bed with a scream, shaking, terrified. In the faint light coming from the rainy windows I could see the covers moving as if somebody was underneath them. I could make out what appeared to be long hair on the pillow, its light-hued color indistinguishable in the moonlight.

The ghost or spirit or whatever you wanted to call it had come to visit for the fourth time. But my terror was quickly turning to anger. *How dare this entity come into my house again, especially now, just after my wife had died.*

In fact, I was downright pissed.

"Get out of here," I shouted. "Leave me the fuck alone!"

The shape shifted slightly under the covers, recoiled.

"I don't know who you are or where the hell you came from, but I want you out of here *now!*"

I could hear soft sobbing noises coming from the bed. A woman's cry.

"I'm sorry," I continued angrily "But I don't want you here anymore. I'm tired of you haunting me or whatever sick supernatural shit this is. And now you have the *nerve* to climb into bed with me, the bed that my wife and I shared until she died last week? I want you *gone*! Forever!"

And with that, the crying stopped.

It finally occurred to me to turn on the light.

The shape was gone. But there was still a depression left in my wife's pillow where its ghostly head had lain. That pissed me off even more. I grabbed her pillow and fluffed it violently, removing whatever trace there had been of the unholy visitor.

I snatched up my own pillow and went back downstairs to the couch. I knew it had been a bad idea to return to our bed so soon.

◉

Two days later I was in my office, trying to get back to some semblance of a routine. I still had a job to do and the company was depending on me. I needed to shake off my own tragedy and come back to the world.

Evidently my temper tantrum the other night had worked. There had been no other visits from the female spirit who had been so persistent with me before and after my wife's death. I guess I had been angry enough to have performed my own little exorcism of sorts. I supposed everything I needed was there: the shouting, the cursing, the admonishment to leave and never return. Everything but the holy water; maybe the rain had been a good substitute.

Mid-afternoon I got a call from Dr. Phillips. I assumed he was calling to check up on me. That wasn't the case.

"Bill," he said. "Can you meet me at my office this evening after work?" He sounded odd. "We need to talk."

"Sure, doc," I said. "Can you give me an idea of what this is about?"

"It's better if I just show you, OK? Six o'clock?"

"Sure, doc. I'll be there." And he hung up.

Needless to say, for the rest of the afternoon, I was even more useless than normal.

◻

"I'll get right to the point," he said, eerily reminiscent of the conversation he had with us several weeks ago when all this started. "I have the results of the examination of your wife's brain."

"Do I really need to hear this?" I asked.

"Yes, you do. You must." This was beginning to get a little upsetting and strange at the same time. "You need to know what we found."

"It's not going to help, if that's what you're thinking, doc." The man had helped me through a lot. Listening was the least I could do.

He went on. "It's called an astrocytoma brain tumor. You saw how big it was in the first X-rays and CAT scans. After a week of radiation therapy it continued to grow. By the time of her death, it had consumed almost forty percent of Judy's brain. That's what caused her to die."

I wasn't interested in this posthumous oncology lesson. My

wife had a brain tumor. It was big. It killed her. What did Dr. Phillips have to gain by telling me all of this?

"Where are you going with this, doc?"

"Bear with me, Bill. Just hear me out." He seemed almost to be pleading with me. "It's important." I nodded and he continued.

"Yes, the size of the tumor eventually got the better of your wife's brain, shut down her systems and she died. But it's not her passing that I want to talk to you about. I want to discuss the weeks leading up to her death, after the diagnosis was given and treatment was started.

"We didn't know just how much it had spread until we were able to physically *see* the tumor itself. It had tendrils, hundreds of them, running out from the central mass, almost like an octopus with dozens of tentacles branching into dozens of other tentacles. It spread throughout Judy's brain, stimulating unknown areas whose functions scientists can only speculate about. We still know very little about the human brain and its connection with the mind and soul. That tumor was likely awakening parts of Judy's mind which had been dormant all her life."

I continued to be patient but he could see in my face that he was losing me.

"Listen to me carefully, Bill." he said. "Was there anything unexplained going on in your house since you moved to Seattle? Things out of place, objects moving on their own, apparitions appearing suddenly..."

That got my attention.

"What do you mean by 'apparitions'?" I asked in a whisper.

"You know, spectral images, ghosts, shadows. Electronics going haywire. Anything like that." He could see he was finally making an impact.

"Why are you asking me this?"

"Because that was *Judy*, Bill. Her mind was reaching out to you, probably while she was asleep or at least very relaxed. In these rare cases, research has shown that usually there's a catalyst, like wind or rain which enables the mind in that state to become strong enough to–"

"Oh my God," I said, standing. "Oh no."

"What is it Bill? What's wrong?" His concern had shifted to me now.

It was too much to explain, too much to believe unless you had experienced it yourself. The hands in the basement, leafing through pages of a book. The eye in the TV, a single tear escaping. The familiar touch in the downstairs bathroom. And it was raining *every single time* those things happened.

My God. It was Judy. She was reaching out to me with her mind, literally *haunting* me before she passed away.

But that wasn't all. The night she died I saw her get up and go into the bathroom at least *three hours* after the doctor told me when her time of death was.

And the shape in our bed only a couple of days ago, after she died... The entity I cursed and told to get out. The spirit that I had run off and expelled. Her true and final ghost, trying to contact me, now pushed away. *By me.*

Oh no. *No.*

"I have to go. *Now.*" I started toward the door.

"What is it, Bill?" He was truly concerned about my sanity now. He would be even more concerned if he knew what I was thinking.

"If I'm right, doc, I'll tell you about it later."

And I was gone.

◉

It is a thirty minute drive, especially on a Friday evening, from the doctor's office to our home. Despite the rain coming down in sheets, or perhaps because *of* it, I cut that in half.

It was nearly seven o'clock when I unlocked the door and stepped into the foyer, clothes soaked through and dripping water on the floor. It was dark. The rain had set in and with it a chill in the air. All I could hear in the house was my breath, raspy with anticipation.

Was I too late? Had I run Judy away, not understanding the miracle that had happened?

Without thinking I ran to the hall door, down the steps, into the basement and over to the corner where I'd seen her hands, weeks ago, reading a book. Drizzly blue light once again illuminated the downstairs. There was no amber light. There were no otherworldly hands floating above the concrete floor. No astral book being leafed through.

I turned, went through the Man Cave and into the half bath. I approached the mirror, hopeful to get a glimpse of her spectral arms and hands, longing for their caress. Nothing.

I sprinted back up the steps and into the living room, grabbing the remote off the end table as I passed. The TV and cable box came on in seconds. I was praying for no picture, for the snow of static. Instead I was greeted with a panel talk show discussing the upcoming Seahawks football season. Not what I wanted to see.

Upstairs. I flew up the stairs and into our bedroom, hoping to see the shape under the covers and the long hair spread out over the pillow. Instead I saw an unmade bed, crumpled pillows and clothes littering the floor, remnants of a new widower.

I was frantic now, upset at myself for not seeing the signs which were right in front of me the whole time. *How could I not recognize my own wife?* I sat on the bed, bewildered, confused and hopeless.

I didn't know it was her who I ran off the other night.

Sitting on the bed, I felt helpless in a way that no man should. My face was buried in my hands, sobbing. I had lost my wife to death. Now I had lost her *beyond* death as well.

Time passed. I'm not sure how long.

The ticking of the clock, the rain thrumming on the roof… She wasn't coming back.

Eventually I rose, numbly walked to the bathroom and turned on the shower. I needed to calm down, relax. Being uptight about something I couldn't control would get me nowhere.

I put the water on as hot as I could stand and stayed under it until my skin was beet red. More tears flowed and washed down the drain along with the shower water. It was as if they never were.

I finished up in the shower and got out. I looked to the mirror, fogged over completely and decided against wiping it off just to stare into my own haunted eyes. I was better off not seeing the reflection of the man who had lost his wife. Twice.

Turning back to the shower, I grabbed the towel from the rack and began drying off. Still lost in thought, I turned back to the sink. Above it, two words were on the mirror, visible only because of the steam from the shower. The words were so fresh that beads of moisture were still running down from them.

D a t e   n i g h t ?

Dear Lord, it was Judy. She was still here.

◉

The forecast is for rain tonight and all weekend long; this is Seattle, after all. I've already chilled a bottle of wine and have prepared candles for the evening. I plan on building a fire and to have Judy's favorite music playing. I have faith she will be joining me tonight.

As I look back on what happened, from me choosing to relocate in Seattle, the rainiest city in the country, to us moving to a house surrounded by water, Mercer Island, it's as if there was a purpose to it all. They say the Lord moves in mysterious ways. Whether this is His doing, or just a freak of nature like many say we, as humans, are - an accident in the whole cosmic mess - I am thankful.

Thankful for the life Judy and I shared, physically on this earth.

Thankful for this house we together made into a home, if

only briefly.

Thankful that Judy didn't share my doubt of an afterlife, making the impossible possible.

Thankful for this second chance.

And thankful for the rain, as it serves as a conduit between worlds.

I was wrong about rainy days not being good for anything. I now realize the rain, those literal tears from heaven, help things grow.

And our love continues to grow, death be damned.

MOMMA'S BOY

HE HAD JUST PUT the finishing touches on what would be the inaugural display of the New Mars History Museum. There would be many exhibits to follow, but this one had a special place for him. There would never be another artifact like it.

After nearly four years of colonization on the red planet, the leaders had followed his advice and put aside enough credits to start this museum, naming him curator as an added bonus. One day, his children's children would visit this place and see what was endured to tame this hostile world.

Securing the aged and rusted metal onto its base, he was overcome with a sense of melancholy unlike any that had come before. The golden-grey alloy was pitted with green Martian rust; a rust looking vaguely similar while at the same time strikingly different than its Terran counterpart.

On the exhibit's plaque, Dean Bishop's name stood in relief as the contributor. He smiled to himself, a sense of pride in seeing his name on something so prominently featured. There were plenty of times he had remembered, regretted and thought twice about the course of events which brought him to this moment on this new world.

They were the first, the colonization parties which landed on this bleak and desolate planet to make a new home, not only for themselves, but for the people of Earth as well. The colonists had chosen a one-way ticket to, for all they knew, certain death. Nothing of this magnitude had ever been attempted. Not even Columbus, in his quest for the new world, had gone up against such insurmountable odds. But they did.

And they persevered.

Not only did they survive, they found a way to make the impossible possible. Thanks to a multi-national consortium, the group had unlimited funds and was able to put the best minds on the planet onto some pretty unsolvable problems. Answers were found to questions they didn't even know they had.

Dean was on the third of nine spaceships launched from

Earth beginning in 2022. There were twelve astronauts on each ship, all with non-refundable tickets to the unknown. There would be no return trip to Earth, no matter what happened. Each of the expeditions could crash upon arrival, and every one of the succeeding launches would still take place.

It was their fate, their destiny.

The colonization of Mars.

Other than the purest spirit of discovery and curiosity, there was no immediate need to leave the comfort of Earth and reach out to Mars. There wasn't a worldwide famine, zombie apocalypse or nuclear holocaust which was forcing mankind to abandon their home world. On the contrary, Earth was becoming a much better place to live. Environmentalists and capitalists were finally working together, coming to a balance between ecological disaster and human advancement. Earth was as much of a home as it had ever been. Nevertheless, it is human nature to explore.

Each colonist left behind loved ones, family and friends. Each had left humanity behind as well. And each had something to look forward to: establishing life on another planet.

It was important for everyone involved to remember where they came from. Each person, in essence, had taken a piece of what made them who they were and planted it in the alien soil. Each colonist had a unique path which had led them here.

Dean, like everyone else, had a story to tell. There were reasons and motivations galore which drove each to make this momentous decision and risk it all. His was just as personal.

While the other colonists were looking for reasons to go, he was looking for meaning in his life, a purpose to define his existence. And the answer came from the most unlikely of places.

◉

April, 2017

"Have you ever thought about going to Mars?"

The question caught Dean completely off guard. His mom had always kidded with him about the most bizarre things at the oddest of times, but this one was out of left field. He swallowed the bite of cake before replying.

"OK, mom," he replied. "I'll catch the next flight out."

"I'm not kidding, kiddo."

"Neither am I."

"No, seriously. I think you should go to Mars. And, better yet, stay there." She said all this with the straightest of straight faces. Something in her eyes told him she was on the level.

"Mom. What are you talking about?"

"Well… there's a project called Mars Prime. A multi-nationally funded group proposing a manned mission to Mars. They are looking for 108 young men and women who are willing to risk their lives for this project. They train for a year and a half and then groups of twelve launch for Mars six weeks apart."

Yep, Dean thought. She was definitely on the level. Nobody could make up something this detailed and pass it off as a joke. Not even mom.

"Mom," he said, looking ever so serious, "I'm sure whoever is recruiting people is looking for specialists, doctors with Masters and scientists with PhD's. Not some Joe Blow who can't even get his life in order."

She grinned. "You know, I thought the same thing until I looked into it. Sure, they're looking for those types of people. They'd be fools not to and, quite frankly, I wouldn't want to go somewhere like Mars without one or two of them with me.

"But what's interesting is that they are also looking for regular people, just like you and me. People with a little common sense, good work ethics and a sound head on their shoulders."

"So you're thinking about going too?" He was wondering if this was shaping up to be the ultimate mother-son bonding experience. Now it was apparent why his mom insisted on taking him to lunch today to celebrate his eighteenth birthday.

"No, kiddo. Too old." There was a hint of regret in her eyes. "They're looking for people in their late teens to late twenties only. Old folks like me would be a waste of time and money."

Dean's mom was only forty-three and was in great shape, both mentally and physically. If there was anybody who could take on something like this and succeed, it was his mother.

"You're serious, aren't you?" He was beginning to think she really was.

"As a heart attack, son. And I wouldn't even mention it if I didn't think you'd be perfect for this project." Her eyes glazed for just a second and Dean knew there was more to this than she was letting on.

"Mom, what aren't you telling me?"

She paused, as if unsure how to answer. Not having a response to anything was uncharacteristic of her. She always knew what she wanted and how to get it.

"It's a one-way ticket, kiddo. You leave and you never come back."

He was stunned. That wasn't what he was expecting at all.

"What do you mean 'never come back'?" Even as he asked, Dean already knew the answer.

"Once the candidates are chosen, you go through a rigorous eighteen month training in Iceland. The field is narrowed to the final 108 through a selection committee and internet voting. Yes, it'll be the epitome of reality shows. Spacecraft are built. You go to Mars. You stay there. You leave Earth and make your home and the rest of your life on another planet. Simple as that."

Simple as that? He really didn't know what to think. His mother was essentially telling him that, if he did this, they'd never see each other again.

"Oh, and by the way," she added, "Happy birthday."

◉

His thoughts interrupted by a couple of technicians bringing in another exhibit, Dean got back to work prepping the display.

The artifact was about the size of an old manhole cover which lined the streets of his Kansas hometown, but it was much lighter in weight and conical. The edges were worn and eroded. There was printing on the metal, but most of the words had been obscured by the Martian wind and years of exposure. The NASA emblem was partially punched through by what was probably the entry hole of a small meter. Part of the distinct blue disc, slicing red ribbon and iconic white lettering still stood out against the dirty gold of the metal.

He had gotten offers of help from his colleagues, but this was one exhibit Dean was determined to take care of on his own. It was personal.

The light Martian gravity, only about a third that of Earth's, made adjusting the object fairly manageable. It was funny that, even after several years, the colonists still retained their Earth-Mars strength ratio. Of course, routine exercise and tough manual labor kept everyone in top physical shape.

Of the original 108 colonists, 106 were still alive. *Remarkable*, Dean thought, *considering the extreme obstacles the missions faced.* Neither of the two deaths was mysterious in any way. No rumors of aliens or extraterrestrial viruses. It was just damned bad luck in both cases.

The first one, geological scientist Loral Havelock, was part of a team exploring the underground caverns discovered near the Tithonium chasmata. All safety precautions were taken; there was no person at fault for what happened. The seismic surveys in the area showed no weak spots where potential disturbances could occur. Nevertheless, during the excursion into the caves, a small tremor occurred, barely even noticeable. Part of the roof where Loral was standing came down on her, barely missing two other scientists at her side. Mercifully, it was quick.

The second casualty was the commander of the first mission, Jed Jones. For a person who oversaw the ultimate fate of his first eleven astronauts, as well as the following landings, he preferred being called J.J. And he insisted on remaining just one of the cogs in the machine, helping to make the project successful. One morning after not showing up for his daily briefings, he was found in his quarters, on his elliptical, dead of a heart attack. A medical exam showed that he had a hereditary aortal valve defect; nothing about Mars Prime had anything to do with his death.

Colonists had also added one child to the mix with another three babies expected soon. Dean was proud to say that he was the father of the first true Martian-born baby. They named him, fittingly enough, Adam. Officially the result of an on-line poll, the boy's name was already chosen by Dean and his wife before they had even gotten pregnant. *The joke's on both worlds*, Dean thought.

His wife was second in command of the third mission, the one of which Dean was a part. Her name was Gillian Maxwell, British and also a hell of a Scrabble player. They managed to keep it strictly professional through the training and the ten-month long trip to Mars. But once they got settled in and, well, basically survived, they started paying more and more attention to each other.

The couple was married on the edge of the Valles Marineris with just a handful of witnesses and the resident minister, sent along to Mars just in case. Fortunately, NASA had planned on the inevitability of such an event. They were colonizing a whole new world; it would have been counterproductive to ignore the facts of life.

Dean's only regret was that his child would never meet his grandmother. Over the delayed telecommunications from Earth, his mother's reaction was a mixture of pride and sadness; on the flip-side, she'd never get to hold her grandson.

Despite the sacrifices made in the spirit of exploration, humanity presses on.

◉

April, 2003

"I have a surprise for you, kiddo."

On his fourth birthday, Dean uncovered his eyes and looked at the flat packet his mother was proudly displaying for him. This was his final present. He had already opened the other gifts all wrapped and bowed proudly by his mother. He'd gotten most of the things he'd asked for: cool pajamas, a remote-controlled Batmobile, several books about explorers and talking animals, a set of water colors and three of his favorite Disney DVDs. His mom usually saved the best for last, so that was why he was so perplexed by the sight of a thin envelope which couldn't hold much of anything. Trying to figure out the proud look on his mother's face, Dean carefully opened the envelope and removed a sheet of paper, heavily matted. It read:

This Is To Certify That The Name
Charles Dean Bishop
Has Been Recorded On The Data Disc Aboard The
Beagle 2
Scientific Mars Express Planetary Lander
Launched 2 June 2003
Landed 25 December 2003

Dean was excited now. Already in his young life, his mother had exposed him to Star Trek, Star Wars and many other space-based TV shows and movies. While he appreciated the usual boy things, Dean, like his mother, had a special place for science, space exploration and science fiction. Even at this young age, she kept challenging his imagination with technical books and scientific documentaries purporting all things fantastic and incredible.

Dean's father was never in the picture, being more of a sperm donor than a dad. Parenthood was never something he had wanted and within a year of Dean's birth, his father was gone. Dean's mother never bothered tracking him down for child support or help with raising a baby. She knew Dean would be better off without that distraction in his life.

His mom had seen an advertisement on the back of Scientific American in collaboration with the European Space Agency. A five dollar donation assured the name of your choice would be made a permanent part of the Beagle 2 exploration lander on the Martian surface, launching later in the year. How cool was that? His mom knew how much he would love this gift.

And he did.

His mother had the certificate matted and framed. It would hang on a prominent part of Dean's bedroom wall as long as he was on Earth.

◉

Dean secured the second part of the exhibit, a flat, a similarly rounded piece of green rust-pitted light-weight metal.

A special base had been set up for the display in the museum, one which held approximately two hectoliters of Martian soil and rock. The artifact would be placed on it, replicating exactly how it was discovered in the Isidis Planitia basin. It was painstaking work, but an effort which Dean savored.

He ran his fingers over the scaled, weathered surface. It was odd, he thought, being able to touch the shell of this object which had travelled through the gulfs of space and lay in wait on the Martian surface for more than two decades.

On this planet at this time in human history, Dean was one of a select few who would be able to document their colonization of Mars. It was a weight he had accepted and a responsibility he took on happily.

As far as this exhibit went, he was the only human on Mars uniquely qualified for the task.

April, 2021

"Number thirty - Charles Dean Bishop of Cottonwood Falls, Kansas, United States of America."

On his twenty-first birthday, Dean was officially named as one of the 108 finalists in the Mars Prime project, placing him on the third colonization flight. He had gotten through the initial training and endurance testing, had persevered over other equally qualified candidates, and had been one of the more popular 'non-specialists' in the internet polling. He was unofficially dubbed the 'Best of the Rest of Us' by the voting public.

Now the real fun began.

Over the two years, the teams would be split off into the twelve mission designations and flight training would begin. It would consist of trips to the ISS for weightlessness drills, machinery and equipment preparation, medical and emergency instruction. He would become proficient in communications, computer technology and technical procedures. If anything, the training going into non-specialists was even more rigorous; these people would be the backbone of the missions. Success or failure would depend on the smallest of gears in the wheel.

Dean was ecstatic to be chosen. His mother was in contact whenever possible, giving her full support and encouragement. It's not every day that people are given this opportunity, a chance to place oneself into history, she would say in different ways, always the optimist. Neither of them talked about what would happen if the missions failed. The dismal failure rate of unmanned Mars launches was never mentioned.

As the launch dates approached, Dean became more and more confident in his abilities. He was able to endear himself to the command crew and was given responsibilities beyond that of his title. His eye for design made him a natural to conceive the internal reporting systems and commentaries which would be broadcast back to Earth, informing the world of his mission's status. He became an essential part of the crew.

◎

As Dean was continuing to prepare the display for the grand opening, he thought about the improbable events which led him to bring this unique piece of history into the museum.

In 2015, after several improvements made by NASA and Earth's space surveying community, this artifact was finally located. Using the Mars Reconnaissance Orbiter, across the vast 120 million miles of space, scientists were able to pinpoint the two meter wide piece of equipment to within a one meter location.

Dean insisted on being the leader of the recovery mission that would take a team of explorers more than 3,000 kilometers from their base in the deepest part of Valles Marineris to the edge of the Isidis Planitia basin. He hand-picked his team, making sure they volunteered freely. This was not a life and death mission; it was a recovery expedition. One especially important to Dean.

The team consisted of himself, the site geologist, the local medical intern and an astrophysicist. His wife Gillian would have to sit this one out and stay home with Adam. With the current technology, the round trip was not likely to take more than seven days. They made sure to make several exploratory stops along the way in order to justify the trip and satisfy the bean counters.

At the recovery site, it was fairly easy to locate the object, only partially obscured by wind-blown Martian sand. The batteries were long dead, of course, making the relic more of a curiosity than anything else.

The team successfully loaded the item onto the flatbed of their transport and made their way back to base. This would be the first of many such trips which would be made to recover scientific apparatus strewn across the face of this new world. Each had a story and the New Mars History Museum would be the medium through with their tales would be told.

Starting with this one.

◎

April, 2023

For something so audacious, the 221 day journey to Mars was routine. Mars Prime 03, Dean's ship, was not launched during the Hoeman Transfer Orbit for the optimal trajectory and shortest travel time. Therefore, his team spent the additional time running tests, preparing for the landing and planning the groundwork for their settlement location in the deepest accessible part of the Valles Marineris. This geographical landmark was the scar which ran along the Martian equator, extending across almost a third of the planet's surface, going as deep as seven kilometers. It was chosen as the primary settlement location specifically because of its depth, approximating as closely as possible the Earth's atmospheric pressure. Also, it was widely thought that, if microbial life existed on Mars, it would be near the deep gullies where liquid water was sometimes observed.

As the mission wore on, the most dispiriting part was watching Earth recede, slowly reducing to just another bright star against the blackness. The communication delay also gradually got longer, making dialogue with Earth more and more difficult. He missed the off the cuff exchanges with his mother.

During his last real-time conversation, on his 23rd birthday, she made sure he knew how proud she was of her little boy.

"Getting to know your fellow colonists?"

"Yep. There's this one lady who's really special."

"Oh, yeah? Who?"

"Can't say. You know these communications are monitored."

"You mean you had to leave Earth to find a gal who would keep you?"

"Yeah, pretty much, Mom."

"Does she know what's she's getting herself into?"

"She has no idea. But she'll be stuck with me millions of miles from home. I think she'll get used to me."

Just then, his crewmates showered him with a spray of water, drenching him and splashing to the floor in the artificial gravity created by the spinning of the main habitat.

"What the—", he said, surprised. "How did you guys—?"

"A little bird told us," the second in command, Gillian Maxwell said, winking at the monitor on which Dean's mother's face was beaming.

"Hey, kiddo," his mom said, knowingly. "You're not the only one who can keep a secret."

Together with his mother, Dean's crewmates began singing Happy Birthday, off key and awful. And beautiful at the same time.

Dean felt Gillian's hand lingering a moment longer on his shoulder. He gave her a quick wink.

◉

Just as he was placing another of the display components onto the diorama, Dean's three year old son Adam came bounding into the exhibition hall, trailed by his wife Gillian. Dean grinned at the sight of his boy, the first Martian-born human in history.

"Daddy! Daddy!" Adam said, running and jumping into his father's arms. Dean gave his wife a kiss as he always did when seeing her.

Dean had always been fascinated by the interesting effect of being a human born on the red planet. Adam was tall and slender, his legs and arms noticeably longer than normal. At only three years of age he stood almost to Dean's chest. Adam had learned to walk before he turned one year-old. His capabilities had been enhanced, either by the weaker gravity or the consumption of the only food he had ever eaten, grown in the Martian soil, or both. While he still had characteristics from his mother and father, Adam's face was quite different in appearance than that of the other colonists who were not native to this world. His skull was elongated and sloped to the back. His long hair was a fiery red. His grey eyes were almost twice the size of his parents', but his nose and mouth were definitely Dean's. Everything about Adam was alien, but at the same time everything about him was all too human. He was an interesting combination of Terran and Martian. Adam was a new breed, essentially the first of the next Martian race.

"What are you doing, Daddy?" he asked, his big grey eyes looking over the display. "What is that thing?"

"It's something very special," replied Dean. "Once I get it all set up we'll come back and I'll tell you a story about your grandmother and how she talked me into doing something crazy a long time ago. How's that sound?"

Dean put the boy back on the ground and turned to his wife. "Give me another hour and I'll have it set up and ready, OK?"

"No problem, Deano," she said, riffing on his mother's nickname for him. "We were on our way to the observatory and thought we'd surprise you."

"Love it when you guys do."

"No plans for later, though, right? I'm cooking your favorite meal for your birthday." She grinned, knowing how Dean loved her cooking.

"No plans. Bring Adam back in a little bit and we'll get this party kicked off right." He gave her a kiss and mussed up Adam's red hair.

Dean watched the two of them leave the exhibition hall, Adam making impossibly lengthy strides on his long legs, seemingly suspended in air between each step.

How did I get so lucky? He turned back to his work and continued to position the pieces of the past into place.

◎

April, 2008

Dean's mother threw him a small party for his eighth birthday. He only had a handful of classmates come, which was fine with him. He didn't have that many friends, but the ones he had were for life. Even in his teens he would still be close to each person at this party.

All of them were science and space geeks as well. They each had their own collection of comics and sci-fi movies, models of spaceships and movie dioramas, favorite books about other worlds and fantasy lands. They took field trips together to the Powell Observatory and his mother even organized a trip for them to the Science City museum where an actual recovered meteorite was on display.

But Dean had one thing up on all his friends: His name was on Mars. He was proudly showing off the Beagle 2 certificate his mother had printed for him on his fourth birthday.

"Tell them, mom," he said. "Tell them how you paid five bucks for my name to go to Mars."

Collectively, his friends all rolled their eyes; they'd heard this several times already.

Dean's mom didn't have the heart to tell Dean, especially in front of his friends, that the spacecraft was lost when it entered orbit back in 2003 and was never heard from again. He would be devastated to know that there was no way of knowing whether or not the vehicle had made it to the surface of Mars intact, or if it had bounced off the atmosphere and was still sailing through space. Statistically, the latter was more probable; only about one out of every three exploratory lander missions to Mars were successful.

"You're right, kiddo," she said, smiling. "The face on Mars is probably reading the list of names as we speak."

It wasn't until several years later that his mother finally broke the news to Dean of the failed Beagle 2 mission. Despite knowing the truth, she insisted on fueling his dreams in those early years. You never knew where they could lead.

With all four parts of the exhibit now secured, Dean stepped back to inspect his work. It had taken hours to get right, but he was convinced it was all worth it. It was a kind of birthday gift to himself on this, his 27th.

Approaching the computer display set up next to the exhibition, he keyed in his password and hit Enter. On the large wallscreen a list of names appeared, filling the display. One by one they scrolled across, highlighted individually, with a short biography following each. There were a total of 2,337 names on this list. Each was a real person who would be remembered in this exhibit. It was a minor miracle the technicians were able to restore the drive and access the data.

He removed a flat box from his backpack. This was the piece of the puzzle which brought it all back home to him. This was the personal part.

Opening the box he gently lifted out an old, beat up frame. It had been professionally matted and encased in Acrylic to protect it from time. The paper inside was brown with age and exposure to harsh lighting. The frame had dings and dents from wear and the innocent neglect of children.

A hanger had been fashioned from Lucite and was positioned next to the wallscreen. Dean carefully placed the frame into the holder. Now the exhibit was complete. He stepped back to take it all in.

The wallscreen continued scrolling names. Below it, a diorama had been created from the red soil depicting a small area of ground. Placed on the red soil was a Martian exploratory lander, weathered and beaten by the alien elements, displayed in exactly the condition in which it was found. Next to the blue stylized NASA circle and ESA symbol, letters could still be made out, despite the weathering:

BE GL 2

He glanced at the wallscreen just as the name Charles Dean Bishop scrolled across. The featured mini-biography, trailing his name, read: *Member of Mars Prime 03; technician & explorer; the only colonist who participated in the Beagle 2 data disc project launched from Earth June 2003; Beagle 2 was lost upon orbit insertion December 2003 and presumed failed; it was later discovered in 2015 by the MRO at target's landing site Isidis Planitia basin and posthumously considered a successful mission; Beagle 2 spacecraft recovered 2026 by Charles Dean Bishop, curator New Mars History Museum.*

And the framed certificate hanging next to the wallscreen was a testimony to the love of a mother for her four year old son.

RITUAL

THE NORTH WIND BLEW
On its way down through
The god-forsaken Valley of the Dead.
And the icy, brittle rain
Battered, but didn't stain,
And spattered on what used to be a head.

The dark clouds gazed,
And the icy rain glazed
The skull peering skyward with sightless eyes.
All its other bones
Were scattered in the stones
With teardrops where its lover still cries.

Lightning split the sky
And something catches the eye
Of the young Indian warrior with his horse.
He utters a command,
Stills the stallion with his hand,
And strides to iv'ry sticks in his course.

Thunder rumbled 'round
And shook the rocky ground
As if it knew what was happening this night.
The Indian sniffs the air,
Looks through his matted hair,
Pushing his senses beyond his sight.

Warily he proceeds;
This last of fateful deeds:
It's time this boy became a man.
In the dark the chain gleams,
He's seen it in his dreams,
'Tis time to conclude the elder's plans.

He kneels down low,
His motions too slow,
And looks into empty eyes of doom.
He handles the old skull
And tries an ancient lull,
Wishing for the safety of a womb.

With hands like a vise
And fingers cold as ice
He pries open the grinning jaws of death.
Probing deep inside
He feels a sense of pride.
He draws out a disc and holds his breath.

The golden doubloon,
Like a yellow moon,
He holds in his strong but quaking hands.
It was pierced upon a chain,
He sees in his brain,
By a man who was killed where he stands.

It's told in ancient tales,
As the wind around him wails,
'Bout a soldier sent from far-off lands of old
To maim and kill the people
And desecrate the steeple,
In search of a worthlessness called gold.

And this, the final test,
"Fetch Cortez' coin by the crest,
Return to the native village and alive."
Preceded by the four,
None had succeeded before,
And he was the curse'd number five.

He tucks the disc away
For the light of the next day
And strides back to his escort, his horse.
He climbs on board,
Says a prayer to his Lord,
And prods the steed back onto its course.

Sightless sockets stared,
As they were prepared
For what happens next in this great scheme.
The broken jaws did grin
At the innocence of the sin;
It was all like a horrible crazed dream.

The rain stopped cold,
And the Indian was bold
To gaze at the thunderclouds above.
Silence stung like death,
The horse, it held its breath
As if it knew what these signs were thereof.

Lightning splits the sky
And the Indian screams a cry
That echoes in the timeless walls of doom.
His body writhes around
As the lightning strikes him down.
The coin hits the ground where life had grown.

Thunder rolled around
And made a deathly sound
As if it knew what its mighty deed had done.
The rain spattered pain
And the wind blew again.
For Nature reigned; it had won.

The horse which was spared
Stood silently and stared
At the rocks where its master's prize did lay.
It slowly turned around,
And the sky, it looked down
On the lifeless body's staring eyes of clay.

The Brave would not return.
In his village they would burn
In effigy, his soul, a warrior hero.
The elders would send another,
Possibly a brother.
To his doom, number six would soon go.

And midst the damned wet dirt
Where the disc lay unhurt,
Gleams an inner golden light from a seed.
The golden doubloon,
Sent from a yellow moon,
Awaiting a young lad to do his deed.

INTO THE PURPLE SKY

THEY ANNOUNCED THE END on radio and TV first, amazingly enough. Then it hit the internet; kind've ass-backward in Pamela's opinion.

Social media began playing it up as a type of contest, seeing who would react how and why. There were polls on Facebook before the virtual ink was even dry: *'What Kind of End of the Worlder Are YOU?'* and *'Celebrity Apocalypse Look-Alike Contest'* and *'What Will Your Last Meal Be?'*

Soon, people finally figured out it was real.

◎

Pamela was at work that morning, a Friday. Ironic, in a way, as Fridays do tend to be when most employees are given their walking papers.

The TV in the break room was tuned to MSNBC. As with most of the main news programs, they like to overplay the Breaking News angle.

Breaking News: *A-List Movie Star Returns To Rehab For Third Time.*

Breaking News: *Congress Can't Agree On Immigration Bill.*

Breaking News: *Water Is Wet.*

Everything was Breaking News.

Not anymore.

◎

Pamela's boss came around about ten o'clock and told the secretarial staff they could go home for the rest of the day, it being the end of the world and all. However, the supervisor smiled and gave them the caveat that they had to be on time Monday morning. Armageddon or not, it wasn't an excuse to just lay out at the start of a work-week. It was probably one of the world's more popular office jokes that day.

Most of the staff vacated fairly quickly. Pamela glanced at the tchotchkes she had managed to place around her cubicle for comfort: little Belle and Beast figurines (Beauty and the Beast was her favorite, especially after the recent Disney remake of the musical), a fifty year-old photo of her mom and dad on their honeymoon in Gatlinburg, a 1:24 die-cast replica of Junior's number 88 NASCAR ride... These were just a few of her baubles, little pieces of a mundane personality. *I am as eclectic as I am boring*, she thought.

She briefly considered packing everything into a box and taking it with her for safe keeping, but then realized it would be pointless. Removing her dad and mom's picture from its frame, she placed it into the side pocket of her windbreaker, the lone exception.

Pamela walked out of the Blake Insurance Underwriters office just before eleven o'clock on the next-to-the-last-day of the world, wondering what to do next.

◎

Until now, black holes had been strictly theoretical. Never had one been visibly captured by Hubbell as a pinprick against the star field of the Milky Way. There had never been any hard evidence, no shift of light from stars or no warped photon path. It was all calculus and concept, speculation and supposition. As long as black holes continued to be conjecture, they remained safe and harmless. And not worthy of attention.

Yesterday, theory became fact.

An anomaly had been detected approximately 150,000 miles from the surface of the Earth. One day it wasn't there; the next day it was.

Scientists tend to overuse the word 'anomaly' to describe something they don't know anything about. Anything which had an incongruity or inconsistency, well that was an anomaly.

It makes sense, in a way: if scientists had the proper vocabulary for half their discoveries, there would be no innovations. It was all about usefulness and value.

For the first time in human history, a black hole was now visible. It floated between the Earth and the moon, looking suspiciously like an old fashioned baby's rattle; one made from leftovers found lying around a rustic country cabin, warped and asymmetrically shaped, a bulbous mass on one side connected by a rod to a smaller ring on the other.

Ironically, it was also about the same *size* as a baby's rattle.

How the Space Defense Grid managed to detect it was anybody's guess. STARWARS had been designed to pick up on ICBM missile incursions and orbiting bomb platforms. NASA was proud of the fact they found a literal needle in a haystack, pinpointing the miniscule void down to within twenty inches of its position.

Despite all that, there wasn't a goddamn thing they could do about it.

Emergency actions were taken as rapidly as possible. The anomaly was hit with state-of-the-art lasers, the beams disappearing into it without fanfare. A satellite was redirected to collide with it. Upon approach, it was sucked into the black hole like a fat kid vacuuming up Jell-O, leaving just the faintest violet glow. Lastly, the ISS deployed two astronauts to investigate. They didn't even have time to transmit before they vanished, presumably into the abyss. Soon after, the ISS itself stopped communicating and a purple veil was seen radiating outward from its last known position.

As it approached our stratosphere, the lavender glow became more intense. It was as if the more mass it consumed, the stronger the luminosity. That was the only difference, however. Despite the size or bulk of an object, including the atmosphere, the results were always the same: whatever was encountered fed into the black hole, literally like water through a drain.

But the anomaly itself didn't get any bigger with each absorption. It remained the same size, roughly that of a child's toy.

Many intellectuals commented on how fitting it was that something about the size of a Starbuck's tall latte would herald the end of mankind.

Satire shines in the face of annihilation.

Suddenly Kid Rock's Purple Sky ballad became apropos. Wherever there was precipitation in the world, Prince's Purple Rain lyrics could be heard. Purple Haze by Jimi Hendrix was the unofficial end of the world hymn. The group Deep Purple made an admittedly rather brief reunion. Social media dubbed our little world-destroying visitor The Purple People Eater. Everyone agreed, however, that people would just be the appetizer.

It really wasn't a surprise to learn the anomaly was on a collision course with Earth. From the time it was discovered, ETA for an American west coast impact was roughly thirty-three hours away. But that countdown was already a day old.

In less than a typical workday, our world would be a cosmic postscript in the universal comedy.

It gave Pamela just enough time to spend with the one person in her life who mattered the most.

◉

Pamela never had kids. Chalk it up to a failed marriage which mercifully revealed its true colors pretty quickly. Within weeks of consummation, they both knew they had made the biggest mistake of their lives. Two months in, they had already separated, and by the first quarter of their newly wedded bliss, the couple had divorced. There was never any thought of bringing a kid into the world as a vain attempt to save their marriage. *Thank God*, she thought, time and time again.

In fact, they never even had time to bring aboard any pets either. *That should have been a sign*, she thought, looking back. She was a dog girl; he was a cat guy. It was almost a testimony to what would come; a marriage doomed to fail before it even started.

Pamela had no brothers or sisters, either. From the tales of her childhood, she was more than enough for her mom and dad. Another child would have driven her parents into an early grave.

Her mother died too early as it was anyway. She was a victim of premature heart disease, a silent killer among middle aged women. At just 47, she went quietly in her sleep, without warning, spooned up against her father, oblivious in his dreams. The morning came and her dad knew before even waking up that he was alone. He told Pamela several months later that he had dreamed that night of the two of them in their older years, the typical rocking chair scene on the covered porch, watching the sun set on their days. He said it was the most peaceful dream he'd ever had. And he told her that he had not dreamed of anything since then.

She had no children to worry about explaining the oncoming doom to. No pets to consider quickly euthanizing before the end. No siblings demanding any last minute problem resolution. And no mother with which to bond before the end.

But she did have her father. Or rather, what remained of him.

○

The nursing home was about an hour from the city. Pamela had picked it because it was the best. And she had picked her city because of the nursing home. Generally speaking, dads are worth those types of decisions.

Secretarial jobs were easy enough to find, of course. She was trained professionally in the sciences and could have pursued a more lucrative career. But her priorities did not make that an urgency. After her mother died, and after her unsuccessful marriage, she really had no incentive to become anything other than a good person. And a good daughter.

Her father already had a decent nest egg, taking an early pension from the railroad, and really didn't need to work later in life. He was able to retire with some good years still in front.

However, he went downhill fast after her mom died.

Alzheimer's hit with a vengeance. The days in which he would remember her face were fewer and fewer. But she always made a point to visit. It didn't really matter that he remembered her; *she* knew *him*.

Physically, he never changed with the mental disease. Outwardly, he remained strong in appearance, with vitality unmatched by any other seventy year old in the nursing home. It was as if his body was anticipating his mind returning one day, needing a strong vessel in which to reside.

It was an uneventful ride, really, from the city to the nursing home in the country. The roads were not that packed, and people were mostly walking along, enjoying as best they could the last few remaining hours of life. Pamela had to assume those who had a predisposition to pray were in their churches, those who didn't give a crap about anyone but themselves were out plundering and taking advantage of others. And those, like her, who considered someone else more important than themselves, were making that last, lonely visit.

Surprisingly, about half the hospital staff was still on duty when she got there. No doubt many of them considered these patients to be as much their family as their own. It was this mixture of sadness and commitment which spoke volumes about the human race.

Pamela found her father sitting in his recliner by the window, watching swirls of lavender roll across the sky. Purple light reflected on his craggy features and softened them a bit.

"Hey, Punkin," he said. "What's with the weather today?"

"Hey, Pops," she replied. They had these pet names for each other for as long as she could remember.

Evidently no one had told him about the impending disaster, she realized. *Thank God.* He never was one to spend time in front of a TV. He'd told her time and again that Talk Radio had gone to shit. And he never really got caught up in the internet before he started slipping away. He spent most of his lucid moments reading classic novels and looking through old photographs. And the other moments, those times when his mind had slipped into the other realm, well who really knew what he did in there.

From the sound of his voice, it appeared he was having a good day. She wasn't sure if it was a good thing, him knowing who he was and why she was here. But if it was that way, it would also be one of regret, with her dad understanding the enormity of what was about to happen to him, to his daughter and to the world. It was simultaneously fitting and tragic. She almost would rather him be recessed into his own mind this one last time and unaware of the impending doom.

"Is it supposed to rain? Those clouds are looking pretty nasty." His innocent observation brought her back to reality.

"Pops," she said. "Let's take a drive. There's a place on the Parkway that has a great view. I've always wanted to show it to you, and today seems as good a day as any."

"Sounds good, Punkin. We'd better dress for the weather. Hate to get caught out in the storm."

Dad, you have no idea, she thought.

"You're right, big guy." Another affectionate term that never seemed to go away. "Better bring your parka and wear your rubbers."

And they both laughed.

It was a relatively quick drive from the nursing home up to the mountains. The Parkway was a nationally funded road which ran along the ridge of the western California coastal mountains. On one side there were unsurpassed views of the city; on the other was the expanse of the ocean.

Along the way were dozens of cars parked along the road, mostly at overpasses and viewing areas. What Pamela thought was a fairly unique way of bringing in the end of the world, now seemed like a popular choice among the ill-fated.

They drove past most of the onlookers, up to the crest of the mountain, to a place which had an overlook on both sides of the road. Pamela chose the ocean view.

While the skies were churning with indigo rage, the wind was absolutely calm. The tranquil sea reflected the violence of the rolling purple clouds above with perfect symmetry, nary a wave being crested, laid out like a great, flat mirror.

By the time they reached their destination, her father had slipped away again. Pamela was familiar with the furtive looks he would give when he wasn't sure who somebody was. He'd steal a glance her way every few minutes, face full of confusion and shame. In a way, he simultaneously knew *what* was happening to him, but did not *know* it was happening. Aside from the end of the whole human race today, it was the single most tragic thing she'd ever experienced.

Four other cars were parked in the turnoff and six or eight people were either sitting on the guardrail or were standing. Most were holding on to one another, up close, whispering in each other's ears.

Pamela brought up some tunes on her iPhone to play in the background, at least while they could still hear them. Her music choices were as eclectic as the rest of her life: movie soundtracks, country, rock, classical. She set the controls to random shuffle.

What do you say to a loved one at the end of the world? It was a subject she would have to broach with her father momentarily. For the time being, they just leaned against her car and took in the view.

"Thanks for bringing me up here, um..." Not sure of her name, he hesitated.

"It's Pamela," she said, saving him the added embarrassment. "I'm your friend, remember?" Experience taught her it was better to come across as someone other than his daughter when he was confused like this. It seemed to sit better in the long run.

The long run. Like that mattered any more, she thought. *In the scheme of things, the 'long run' today would be only a matter of minutes.*

She took two folding chairs from the hatchback and removed the carrying cases. She didn't think they'd need to put them back when they were done.

Pamela and her dad chose a path which led slightly uphill from where they had parked, towards a small bluff shielded from the gathering wind. It was still much calmer than one would think, with destruction literally on the horizon.

Settling into their chairs, together they watched the ocean for a few minutes, extending the silence as long as possible. *Maybe*, she thought, *this was how it was being repeated all over the world.*

◉

Lost in thought, Pamela reflected that life was like a series of games, small competitions which allowed people to hone their skills, however small and meaningless they may be. The two of them played games all the time. Of all the things in life, they shared a love of the movies.

There were a couple of favorite movie games they always fell back on. One of them was The Quote Game. Each would come up with a quote, preferably from a movie they had seen (but not necessarily; it was their fallback tripping point when they became desperate), and the other would try to guess the film it was from and the actor or character who said it. Her father was really good at this game. She supposed it had something to do with the way his mind worked these days, storing scraps of useless information for future repetition. He even joked with her in those lucid moments, telling Pamela she would have to develop Alzheimer's just to compete with him. She usually cheated by resorting to the quotes section of IMDb, but her father still handed her ass to her more times than not.

Pamela's game of choice was Seven Degrees of Kevin Bacon, only without the Kevin Bacon part. The goal here was to link two actors together through movies or TV shows, preferably within seven steps. They usually threw out the number of steps restriction in favor of a more entertaining route. She schooled him in this game. She was proud to say she could connect Marilyn Monroe to Chris Hemsworth in three steps or Rebecca Ferguson to Mickey Rooney in two. Her father sucked at this game; he usually deferred to being the one who threw the challenges out instead of the one finding the links.

Movies to them were the ultimate distraction, the essential getaway from the real world when it seemed like there was no escape. Many times they served as diversions when life seemed too real. There would be weekends when they took in three, four or even five movies, sometimes not leaving the same Cineplex for hours on end. Redbox became their best friend. They would rent stacks of DVDs, comedy, action, horror, documentaries; it didn't matter.

Films became their reality in a way, especially when her father was first diagnosed. *It was a way of staying anchored,* she often thought. Sometimes Hollywood could be more real to people than life itself. At least in the cinema, one could go back to relive past moments and not have to rely on something as fleeting and transient as memory. These games were especially helpful when her dad started slipping away.

They used to joke and say that, in the next life, they would meet up in the lobby of the Mystery Science Theater 3000 movie house so they could watch bad 'B' movies and make wisecracks for eternity. It was their own special version of heaven.

It would be fitting, Pamela thought, *if black holes somehow had direct routes to places like the MST3K Theater.* She wouldn't be surprised. Not at all.

◉

Her father broke the silence. Her *real* father, not the man who had a memory shell fraught with hairline fractures.

"I never told you how I was before you were born," he said, not looking her in the eyes. "I was a real jackass sunofabitch. I was Melvin Udall on steroids. People liked Jar-Jar Binks better than they liked me. I cared about myself, said I loved your mother but didn't really show it. I lived for my job and my bad habits. Other people were secondary and didn't matter. It was me first, and the rest could go to hell."

Pamela sat there, stunned. This was the longest coherent conversation they'd had in months. And it was something he had never shared with her before now. For all she knew, her father, her perfect daddy, was the most loving person she had ever known. In her mind, he had always been that way.

"I had zero emotions," he said, smiling faintly. "I dared not crack a smile, laugh, show any pain or let anyone know I gave a damn. People who worked for the railroad were cut from that type of cloth. It's why railroaders seldom had families. I never wanted a family myself. But I ended up with one. And with a baby girl to boot. If there was ever any doubt that God has a sense of humor, the fact that he gave me a *daughter* proves it, right up there with the aardvark and the giraffe." He let out a little snort, almost a cough of a laugh.

"But once I laid my eyes on you, Punkin, I was never the same. You were so beautiful it hurt. Hurt my heart, hurt my mind, hurt my soul, hurt my eyes... After you came along I discovered emotions I never knew existed for anybody, much less an old buzzard like me. It was overwhelming. I was glad there was only one of you, thankful we never had another child, because I don't think I could have mustered up enough love for another."

He was looking at her fully now, face on. His eyes were as clear as she could remember ever seeing them. She knew she had to say something. The time would soon be upon them when there could be no more words. Nevertheless, she sat there speechless.

He turned his vision back on the ocean, taking in the growing wind and boiling lavender clouds above their heads. It was like gazing upward from underwater, the types of clouds which looked like waterfalls in reverse, billowing downward as they hit the surface.

Pamela took another moment before she spoke.

"Pops," she began. "Daddy. Do you know what's happening? Do you know it's not just a storm moving in, that it's not just bad weather?"

"Hello. My name is Eugene. And you are…?"

Oh, no, she thought. *Not now.*

"I'm Pamela, your friend." *How could one's mind switch back and forth from coherence to inconsistency so quickly?* She'd asked herself this question more times than she could remember.

"Hi, Pamela. Thank you for bringing me here. There was a famous actress named Pamela, wasn't there? This is beautiful. I think a storm is blowing in, though. The clouds remind me of cotton candy." They did. Pamela wondered how they'd taste if you could take a bite.

"I think I had a picnic here a long time ago. I can't remember who with, but I do remember the PB&J sandwiches." He smiled and glanced at her sideways, giving her the look that she was sure melted her mother's heart so many years ago. "PB&J is my fav."

"Mine too, Eugene. Maybe you were here with your wife and your daughter? This would be a good place for a picnic."

A flitter of confusion creased his forehead.

"I remember a woman with dark hair who smelled like grass," he smiled and winked. "But in a good way. I remember she called me Genie. That seems like a wifey name for a husband, doesn't it? Or a Robin Williams character in an animated movie. I can't remember her name."

He looked at Pamela, studying her features. "If I had a daughter, I would hope she'd be half as beautiful as you."

How many times had he said things like this, so innocent and yet so heartbreaking in their simplicity?

They sat quietly, surveying the impending portent, cobalt and indigo shadows casting over them like a kaleidoscope.

◉

"I never told you how proud I was if you, Punkin." His voice startled her in its directness, only moments later. Her dad was back, at least temporarily. *Maybe it's all we need,* she thought.

"How's that, Pops?" She found over the years it was best to go with the flow and not make anything of his coming in and out of sobriety.

"After your mom - after Patricia died, I felt like I was losing my mind from time to time. It was like I'd be gone on a trip, but not know where I went, how long I was there or when I even returned. It was the sense of missing that I could never get used to. An absence which couldn't be measured. It was like Aaron's character in Primal Fear, always 'losing the time.'"

He continued. "I know you changed your life so you could take care of me, and that you put aside your dreams to be near me. I know you chose what was best for me over what you wanted. I know you moved to this city, sat in a dead end Office Space type job so you would be close by. I know—"

"Dad," she interrupted. "Pops, I—"

He interrupted back. "Punkin, let me have my say. I'm aware enough of the fact that I go missing for minutes, even days, on end. Who knows when it will happen again? Maybe even before I finish my next thought.

"The words I Love You seem so inadequate to me. Always have. Maybe it's because people nowadays, being human and not something beyond, can't fully express themselves when it comes to something as abstract as love. Maybe real and true love is meant for us to experience from another level. Sometimes we get a glimpse of it when we look at our babies, when we see someone sacrifice themselves, or when we sit on a hillside watching the end of the world come in like the tide."

"So you *do* know what's happening? You know we don't have long." Pamela said that more to herself than to her father.

"Yeah, Punkin," he replied. "I do. Did you know your mother's favorite color was purple? Her favorite stone was amethyst. When I see these lavender clouds, the wind starting to build, the violet rays of sun trying to break through the cataclysm, I think it's her way of—"

Pamela waited for him to finish his sentence.

Waited a beat more

And another.

She looked over at him and could see the thought was no longer there. Whatever reflection he had would remain unspoken, buried forever.

◉

Purple neon lightning struck the water less than half a mile out, thunder less. The flash was bright enough that Pamela perceived heat radiating from it.

Something told Pamela this was it. The anomaly had no doubt made landfall by now and was starting its slow, steady consumption of everything called Earth.

She slid over, putting her arm around her father, pulling him in tight so he could hear her words against the growing wind.

"Eugene. I have something to tell you."

"How do you know my name? Do I know you?" She had never felt so lost. She hoped this feeling wouldn't follow her into what was to come.

"Eugene, I'm Pamela. My friends call me Punkin. You are my friend. Please, call me Punkin."

"OK, Punkin. I like that name. Punkin." He smiled.

The wind was becoming a beast of its own, ripping the air in waves, screaming in futility as it was funneled into another dimension through a toy sized sieve. In the background, Pamela was aware of the music coming from the iPhone, trying to compete with the noise of the wind.

- I just wanna drink 'til I'm not thirsty -

"Listen, Eugene. You have a daughter and she sent me to give you something."

"A daughter? I have a daughter? Yes, I have a daughter. I

imagine that I would have a daughter." Whatever was happening to the earth seemed to be accelerating her father's dementia. The world itself was slipping into another realm and her dad's mind, not to be outdone, was keeping pace.

- I just wanna sleep 'til I'm not tired -

Pamela was praying she was getting through to him. Funny how people pray right up until the end, even if they are unsure of the direction in which the prayer was headed.

She reached into her jacket pocket and extracted the photo of her father and mother on their honeymoon, taken in the middle of a bustling tourist trap of a town, years ago. It pictured two young lovers, smiling at each other with the promise of a long, happy future in front of them. Her father looked at the old, faded photograph and smiled with recognition.

Pamela and her father were now forehead to forehead, eye to eye. One could even say soul to soul. She was vaguely aware their feet weren't on the ground anymore.

Nothing mattered any more. Not the black hole, not the wind, not the swirling colors, not the purple clouds overhead or the plum stained waves below, above which they were now floating.

- I just wanna drive 'til I run out of highway -

The last moments of the world paled in comparison to the last moments between a father and his daughter. Even as an uncertain eternity approached, they both knew they would have each other.

Pamela's vision was becoming distorted as the pressure from the black hole's vacuum increased. The amethyst light danced brilliantly, searing imprints into her eyes. She looked once again at her father.

"Hey, Punkin," he said, now smiling with full knowledge of who she was and what was happening. "Look."

She followed his gaze and saw a large white rectangle, flickering against the dark violet backdrop. A dozen or so black semi-circles were lining the bottom of her field of vision against the silvery box. She saw odd shapes at the top of three of the arcs. In the middle was the silhouette of a man pointing upwards with his left hand. One of the flanking shapes looked like a thick stick with a ball at the end. The other resembled an old fashioned radar grill with a bird beak attached to it.

- Into the purple sky -

Pamela smiled. Perhaps everyone's eternity is different, tailored to the things that were most important in their lives.

Her dad said, "I'll sit next to Crow, Punkin, and you grab the seat by Servo."

Suddenly this end wasn't so terrifying.

Pamela had her dad, and he had her.

But there was more.

They would always have the movies.

UNDONE

MY HEAD SAGGED AGAINST the airplane window, contemplating the devastating effects of a fall from our cruising altitude of thirty-five thousand feet. There wouldn't be anything left. It would be as though I had never have existed. It was a strangely comforting thought.

I was looking for a way to change my life, but I had no idea the answer would come from the back of a Good Housekeeping magazine. I saw a small, seemingly innocent advertisement in the lower left-hand corner of the third page from the back. The simply worded ad read:

> *Need to undo your life?*
> *Take a chance. Believe in PHATE.*
> *Call 555-6523.*

After considering this was undoubtedly a futile attempt at shock value, I figured the worst thing possible would be a wasted phone call and maybe a good laugh. I tore the ad out and stuck it in my money clip. Forgotten so quickly, it stayed there for several days while I flailed and struggled and wasted more of my life.

It didn't register at the time. Life changing events, contrary to popular belief, rarely do.

○

For the record, my name is Josh Childers. I am one of those guys you have met on the street time and time again and would not recognize from one instance to the next. I was that unassuming.

I was living one of those lives which would never amount to anything. I was destined to work my entire career in a hated dead-end job, endure a miserable marriage, and be the worst father imaginable. I would live a dismal life and die without fulfilling any true potential. The best thing I could pass along to my kids was a hefty insurance payout. I was also an organ donor, turning me into a liability every time I took a breath; I was literally worth more dead than alive.

I'd grown up in a Carolina backwoods country town and had become a big fish in that small pond. I was an All-State tennis player in high school, parlaying it into a promising education at a mid-level university. My plans for the future were optimistic early on. However, in my youthful exuberance, I mistook college life for a big party like so many. It took slightly less than two years to flunk out and kiss a full athletic scholarship goodbye.

I snuck back home and took a menial position at a local manufacturing company, secure and dependable, working for The Man. Dreams of the future flushed away along with any chance of being truly happy. I had been thwarted at every turn, passed over for promotion, ignored by my superiors, and had generally reached the pinnacle of my career as a machine repair technician. My company loaned me out to other facilities, basically whoring my talents, sending me on the road several days a month.

I was fed up with my career, my marriage, my life in general. I had, in the past, contemplated leaving on a business trip and just not returning, favoring a new start over the stale life I was living. I'd also thought about suicide more than once, but decided that I was way too much of a pussy to face the consequences.

If not for my kids, I would have done something drastic a long time ago. My home life had become a joke. My wife and I had not had sexual intercourse in over a year, had not engaged in any kind of sexual relations in half a year, and we had not been even the least bit intimate towards one another in probably both those time periods combined. You don't have to be romantic to get your rocks off.

The source of grief at home was my wife, Darlene. She was overbearing, verbally abusive, negative and socially retarded. She was also a chronic hypochondriac, forever convinced she was continually suffering from some exotic disease. She was the only person I'd ever seen who had literally worn out one of those medical reference books, the kind designed to aid people in emergencies. This illusion also bled over to the kids. She would not allow them to participate in normal activities as they were growing up.

But my children were what held me together. The older, my boy Steven, was destined to be an athlete who would excel above his peers, hopefully having his college tuition paid for in scholarships. Also like his old man, he could care less about making an effort in school.

My seven year-old daughter, Emily, was an angel sent from heaven. But one with broken wings; she suffered from spina bifida and could not walk without the aid of leg braces. What she lacked in physical prowess she made up for in her art. She worked wonders with pastels, water-colors and charcoal.

In their own ways, both kids were wonderful, both kids were tragic.

My thoughts were interrupted by the flight crew preparing the cabin for descent into Atlanta International. I had been on a business trip for three days and was on my way back home. I was also stressed out as usual.

My boss had called bullshit on the trip, saying I was dragging it out just to play golf. Maybe I had extended my trip just a little. But, you don't understand. It was the number one rated golf course in Arkansas. I love that course. And I played halfway decent.

I had originally scheduled myself on a return flight timed so I would be able to get into the office for the last half of the day and at least put in a good showing. But after having words with my boss over the phone, and arguing with my wife the night before, the last thing I wanted to do was to go into work after flying in on a white-knuckle commuter.

The first leg of my return flight was delayed about half an hour due to severe thunderstorms. I decided to turn that half hour into two by telling everybody I had missed my connecting flight. Instead of touching down in Atlanta in the morning as scheduled, I was now not supposed to arrive until well into the afternoon. Obviously, I'd just waste my time coming into work so late on a Friday.

I left my boss a voice-mail during his lunch break. It was easier that way.

I also called my wife while driving home from the airport and told her I was still delayed. *Yeah, sorry, I know, but it's just one of those things.*

She bitched. She usually does. She likes to find a reason to bitch. She makes an art out of bitching.

I thought about going and playing some golf or maybe even taking in a movie. God knew I didn't have any time to myself, what with trying to make ends meet. Any time alone at all would be welcomed.

But I was depressed and didn't want to *do* anything. I just wanted to throw off all responsibilities and go away someplace distant where no one could find me. The sense of needing to get away was so overwhelming that I felt a tear trickle down my cheek. It was followed by an ocean. Twice I had to pull off the road and bury my face in my hands.

Finally I got home. It was almost noon. Nobody was expecting me until after three. For a while, at least, I was accountable to no one. Still, I felt trapped. I sat in my car, hands still on the wheel. Chained.

I had thought about ending it all several months ago when my wife and I first started having arguments and fighting. My job was, as usual, shitty. And my life followed suit. Basically, I just never found a convenient time to slit my wrists.

But *this* time was different. I had the time. I had the reasons. *Did I have the guts?*

We'd see about that.

I had some prescription sleeping pills which I used a couple of years ago when I was fighting insomnia. I kept them hidden even after my wife told me to throw them out. You never knew when things like that might come in handy.

The way I figured, I could take off in my car and find a remote place somewhere away from the city which had a spectacular view (I knew a place which overlooked a local theme park), a place where my car would not be found for hours, maybe even days.

I had already said goodbye to my wife: a nice, quick, curt, cold, *bitchy* kiss a couple of days ago when I left on my trip. I wasn't sure she'd even know I was gone. And of course, she'd find *something* to complain about, even if I wasn't there.

I had said goodbye to my kids as well. Although I longed to see and hold them again, I knew if I saw them there'd be no way I'd go through with what I was planning. By now, they were getting used to me being out of town every couple of weeks anyway. They'd just think I'd taken an extra-long business trip. Maybe they'd be right.

Finally, I got out of the car and walked to the end of the driveway to check the mail. Nothing but bills. It depressed me even more.

I let myself in the house and set off the goddamned alarm system my wife *insisted* we install. She was so fucking paranoid it was a wonder she even got out of the house. She was afraid of life and I was concerned she had irrevocably affected the kids. They were already starting to show signs of being neurotic as well.

I turned off the alarm, stifling an impulse to smash the control face with my fist.

I walked to the bathroom and retrieved the bottle of sleeping pills from where I'd stashed them behind a spray can of jock itch medicine. I sat on the closed toilet lid for several minutes, leafing aimlessly through the latest Entertainment Weekly. *Was this the last magazine I'd ever read?*

I silently prayed that I was hallucinating.

I returned to the den and sat in my office chair at the computer, switching it on. It booted up in less than a minute. I brought up Word and clicked on File, New. I immediately saved the document to a jump drive titled 'Goodbye.' The virgin cyber page was ready for insight, my final words to this world. I typed:

My job is taking me nowhere. My marriage is a joke. I wish I could be the father my children deserve. At least Pepsi will miss me. I'm checking out. Josh.

Pepsi was our cat. He was slinking around my legs as I wrote the note. I briefly thought about taking him with me, slipping him a couple of sleeping pills, too. But I couldn't do that to a noble creature like a cat. I let him live.

I read the note again. It wasn't Homer, but I figured it would get the message across. I hit Save again and removed the memory stick, planning on tossing it in the mail on my way to eternity. It was warm with the power of computation.

I turned from the computer and sat there. While I've contemplated this before, I'd never been so close to actually doing it. My breathing was accelerated, my heart was racing.

Now, don't get me wrong. I'm a sinner. In my time I've committed some doozies, believe me. But this one. *Suicide.* The beauty-slash-terror of this sin was its *finality.* All the other transgressions, no matter how bad or how often or how enjoyable, could be forgiven if you lived long enough. Chances were, with suicide, you'd pretty much squelched your chances of getting exonerated by the Almighty.

I thought deeply about that last, profound concept.

Heavy sigh. Did I mention I was a coward?

I slipped the jump drive back into the USB slot and calmly reformatted it.

I flushed the sleeping pills down the toilet. The entire bottle.

Instead of committing suicide, I watched *Jerry Springer: Too Hot For TV*. Twice.

In retrospect, after watching the DVD, I probably should have gone ahead and killed myself. It would have been less painful.

There are some hells from which you can't escape.

○

Three days later, I stumbled across the crumpled advertisement in my money clip as I was settling my bill at the bar across from work. I read the words again and had the same confused reaction inside my head: a mixture of puzzlement and longing. Those feelings intermingled with alcohol aided my decision to make a slightly drunken phone call to the number in the ad.

I was pleasantly surprised to hear a very sultry, sexy female voice on the other end of the phone, even at this late hour. I wish I could recall the details of that conversation, I honestly do. Before I knew it, I had made an appointment for God-knew-what the next afternoon at the offices of PHATE, Inc. on the outskirts of Atlanta.

○

I was unable to sleep that night. The potential of something wonderful happening instead of the usual insomniac dread of the next workday was what kept me awake this time. I felt like I was about to be released from my prison.

I took a half day vacation the next day, had a long relaxing lunch, and showed up for the meeting five minutes earlier than the appointed time. The directions given over the phone were flawless. I found the place on my first try.

The building itself, obviously a remodeled convenience store, was set a good block away from any other structures. The outside was well maintained, landscaped, and had a professional look. But even a polished turd is still a turd. It remained what it was: a remodeled convenience store.

Inside, I was greeted with luxurious burgundy carpeting, low lighting coming from behind black oriental metal shades, and rich mahogany furniture. The interior belied the exterior to the extreme.

The receptionist embodied every bit of the fantasy that I had imagined after hearing her voice on the phone. She could have been the sister of the chick from the Big Bang Theory; the pretty blonde, not the frumpy ex-Blossom actress. After registering my name, I settled into a comfortable, oversized stuffed armchair and waited.

A few minutes later, the receptionist glided over to me and whispered my name as if we were in a library. She led me through the only door in the room and into an office decorated to compliment the waiting room. Obviously the proprietor had done quite well for himself. The receptionist said the 'Doctor' would be with me in a moment.

After she left, I looked around at the certificates and honors which were framed and hanging on the walls. The amount of credentials was impressive, the distinctions obviously varied and eclectic, and the writing very elegant. Curious though: none of the certificates were in English.

Just then a smallish, rather unassuming man walked in. He smiled and offered his hand immediately.

"Hello. I am Dr. Von Ramm," he announced. He was several inches shorter than me, stout but not heavy, and had obvious Eastern European blood in his veins. He gave off an air of authority and spoke with a heavy Slavic accent.

Briefly, Dr. Von Ramm explained that he was a German transplant who had been in the states for just under five years. He had a wife and two sons, lived outside Atlanta and he loved his newly adopted country.

I introduced myself and told him that I had seen his advertisement and was intrigued by its directness. He told me that it was his receptionist's idea.

The nature of his business was called "Psionic Resonance." It was an off-shoot of a scientific principle first explored by the American-funded WWII Russian scientists who were trying to beat the rest of the world to the atomic bomb finish line. It was the same science which had been explored by Dr. Niccoli Tessla and made famous by the fabled 'Philadelphia Experiment' of 1943.

In short, it had to do with time travel.

At first, I wasn't sure I had heard the doctor correctly. *Time travel?* Obviously, I had wasted my time. In my opinion, time travel was merely a science fiction writer's vehicle used to entertain. It had nothing to do with reality.

I politely excused myself and moved to the door.

It was locked.

I turned, more surprised than frightened. Dr. Von Ramm explained that my reaction was textbook. Almost all clients who had come to PHATE had exactly the same initial reaction. The locked door, while imposing, was merely a device he used to allow his presentation to be heard. He further explained that rarely did his potential clients panic or get hysterical, demand to be freed or use threats of law enforcement. Only once had he gotten a return visit from a scared customer with the police in tow. A quick explanation quieted the officer's questions and, by the time the two had left, the policeman was beginning to suspect the complainant was a little off-balance, not the good doctor.

He asked me whether I would fall in the majority or minority.

I stayed, if only out of curiosity to see how this money making scheme could possibly produce enough legal income to afford the rich tastes so readily displayed in the office. The door unlocked with the click of a remote device on the doctor's desk. I opened it and then closed it, if nothing else than for my own reassurance.

Dr. Von Ramm continued. "By using certain medicines in conjunction with older power sources, the scientists of the forties discovered they could produce certain temporal displacements which effectively caused rifts in time. Ultimately, the experiments were abandoned by the end of the decade due to environmental and ecological concerns. However, with the recent advent of micro technology and the onslaught of cybernetics in the early twenty-first century, the theories had been revisited. Certain investors preferred a more private and a more profitable approach.

"As a result," he concluded, "it was now possible to 'travel between the moments'."

He waited for my reaction before continuing. I remained stone-faced.

Von Ramm went on. "PHATE does not have any interest in changing the scope of humanity. My company is not intent on going back and saving Jesus from His duty to mankind, murdering Hitler before his rise to power, or stopping 9/11. PHATE is here to provide a consumable commodity, and, in turn, make a modest profit. Period."

He smiled and continued. "The service is, in a nutshell, to give people the ability to travel back into their *own* lives to one specific moment they needed to change. Even I do not know *when* the person would go. Only the patient knows the exact moment which changed their lives and often, they themselves don't even know the precise event, but their subconscious does."

Anticipating any questions, the doctor went on. "The procedure is irreversible, of course. Once someone undergoes the process, they are never heard from again. Nor is there any memory of the client to the PHATE staff, including myself. This is because the client has changed their life in such a way that they would never need to consult with PHATE in the first place."

I tried to get my mind around the concept.

He explained that the only record was a signed release and a monetary deposit into PHATE's bank account. Video and audio recordings, as well as any other type of 'hard' evidence were not to be found. Only 'soft' signs like graphology remained. Complaints, understandably, were nonexistent.

The doctor even went so far as to conjecture that there was no way of knowing if the patients retained their present-day memory or not. If someone had come back through PHATE more than once, the doctor and his staff would have no memory of their initial visit.

Again, I wrestled with the idea. It really appeared that Von Ramm actually believed what he was preaching.

In the back of my mind, a plan was slowly forming. If this guy truly had the ability to do what he claimed, then I might finally have a way out of this miserable existence. God knew I didn't wish any harm on my children. When I got right down to it, I doubted that I really hated my wife as much as I thought.

I just needed out. Out of my life and, more immediately, out of this office. I thanked the doctor, took one of his cards, and left.

The rest of the day went relatively without incident. I went home, had no interaction with my wife or kids that night, and fell into a dreamless sleep in a lonely bed.

◉

"What the *hell* have you done?" Darlene's face was inches from mine, screaming at me.

I was awakened before six the next morning by a furious wife, hovering over the bed, grilling me about why I had taken half a day vacation without telling her. With two kids and the flu season right around the corner, how could I justify wasting *any* vacation and not save it for emergency medical days?

I did my usual head bobbing and mumbled apologies, all the while seething with rage.

Something inside me snapped.

A ganglion joining brain regions had worn too thin; a synapse didn't quite fire; a gland didn't secrete a chemical.

A straw broke a camel's back.

◉

I was waiting outside the convenience store office of PHATE, Inc. when the secretary finally showed up just before eight. I managed to talk her into letting me wait for Dr. Von Ramm in one of the overstuffed chairs in the corner. At exactly 8:32, I was shown into the inner office where Dr. Von Ramm sat waiting behind his desk.

I explained what had happened and that I was ready to do whatever it took to change my life permanently. Von Ramm asked several questions, but the most disturbing inquiry had to do with whether or not I had thought to say goodbye to my children. It was almost enough to make me change my mind. *Almost.*

Documents were produced and signed, transferring an ungodly amount of money to an off-shore bank account. *Darlene will kill me*, I thought. Then I smiled. *Maybe not. There will be no 'me' to kill.*

The doctor led me through a back door, down a flight of stairs, and into a large room containing a dozen hospital beds. Everything in that room was a muted shade of burgundy. "No reason," explained the doctor without me having to ask. "Just a favorite color."

I changed into burgundy hospital scrubs and cap of the same color. I was given *six* extra strength Tylenol to wash down with a two liter bottle of lemon-lime Gatorade.

Ten minutes later, I was strapped crucifixion-style to one of the hospital beds with an IV in my arm. Dr. Von Ramm and two other masked technicians stood over me.

"I am going to give you a couple of drugs," Dr. Von Ramm said in the usual halting manner, belying his native language. "A special cocktail of my own invention. You will have slight tremors for a few minutes. I will be back after they have passed."

The 'slight' tremors nearly broke my back and sent me into stomach-churning convulsions. The 'few minutes' were lost in a haze. All told, it was a half-hour that tested my very will to live. When the shakes finally subsided, I felt strangely calm, oddly at peace.

The technicians hooked another splice into my IV which led to a smaller packet of a deep burgundy-colored liquid. Dr.

Von Ramm reappeared, poker-faced as ever. He placed into my hand what looked to be a small toggle switch topped with a bright red button.

"In that bag," he gestured to the solution, "is the core of the, shall we say, *transformation*. Have you ever heard of nano-technology? It is a microbiological wonder which gives us an edge over the crude experiments Dr. Tesla toyed with in the forties. The switch in your hand will release them into your IV. It is all up to you now. Deep down, you know the point in time in your life which needs to be changed. You will arrive within a day of the moment when your decision, or lack thereof, will make a difference for the rest of your life. When you are ready, *if* you are ready, push the button and it is, how do you say, a done deal. No way back"

I looked at the toggle switch in my hand. The scary thing, I thought in retrospect, was the fact that there was no second thought, no hesitation.

I pressed the button.

I watched the ruddy liquid invade the external catheter, mixing with the saline solution in the IV. I watched the wine-red fluid snake through the small clear tubing, disappearing into my vein.

Warm, tingling, itchy feelings started in my arm, and then quickly spread to the rest of my body. My vision blurred and a bright light washed over me.

Of course, the color of the light was burgundy.

◎

I gradually came awake, the sun peeking through the blinds. It felt like morning. My eyes were blurry, my head groggy. It was like I had lost a fight with Mr. Jack Daniels. The fact that I couldn't remember the night before was a good sign; I had must have somehow staggered home from the bar down the street.

It was probably Saturday because my alarm hadn't gone off. I felt beside me and the sheets were cold. Darlene must have already gotten up (or had never come to bed) and was planning my Honey-Do list for the day. I rolled to my side and promptly slid off the edge, hitting the floor. Even in my sleep, even in a king-sized bed, I must have been getting as far away as possible from the bitch.

Picking myself up, I turned back to the bed to pull up the covers and froze. It was a single bed. I was in a smaller room than our master bedroom. *Had I fallen asleep somewhere else? Lord, Darlene is going to be...*

It hit me like, well like reality hits you: square and hard and brutal. All of a sudden I remembered what happened, the doctor, the color of burgundy everywhere, the deep red liquid in the IV, the toggle switch, and...

I was there. Or, rather, I was here. But *when* is here?

Looking around, I realized I was in my parent's garage apartment in Pineville, a small community just south of Charlotte. This was where I had secluded myself after my failed college days. My folks had let me move in here until I got my act together. It must have been at least twenty years ago.

One question had been answered: I could remember everything. All those years cow-towing, walking on eggshells around Darlene. The crappy job, my transgressions, my unhappy children. Everything. The memories were as clear as if they had happened yesterday. They had. But technically, they wouldn't happen for several years. If at all.

I needed to know exactly when it was. If there was some critical moment I needed to embrace or ignore, I couldn't afford to get caught by surprise. In awe, I looked around the apartment.

Everything was just how I remembered. This place, the house, the garage, everything had been sold shortly after Mom passed, a year and a half after Dad died. So the fact that I was here made this around 1998 or '99. If that was the case, I was between jobs for the third time and wasn't looking very hard.

I looked down. What I *didn't* see was the beer gut I had developed over the years. I was lean and fit, only a year or so removed from playing college sports. I also realized the usual pains and achy joints were, not only gone, but were replaced by a sense of vitality I hadn't felt in years. *My God, I was young again.*

Mom. Dad. The realizations kept coming. *They were still alive.* I had a chance to see them again, to help them like I hadn't before, and to make a difference with them near the end of their lives. *This is a miracle.*

Simultaneously the knowledge of exactly when and how they would die also hit me. Dad would have a heart attack in the garage right below my feet. I would find him looking like he had gone to sleep and had never woken up. Mom would follow months later from complications of pneumonia. Her death would take longer, and be more of a goodbye than Dad's.

I looked around to find a pair of raggedy jeans and t-shirt, both impossibly small. But I had to remember that I was impossibly small as well. I dressed and everything fit perfectly.

Opening the door and slipping down the stairs into the garage, I half expected to see Dad in there, tinkering with some hobby of his. I could tell where he had been working earlier, his tools arranged next to a half-built car engine. *I remember that engine.* It was given to him to rebuild as a project. If I had my timing right, he would sell it in a few weeks and the car in which it would go would win the Labor Day race at the local speedway. Dad had a way with making things better than they already were.

Well, most things. Then there was me. The *old* me, I reminded myself. *I had a secret.* I was literally not the same man I was yesterday. But as far as anyone else was concerned, it was just the next day. Josh Childers, as everyone knew him, was still the same loser-come-home failure. And I knew that. It was the knowledge which would give me the edge I needed to *make* something of myself this time.

I crossed the driveway to the backdoor which opened into the kitchen. There was Mom, slicing apples for a pie. *How Norman Rockwellian iconic.*

I nearly teared up at seeing her. However, I knew I couldn't let her see that, or do anything she'd think was out of the ordinary. As far as she knew, I was the same troubled young adult who had put her and Dad through hell when I was in high school. To my mind, it was twenty years ago; to her, it was just a couple. I needed to act the part, if only for a while until I got my bearings in this strange past world I knew only from faded memories.

"Hi, Mom," I said, ducking into the refrigerator and wiping the wetness from my eyes. "Where's Dad?"

"Oh, he had to go across town this morning and help Carl Richardson help get a riding tractor started. He'll be back soon. You know him, it'll only take a few minutes to work his magic." Her voice, a voice I hadn't heard in decades, was like proverbial music to my ears. "Why? You need him for something?"

"No," I lied. Of course I needed him, needed *her*, for *everything*. It's always been said, and now I knew it to be true: you really never miss someone until they're gone. "Just checking. I figured he'd be messing around in the garage on something. I saw he had the race engine half apart and—"

Mom was looking at me, puzzled. "Race engine? What race engine?"

Damn. I'd forgotten Dad had only just gotten it and its future was as yet unknown to everyone but me. As far as anybody knew, this was just another rebuild for a regular car.

"Not race engine," I said. "The car engine in the garage. I guess I had racing on my mind."

She snickered. "You and your single-mindedness. You've always been like that. You get something in your head, there's no going elsewhere."

I realized I had to get out of here before I said or did something which would betray what I knew and would have to answer some uncomfortable questions. I grabbed the newspaper off the table, still rolled up in its rubber band. "Tell Dad I'll bring this back when he gets home, OK?"

"Still looking in the want-ads?" She didn't mean anything by it, but her words brought back memories of when I was adrift, jobless and living off my parents years after I should have been.

I nodded and headed out the way I'd come in. Passing through the garage, I looked at the place on the oil stained floor where I would find Dad in a few years, vise grip in one hand, ratchet in the other, looking like he had decided to take a nap on the cement.

I wondered to myself if it could be prevented somehow, this time around. I wondered if that was part of the new plan.

I ran up the stairs and back into my old apartment. I slid the rubber band off the paper and plopped down into my over-stuffed Lazy Boy which was coming apart at the seams. It would end up in a dumpster soon.

Unfolding the paper, I looked at the date next to the headline. Saturday, August 1st, 1998. That was twenty years ago, almost to the day. Only it wasn't 'ago' anymore. It was *now*.

August 1. That date meant absolutely nothing to me. I was racking my brain, trying to find some significance, but I couldn't. *Something* was going to happen, or *not* happen, sometime today and I didn't have a clue as to what it was. *Wouldn't that be a heck of a note?* Travel twenty years back in time to fix something which got broken and miss the whole damned thing because I was taking a nap or driving around town? What kind of messed up time travel scenario was this anyway?

I realized I was being irrational about it. As if something like what was happening was anything to be rational *about*.

I opened my empty mini-fridge and looked at the clock above the stove. Ten in the morning. If I couldn't figure what was going on by this time tomorrow, nothing would matter and I'd be right back in the same hell I'd lived for the past twenty years.

I slammed the refrigerator door and all the magnets and their captured contents spilled onto the countertop. I gathered up the mess to throw it away because at this point, none of them meant anything to me anyway. I looked at the trash in my hands and something caught my eye. It was a handwritten note on the back of a bar tab:

Party Sat Aug 1 - Tony Ballard's 8:00 BRING BEER.

I froze. I knew what was happening now. I knew the moment in question. I knew why my drug-induced subconscious mind had picked this day to return me to.

Tony's party was where I had first met Darlene, tonight, twenty years ago.

No. Again, I reminded myself, not 'ago.'

Now.

◉

I spent the rest of the day reading every story in the newspaper to better orient myself. It was still hard to believe I had awoken in my past, twenty years from what I considered the present. All my thoughts were intact. I could recall everything about my pitiful life, right up to the point where Dr. Von Ramm spoke his final words to me: *No way back.*

My immediate concern was tonight, Tony's party and how *not* to meet the future bitch of my life. While the answer seemed easy enough, *don't go*, it wasn't all that simple. Being the local ex-jock, albeit a failed one, I had a certain reputation which needed to be upheld. Missing the party wasn't typical of the arrogant prick I was in the nineties.

So, I had to go; that was a given. But I didn't have to make the same mistakes.

Dad came home late morning, but I didn't dare go down and talk to him. I had come close to tipping my hand with Mom earlier, and I knew, given the chance with Dad, it was likely I would say or do *something* which would make him question my sanity. Besides, I had plenty of time to spend with them after I took care of business tonight.

Morning turned into afternoon and before I knew it, evening had slipped in and it was time to go to the party. I dressed. *Was I wearing the same thing that I wore twenty years ago when I did this the first time around?* I headed down through the garage to my car.

My car. Wow. I had forgotten what I drove back in the day. But there it was, my old 1973 Opel GT. I remembered loving that car. It looked like a miniature Corvette. I had bought it in high school and Dad and I restored it from the ground up. I was thinking there was no way I would fit in it with my current weight before I remembered I was literally half the man that I would be in the future.

Remembering I kept my spare money in the ashtray, I was relieved to find a twenty stuffed in there next to my driver's license. It was good to have cash because I didn't have a clue what my 1998 PIN number would be at an ATM.

I took a quick look at the picture on my driver's license. A young punk dickhead stared back at me. *How did I ever let myself turn into such a prick? It won't happen this time around.*

Grabbing a case of Budweiser from the convenience store (where I was carded!), I made the fifteen minute trip across town to Tony's. It was exhilarating to be driving my old car. I wanted to take it on the road and never look back. I knew I'd have that chance if I could just make it through this evening without committing the same mistake I'd made before.

◎

I was fashionably late arriving. There were already a dozen or so cars in Tony's front yard. He wasn't rich, but he wasn't poor either. His dad had a local insurance business and his mom was a secretary at an accounting firm in the city. They were cool folks and were OK with Tony throwing this party... as long as the place didn't get trashed.

Taking the beer from the passenger seat, I hesitantly made my entrance. Slaps on the back and handshakes galore, I was the closest thing to a local celebrity this small town had. In another life, *this* life, I would have eaten up the attention. Now, with a devastating alternate life experience under my belt, I was more embarrassed than anything.

Still, I had to make my rounds and act like I normally

would, at least in general. I struck up conversations with people I hadn't seen in years, acting as if we'd only hung out a few days before. It was scary how effortless it was to fall right back into my old routine. I could easily stay the same person I'd come to hate twenty years from now.

Darlene arrived about a half hour after I did, along with a couple of her girlfriends. She was beautiful, just like I remembered, so full of life and carefree abandon. If I allowed things to continue the way they had, in a few of years we'd be married, with children following soon. All the while my life would be spiraling downward and out of control. She would end up an overweight bitch who hated everyone and everything and I would be compelled to try *time travel* as a last resort. It was almost comical if it weren't so tragically true.

Loosely, my plan was simple: just steer clear of Darlene the whole night. With any luck she'd get her talons into some other unsuspecting guy and never give me a single thought. Distantly, I felt a little guilty about what would happen to the poor sucker she would end up with. I got over that thought rather quickly.

As the night wore on, despite my best efforts, we kept running into each other. It was almost as if it was inevitable that we meet, regardless of my efforts. In my past, we first met in the kitchen as I was fixing a drink. She had sauntered up to me, struck up a conversation and never left my side the rest of the night, all the way until morning. *This was going to be tough*, I thought.

I was able to duck out if the kitchen as I saw her approaching, dark hair flowing behind her. I went into the backyard and watched a riveting game of badminton for a few minutes.

As I was returning to the house, she was coming out the back door. I quickly raised my red Solo cup to my lips and took a big swig of beer, essentially covering my face and showing her I was preoccupied. It looked like she slowed to say something to me, but hesitated. I walked past her without a second glance.

An hour later, I was exiting the bathroom and again ran into her in the hall. Our eyes met and I knew I had to do something which would head off a conversation of any kind. I came up with the only solution I could think of, and I'm not very proud of it.

"Whew," I said, waving my hand side to side in front of my face. "I wouldn't go in there if I were you. At least not without a gas mask."

Whatever eye contact she might have made was quickly replaced with a look of revulsion and disgust. She was shocked to hear someone so blatant about stinking up the bathroom at a party. I decided to go for broke and make an impression she'd never forget, essentially severing whatever fate there might have been between the two of us.

"Well, hello there sugar britches," I said, putting on my best drunk voice. "I bet your name's Angel."

"No," she replied, uncomfortable from the start. "I'm—"

"I guess you know who *I* am," I rudely interrupted. "Josh Childers, star athlete." I made a big display of formally bowing to her. "Now, what would you like for breakfast in bed?"

"I know who you are," she said, horrified at my performance. "And as far as breakfast in bed with you... not if you were the last man on earth."

I smiled. *Mission accomplished.*

I saw her only one more time that night. She had some guy cornered in the living room, obviously working him over with her womanly ways. She glanced up just in time to see me come into the room, took one look at me, whispered something to the guy she was with and they both looked my way and laughed. I really didn't care at that point. If she was out of my life forever, I could withstand a little embarrassment. Besides, I'd never seen that guy before.

And I'd never see Darlene again.

I left the party not long after, alone, exhausted and spent. It can be bittersweet, changing the fate of yours and others' lives. I remember driving home and collapsing into bed. My last thoughts, before fading into sleep, was wondering what tomorrow would bring.

A new life, new future new potential.

As always, I don't remember falling asleep. *Does anyone?*

◉

Over the course of the next twenty years, my life was a mixture of memories of how things used to be contrasted against things I'd never experienced.

Before I lost my parents, I made sure to right many of the wrongs I was guilty of up to that point in that life. While they were still alive I purposely didn't use my awareness of what lay ahead to profit. I was determined to become the man my folks wanted me to be, all on my own, without cheating. For a while there, we were a family once more.

The anticipation of Dad's death, followed by Mom's a year later, was grueling. When I finally found Dad on the garage floor it was a mixture of sorrow and reprieve, finally freed from the burden of knowing it was coming. And Mom, bless her heart, didn't linger as long as I remembered the first time around.

After mom passed, I took what little life insurance had been paid out and headed to Vegas. Being an avid sports fan, I knew who would win each of the World Series for the next two decades. Bets placed correctly during spring training would net me a fortune by October each year. There were also Superbowls, The Masters, NBA Finals… My head was spinning with possibilities.

Within six months I had multiplied $25,000 a hundred fold. Two years later, my net worth was north of five million dollars. Not bad for an alternate universe screw up.

I was able to parlay my knowledge of the future into a multi-million dollar estate without having to do any *real* work. I invested in specific stocks which flew under the radar, but I knew were poised to explode: Green Mountain Coffee, Southwestern Energy, Decker's Outdoor, just to name a few. These companies started out in the stock market basement and had soared beyond expectations in the early part of the new century.

I was able to do the things rich people did: Fly to another country for a round of golf, get red carpet treatment at Hollywood premiers, connect with the elite, have tea with the snobs on Martha's Vineyard. All the while I made sure not to influence anything which would alter the course of anyone's history but my own.

I didn't work, I just played. I didn't make decisions; I hired people to do that for me. I made contributions to all the usual charities and causes. I was widely recognized as someone who took care of the people who worked for him. I became the person I'd always wanted to become.

Through it all, it was just me. I could have companionship anytime I wanted, an unspoken privilege of the rich. I could buy any woman I wanted (or two - which I did from time to time), never letting any of them get too close. But there were no girlfriends, no wife, no children. Hell, I didn't even own a dog or a cat.

It was by choice, though. After I had narrowly escaped my former life and the hell I went through with Darlene, I could never bring myself to trust, much less love, anyone ever again. *It was OK*, I would tell myself over and over. *It's better like this.* After all I'd learned from before, I knew what I was doing this time around.

There's a line from an old Van Zandt song that goes something like this: *If you want to hear God laugh, tell Him your plans.*

Funny. I could hear Him laughing already.

◎

I saw my *never-was* wife and *never-will-be* children downtown the other day. It was completely by chance. At least that's what I keep telling myself.

I was walking from the bank to the parking garage and glanced across the street. There they were. Darlene looked the way I remembered her, even after twenty years and another life ago. She had shopping bags in hand and the kids trailing behind.

Her children.

Not *mine*.

There was enough of Darlene in them that they were still recognizable. They looked to be about the same age as when I last saw them: They had the same features, or at least the basics of those features. The eyes were the same, but not. Their noses just different enough to give them a dissimilar appearance than what I remembered. Steven's brown hair was now blonde and Emily's flowing blonde hair had been replaced by shorter curly locks of fiery red. Steven still walked with that athletic swagger and Emily, *Lord help me...* Emily was walking without the use of braces. She had two strong legs which had not been ravaged by the curse of birth defects.

It was a jolt to my system, not *just* seeing them but seeing them as they would have been without me as their father.

Without me as their father. Those words were haunting.

It occurred to me that I wasn't there when Steven took his first step, when Emily lost her first tooth. I probably wasn't there the first time around either, in the other, failed life. I was likely on some business trip and missing out on my kids' lives. As usual.

But there were other recollections I *could* place from before. I remembered watching Steven play Little League baseball, and attending Emily's piano recital. I was there when the ballet troupe made a special part for my crippled Emily in the Nutcracker. I remembered giving Steven advice on his first date and feeling the sting of his fastball as we played catch in the back yard. I suddenly realized I would never experience any of these memories with my children.

It took seeing my never-to-be wife and her children to make me appreciate just how lonely I really was. I found myself standing on the corner of one of the country's largest cities, at a busy intersection, staring at a family I never knew with tears running down my cheeks. People stared as they passed, only briefly, too caught up in their own lives to worry about some stranger having a meltdown.

Impulsively I started across the street. The pedestrian crossing sign was still telling me not to, along with my subconscious yelling the same. Nevertheless, I crossed, dodging cars and angry drivers, not knowing what exactly I would do when I got there.

Darlene, Emily and Steven were still standing in front of a large plate-glass window, watching an elaborate toy train set chug its way around and through a papier-mâché mountain. They never gave me a second thought as I approached. I still didn't know what I was doing, but I knew I had to see them up close.

Emily had a stuffed Winnie-the-Pooh rabbit in her right hand and was holding the hand of her big brother with her left. As she went to point at something in the window, the stuffed toy came out of her hand and dropped to the sidewalk below.

It was almost as if it were planned.

Before she even knew she had dropped it, I was already there retrieving it for her. As I squatted down, eye-level with her, she turned to look at me. It was all I could do to remember to breathe. Her eyes were so blue, so piercing. I had to look away.

I handed the stuffed rabbit back to her. "Here you are sweetie," I said. "Don't want to leave this little guy lying on the sidewalk, do we?"

Steven was looking at me now, as was Darlene. Immediately she took a defensive posture, a good mother protecting her children. I could tell immediately she was a different person from the one I'd known. She was confident and sure of herself, but at the same time I recognized the woman she was always meant to be. Without me in the picture for twenty years, Darlene had remained the decent person she always had been. *Was it possible it wasn't Darlene who was the problem in that other life, but maybe it was the college dropout fuck-up from twenty years ago who shaped her life into the miserable one I had given her?*

"Thank you," she said, instinctively stepping between her

children and this stranger on the street. "Tell the nice man thank you, Emmy."

"Thank you, sir," the sweet little girl said to this man she had never known.

"Are you all right?" asked Darlene. I realized I still had wetness on my face from the tears I was crying a few minutes ago.

"Oh… yeah," I said, wiping my face. "Allergies."

"OK. Well…, thanks again," she said, ending the conversation the way we all do when we're talking with someone we don't know and are ready to move on.

"Glad I could help," I said, trying to walk away but not succeeding.

Finally, Darlene gathered her children and whisked them off, away from the strange man on the street who was obviously lying about the tears on his face, who had just conveniently shown up to pick up her child's toy and had struck up a conversation. She'd evidently gotten curious vibes from me and was moving on.

My mind was racing. Was Darlene *really* the one to blame for my failed life in that alternate reality? If I could change my path, make myself a better person, would the effect of such changes rub off on people with whom I was associated? With what I knew now, would it be possible to salvage a life apart from the one I had cheated? Had I conned the universe into changing everything except the *real* offender - me?

I stood there, rooted to the sidewalk, afraid to move for fear I would follow that family down the street. I watched them until they turned the corner.

None of them looked back at me like I hoped they would.

At the same time, I couldn't look away.

My God, I said to myself. *What have I done?* Suddenly the petty, selfish memories of a hellish life were outweighed by the reality of a life unfulfilled.

I needed my family back.

It took only three days from when I saw them to find what I was looking for. I perused every library, every bookstore, every gas station that had a book rack on a quest for the *one* thing I knew I could find to set things right.

I hardly ate. I barely slept. I let my company run itself.

Finally, late one evening at a sidewalk newsstand, I found it. I paid the vendor while he looked on with questioning eyes, no doubt wondering why this haggard man was buying such a feminine periodical.

With the magazine in a plastic bag, and securely tucked under my arm, I walked back to my penthouse apartment. The doorman let me in, greeting me warmly by name. "Evening, Mr. Childers."

I didn't raise my head to him. I didn't glance up at the wall in the lobby which bore my name as the building's owner. I didn't look at my face on the covers of *Inc.* and *Success* publications resting on the side tables. I kept my head down and intent on what I needed to do. I was afraid that if I didn't, I'd change my mind.

Once I got to my rooftop penthouse, I went straight to the Nuevo riche roll top desk from where I ran my empire. I sat down heavily into the fine Italian leather chair, simultaneously fatigued and excited.

Sliding the copy of Good Housekeeping from the plastic bag, I leafed straight to the back section where the advertisements were displayed. There it was, in the lower left-hand corner on the third page from the back cover, innocuous to the everyday reader:

Need to undo your life?
Take a chance. Believe in PHATE.
Call 555-6523.

I ripped the page from the magazine, carefully folded it and placed it deliberately in my money clip. It would not stay there long. Not this time.

I had a doctor's appointment to make tomorrow morning.

SENSE/LESS

I HAVE SOMETHING IN my eye, Shawn Cody says to himself.

He remembers back to the day before, to just as he is glancing up at the overhead lines on which he is working, a drop of fresh rain strikes him square in the eye. *It's not like I've never gotten a raindrop in my eye. It probably happens more times than we realize*, he thinks. *Nothing to worry about.*

But this morning, it is definitely bothering him.

Upon closer examination in the bathroom mirror he begins to think he's left his contact in his eye overnight. It sometimes happens when he's had too much to drink, or has taken his Ambien a little earlier than normal. While neither of these he remembers doing last night, it is still possible, even likely.

Pulling his right eyelid down, and reaching in with his left index finger, Shawn is able to pluck the contact lens from his eye with one fluid, practiced motion. The sting is the usual nuisance and temporarily makes him squeeze his eye shut.

Reaching into the top drawer of the bathroom cabinet, he removes the contact case and places it on the counter. Opening the twist off lid with the big "R" on top, he starts to place the lens he's taken from his eye... and stops.

His contact lens is *already* in the storage container.

So what's on the tip of my finger?

Squinting through the one eye which isn't watering, he examines what he's removed from his other eye.

It is a similar in thickness to his contact lens. That's why he doesn't examine it further after it is removed. But the similarity ends there. It is the same hazel-brown color as his own iris with the familiar radiating striations. The only thing not identical is a clear center where the pupil should be.

It's like he is balancing the *skin* of his eye on the tip of his finger.

What the—?

Quickly pooling some tap water in the plugged sink, Shawn

gingerly places the foreign object into the temporary bath.

Looking back into the mirror, drawing the lid of his left eye down, he slides a similar membrane off the other eye. Steadying it on his fingertip, it looks indistinguishable to the other, now floating in the sink, looking up at him.

He places it in the water next to the other and looks back into his reflection in the mirror. The eyes staring back look just as normal as they ever have, even down to the tiny red veins at the corners.

Strange. He's never been able to see detail like that from this distance until he's put his contact lenses in for the day.

He looks back down at the discs floating in the water and has a thought. Grabbing his iPhone from the nightstand, he snaps a quick picture of the faux eyes ogling back at him from the basin. He stifles a chuckle at how ridiculous they look: a pair of cartoon irises daring him to blink.

Pushing the plunger down to let the water out, Shawn watches them quickly spiral past the stopper and into the drain, washing into the septic system.

Hope I won't need those, he thinks. And he laughs.

◎

After popping in his contacts and going through the rest of his morning routine, Shawn is soon on the road to his job at the phone company.

The sun seems especially bright for this time of morning and he dons his sunglasses. But even with them on, everything still looks washed out, flat and out of focus.

Arriving at the AT&T office, Shawn immediately goes to the bathroom and removes his contacts for rewetting. Before he can replace them, he again sees that his eyesight seems to be perfect without contacts. He decides to try the day without them.

Once on the road for his morning rounds, Shawn notices once that everything seems unbelievably clear. He can see details in things at distances beyond what he can remember. *This is how thirty-one year-old eyes are supposed to operate.* He thinks once again that he is too young for corrective lenses.

The trade off, however, is a bit of vertigo. It reminds him of how your vision is when you stand up too quickly: a slight spinning which throws off your balance.

Then he notices the colors.

There aren't any.

And yet, the grass is still green, the sky is still blue and the fluorescent color of his safety vest is still bright orange. While they don't *register* as colors, he still *recognizes* them *as* colors.

Strange as it seems, Shawn accepts this difference in stride. The foremost thought on his mind is how much money he will be saving in contact lenses.

I'm not cheap, he says to himself. *I'm frugal.*

◙

The next morning, Shawn Cody wakes to the muffled sound of his alarm going off promptly at 6:45.

Muffled? It should be screaming at me.

He reaches over and stifles the alarm by hitting the snooze button. He sits up in bed, swings his legs over the side, stumbles into the bathroom and promptly takes a leak.

His piss falls eerily noiselessly into the toilet bowl.

It doesn't make a sound.

Taking one finger, he digs into his right ear, feeling a slight itch after starting to poke around.

He feels some resistance.

His mother had always told Shawn that you aren't supposed to stick anything into your ear smaller than your elbow. This sticks in his mind because, even if you could get your elbow to your ear (which is physically impossible), it is way too big to stick into it anyway.

Nevertheless, he takes a Q-tip from the glass container on the counter and uses it to continue the detail work his finger is unable to do. After only a few seconds he can feel something start shifting and loosening up. He manages to wedge the Q-tip off to the side and— *phhhit.*

A mass about the size and color of a small dried plum drops onto the counter with a wet splunk.

He instinctively opens and closes his jaw, feeling that he needs to pop his now cleared ear.

To his right Shawn hears a loud scuttling sound that startles him. He looks down at the toilet base just in time to see one of those gross silverfish disappear into the crack under the baseboard. As it squeezes into the crevasse, he swears he can hear its slick sides rubbing against the wood.

He looks back into the mirror, catching a double vision of himself for just a split second. He plunges the other end of the Q-tip into his left ear.

Phhhit.

Another fleshy, dark object plunks onto the counter beside the first one, slightly bouncing as it hits.

From the bedroom he hears the electric current in his alarm clock shift ever so slightly as the minute number on his digital clock changes from a six to a seven. At the same instant, seven minutes after it originally rang, the snooze alarm starts its wail.

Agony splits Shawn's head as the sound is abnormally loud, nearly knocking him off his feet. He sprints into the bedroom and silences the clock once more, this time switching off the alarm completely.

Returning to the bathroom, with the thunderous sound of his bare feet slapping the cold wooden floor, he looks at the goo which had come out of his ears.

He's never seen so much ear wax come out of his head. On top of that, the color doesn't match what he is used to seeing. Instead of the usual golden orange, this wax is a glistening, deep bluish-purple.

It twitches.

At least he thinks it does. Obviously his eyes are still playing tricks on him.

Feeling justifiably troubled, Shawn flicks the wax into the sink with one stained end of the Q-tip. Like yesterday, his morbid curiosity prompts him to take a photo of the gunk, saving it to his iPhone's image gallery. Before turning on the faucet, he prepares himself this time for the sound the water will make as it splashes into the sink and washes the mess away.

It's loud, sure. But he tells himself it isn't anything he can't get used to. *Looks like ear protection will be the way to go today*, he thinks.

◎

The next morning, Shawn Cody opts to be awakened by his cellphone on vibrate. He is exhausted from the previous day's activities. Between having to wear sunglasses all day, even while indoors, he also finds it necessary to keep earbuds in. At the extreme low volume, he listens to an uncharacteristically different playlist of music than he's accustomed:

Bach.

Zimmer.

Mozart.

Elfman.

All orchestral or soundtrack music without words. Song lyrics seem to grate on his nerves.

Shawn's throat seems scratchy this morning, as if he had slept with his mouth open all night. Attempting a breath through his nose, he discovers that he is completely stopped up. *Great*, he thinks. *On top of everything else, I'm coming down with a cold.*

Careful to not stand too fast for fear of vertigo, or make any sudden sound that would split his head, he gingerly places his feet into his slippers and shuffles into the bathroom. The image in the mirror reflects a haggard man, obviously feeling like crap.

Hello, handsome.

He grabs a couple of Kleenex out of the box and blows snot out of one nostril, and then the other. Inspecting the mess as a habit, he is shocked to see, not the usual brownish-green sticky mucus, but rather a grainy, flaky orange segmented worm-like object. *What the hell kind of cold is in my head?*

Nose now clear, even to his own disgust, he takes a smell of the slime which is soaking the Kleenex. It smells like honeysuckle. *Honeysuckle scented snot. I am definitely losing it.*

Repulsed, he sets the tissue on the counter next to the sink, looking like mandarin jam waiting to be spread on morning toast and eaten with a cup of coffee. It even jiggles a bit as it settles.

Leaving the overhead off so as to avoid the same light sensitivity that has been plaguing him for the last couple of days, Shawn starts his morning ritual, preparing for work.

Removing the cap from the toothpaste, and just out of curiosity, he takes a quick sniff. It smells sweet, like honeysuckle.

He unscrews a bottle of cologne and takes a whiff. It smells like honeysuckle.

He squirts some shaving gel into his hand.

Honeysuckle.

He takes a shit.

Honeysuckle.

And yet, as with his eyesight, he is able to distinguish the different aromas of the everyday, despite the honeysuckle fragrance of everything.

Toothpaste is still peppermint.

Cologne is still musk.

Shaving gel is still menthol.

And shit, well, still smells like shit.

But it's all honeysuckle to his nose.

What the fuck is going on?

Almost as an afterthought, Shawn again snaps a digital photograph of the weird secretion from his body, staining the tissue with its orange fluid. He throws the wadded tissue into the toilet bowl, covers his ears and flushes it together with his sweet-smelling feces down into the sewer to mix with his neighbors'.

◉

From his AT&T work truck during the day, Shawn contemplates sending his doctor a request to see her at some point during the day. What is happening to him can't be right. *But*, he thinks, *it feels good.*

Ultimately, he decides to forego a visit to his doctor. He rationalizes his inaction: *What can be wrong with good vision, excellent hearing and everything smelling like flowers?*

With his ears plugged, eyes under the darkest shades he can find, and the window rolled down to enjoy the smells of the outside world, Shawn goes about his day in a much better mood than he can recently remember.

He feels like a whole new person.

◉

After waking the next morning, Shawn Cody expects to see something else leave his body just like the previous three days. There is nothing out of the ordinary waiting for him in the bathroom; no strange mucus or detached irises.

He is slowly getting used to his newfound changed senses. While the lights are still too bright, and sounds are still too loud, he is finding that he actually welcomes the difference. *How did I get along before? Everything is so much more vivid, so much more alive.*

After dressing, he goes to the kitchen and begins his breakfast routine with a bowl of Cheerios and a cup of coffee. To Shawn, it is harder to flavor his coffee properly because he can't discern odors, at least not like he used to. He adds too much sugar, or not enough creamer, solely based on what he smells. Or thinks he smells.

He fills the bowl with cereal and milk, takes it to the small dinette table and begins eating. He stops midway through his second spoonful.

No taste.

And yet... As with his sense of smell, there is a distinct flavor coming through the blandness. Honey. Sweet, syrupy, sugary honey. One of the tastes he hates most in his life is honey. Sickeningly sweet, thick, with a phlegm-like consistency. The thought of eating honey makes him gag.

But not this time.

This time, it is like ambrosia on his palette.

He feels something slip, something grainy on his tongue. Something large which fills his mouth.

Reaching in, he gently pulls at his tongue and something slides off. Extracting it, he sees what appears to be his *tongue* dangling from his fingers. Only it's not. As with his eyes, it looks like the *skin* of his tongue, as if it has molted and has shed its entire surface.

Resisting the natural gagging reflex, Shawn gingerly lays it next to his cereal bowl.

Why not? With everything else happening with my senses, why not?

Taking it all in stride, whether rationally or not, Shawn calmly focuses his iPhone on the gelatinous mass and snaps off a couple of pictures, adding the photos to an already bizarre image gallery.

Almost as an afterthought, he goes over to the counter, grabs a paring knife and returns to the table. With the knife, he carefully slices the molted tongue-peel like fruit. He plops the pieces into his bowl where it mixes with cereal and milk.

Methodically, Shawn completely finishes his breakfast of Cheerios, milk and cut up tongue-skin.

It tastes like honey.

◉

That night, there is a dream of waking up and showering. This is strange because he never dreams of something so odd. *Girls, sure, waking up with a boner. Falling, yes, coming out of sleep with a start. Fear of speaking in public, just like everybody else. But taking a shower? Weird.*

What makes it even more unusual is the shower is precisely

where he finds himself in the morning, as he stands in the steam, hot, scalding water runs off his body.

Loofah in hand, he is scrubbing furiously at his arms and chest and legs and groin, as if he is trying to clean down through his skin. *Trying to get at what is underneath.*

After several minutes and still dazed from sleep, he turns off the shower and dries off. It feels as if he can't rid himself of the dampness from the water. *Must be the condensation in the bathroom,* he thinks. The humidity has obviously gotten everything sticky and wet.

Wrapping the bath towel around his waist, he walks back into the bedroom and stands at his closet, ready to grab his clothes for the day. As he opens the closet door, moisture beading from his forehead stings his eyes. He wipes at it with the tail of the towel. A thought registers within that he doesn't recall having red towels.

Looking into the closet, he sees something hanging between his work shirts and his jeans, but he can't quite place what it is. After a moment, he comprehends what he is looking at.

Hanging like a sports coat in his closet is the skin from his body, draping ever so neatly over a clothes hanger.

Reality sets in. Within days, his senses have been replaced, one by one, with something else. Something unearthly. Something… *alien.*

One thought dominates: *What was in the raindrop that started all this?*

Blood on his macabre tongue is wine.

He feels as if he is standing on searing hot coals.

The dripping flesh is sickly sweet in his nostrils.

The scream from his mouth falls on his own alien ears.

And his eyes… *Oh God.* His eyes really don't do it justice.

In his iPhone's viewfinder, framing the skin neatly suspended next to the polo shirts in his closet, Shawn Cody properly documents the last of his ties to the human race.

For posterity's sake, it thinks.

GOLF IN THE AFTERMATH

AS SHOCKING AS IT sounds, I never thought I'd enjoy the end of the world near as much as I have.

My conservative family is probably turning over in their respective graves or has since disowned me if the former is not possible. The idea that I have reached the pinnacle of my golfing dreams or have been able to make the most of the world's misfortune would certainly eat at their craw like back-to-back bogies eats at your confidence.

Now, just a minute, Pards. Don't get me wrong. Don't think for one minute I'm some kind of inhuman monster or uncaring son-of-a-bitch. Don't think one day goes by that I don't shed a tear for those who died two years ago during the Skirmishes. Don't think that I enjoy my life all alone, riding the roads, avoiding what's left of humanity, picking through the metaphorical rubble for playing partners. Don't you dare let it cross your mind that I'm in league with the devil or even the Antichrist.

I'm probably worse than all of them put together.

I'm a golfer.

◉

My name is David Parr. I used to be an engineer in the automotive industry. I used to work a job I hated forty, fifty, even sixty hours a week. I used to be able to hit the links, maybe once a week in the off-season, three times a week consistently during the summer if I was lucky. I used to have a house and a couple of pets. I had friends, acquaintances and one pretty special golf partner who would tolerate me choking during four-ball season. Now I have none of the above.

But I still have my sticks.

I thank God I didn't have a family during the last days. Mom died about ten years ago, finally caught up from all those packs of cigarettes that she used to smoke. She never quite understood why I chose not to marry, settle down and raise a family. I don't blame her for that one. I don't blame her one bit.

Dad died a year before the bombs hit, before it really got crazy. He coached me in baseball until I couldn't play anymore because of my crappy shoulder. He was one of the most revered baseball coaches to grace the chalk lines of Western North Carolina. He never really understood my obsession with golf, but he did understand my passion for sports.

I was alone, which was no big deal. I was always a loner, never at ease with others, always avoiding a crowd. If I'd had a family, trust me, the tone of this story would be way different.

Amateur. Double-digit handicapper. Hacker, chunker, slicer, hooker, Alice, worm burner, T-Rex arms. Every name you've ever tagged yourself or your playing partner with - that's me. I've been called 'em all. Hated them on the outside, but secretly loved the attention on the inside. Bad thing is nobody's left to rib me. And it's no fun to call *yourself* a chili-dipper.

I don't know what started the Skirmishes. That's what the government called them at first. Even after they got out of hand, the name stuck purely because of how ironic it was. The Skirmishes eventually turned into World War III. World War III eventually turned into the end of civilization as we knew it. Looking back, I really don't *want* to know what started it all, what made some countries lose their shit and made other nations go mad. I feel that if I *knew*, then somehow I'd *understand*. I don't *want* to understand.

Worst of all, the days of golf came to an end.

Golf's been around, some argue, since the days when Asian fishermen swatted ice chunks around frozen fishing holes. The Scotts, of course, claim the *true* game started over in the European Highlands. Whenever it began, however it evolved into the game we used to know, golf has persevered through war, famine and pestilence.

Where there have been greens and tee boxes, fairways and rough, and enough junk balls to keep the shag bag filled, history has found people gathered to pursue the insanity of the competition. Golfers, being creatures of misery, constantly flock together and compare tales of woe, yet distance themselves from others on the course. Those who golf find a way.

Until now.

◉

The day the end came, when the bombs reigned, the US Open had just finished its first round. The amateurs who had ground their way to the top were living their fantasies. Champions from all over the world were present to put their titles on the line, to pursue that one, elusive championship. The old invitees were there, too, wondering if they had what it took to come out on top one more time.

The only notable absences were representatives from some of the European nations. Langer should have been there, having gained exemption with his surprise tour win the year before. Because of the political tensions in Europe, Garcia passed on defending his Open title from the previous year. Fortunately, or so we thought, it enabled some of the others who hadn't shown for months to make it to the festivities: names like Spieth, McIlroy, Fowler, Johnson, Kuchar and Mickelson. The US was well represented, as was the rest of the world. Everybody agreed that *this* Open was a true All-Star event.

Now there are tragedies and there are *tragedies*. I don't want for one minute to downplay the human calamity which impacted the world when the bombs dropped. It's estimated the human race was reduced to less than one-tenth of one percent in about eight hours. But chew on this: *In a fraction of a second*, the professional golfing community lost its entire population.

I wish I could say I remember it well, that I knew exactly where I was when it happened. You know, like the Challenger disaster or Princess Di's death or the World Trade Center attack. All I know is that I went to sleep one night, woke up the next morning and the world would never be the same.

◉

My four-ball partner, Andrew Smith, his wife Terri and I had gone off on an extended golf weekend. It was nothing unusual for the three of us to take off like that. We had a great relationship and always had a spot open in our threesome. A spot which usually stayed vacant.

Andy managed a local machine shop. Terri worked part time for a weekly paper which sold odds and ends. They didn't have kids, but they both had strong family ties to the mountains.

We were pretty much in the middle of BFE, thank God, and had decided on a series of four courses in the mountains of Eastern Tennessee which had small cabins for accommodations. We were planning on playing from sun-up to sun-down, taping the Open and watching it in the evenings until we fell asleep.

We shared a cabin. Terri was a very attractive woman, but I never had inappropriate thoughts about her. It was probably because I respected Andy so much. Aside from my father, I have never had so much respect for one individual. That, and he was one big sumbitch. He could've snapped me like a matchstick if he thought I was even *thinking* about making a move on his wife. So, to say the least, we were cool sharing a cabin.

We had finished playing twenty-seven holes at Graysburg Hills, had ordered pizza from a local pie shop, and were settled in, ready to watch the DVRed recording of the Open's first round action. All we got was static. We tried the cable TV channels and got the same. Snowy static. Eventually, I went down to the local Redbox and rented us a couple of DVDs. I'm not really sure what we watched. Maybe *Ronin* and *Something About Mary*. Two ends of the spectrum.

The next morning, after a great breakfast specially prepared by Andy (he was the cook, not Terri, bless her heart), we showed up at the golf course around ten or so for an eleven o'clock tee time. I was going to work out the kinks on the practice range and get the yips out of my system on the putting green. Andy used to rib me that no matter how much I practiced, I'd always suck because I was left-handed. Hard to argue that point.

When we arrived, there wasn't a soul at the course. There was just a handwritten note on the front door:

Golf is dead. Come back tomorrow.

We had no idea what that meant. All I knew was we had a tee time in fifty minutes, come hell or high water.

"Maybe we ought to find someone, find out what's going on," Andy said, looking just a little worried. I figured he was upset because he wouldn't have a chance to win back those two dollars that I had taken from him yesterday when I striped his ass, one of the few times.

"Looks deserted," he said.

"You look. I'm hitting," I said as I started for the range.

I was just finishing my first bucket when an ashen faced Terri came up behind me, obviously upset, wiping tears from her eyes.

"You'd better come, Dave." Then she just turned around and walked off.

I hit another half-dozen or so wedges before I went back to the clubhouse. We had about twenty minutes 'til we teed 'em up. Just enough time to putt and get the greens' speed dialed in.

Evidently they had found one of the maintenance guys who not only worked on the course, but also had a small apartment above the tractor shed. He was a tall, black, older man, bald and skinny, probably about sixty. What little hair he had left was silvery white. He called himself Max.

He'd been crying, of course. He'd been drinking, too. Probably all night. It was corroborated by the half-bottle of Thunderbird in his hand.

I looked at Andy. He was holding Terri tightly against his chest, not daring to make eye contact with me. It was apparent something big had happened. It felt like somehow it was all my fault. I felt *guilty*.

Max motioned for me to sit in one of the wooden rockers lining the porch of the clubhouse. I could sense he had a story to tell, perhaps his last. I could also see that Andy and Terri had already heard this one. They stayed, though, hands clasped, as if hearing it again would make it seem less real.

I sat there.

Max talked. I listened.

Andy rocked Terri. Terri cried on Andy's massive shoulder.

Not one bird sang in the trees that morning.

Tee times went unfilled.

One of the mistakes, looking back on it all with perfect 20/20 vision, is that the USGA chose to have the Open at The Congressional near Washington, DC. Nobody realized they were playing near one of the biggest air defense bases in North America, one of the top three strategic military targets in the United States. Nobody ever used to think about that sort of shit. They do now.

Max was through with his chores for the day and had retired to the commons room in the maintenance shed with the other groundskeepers to watch the end of the first round of the Open. *It's funny*, I thought, *how even caddies and course maintenance workers have that same dream about playing in the Open, in the Common-man's tournament.* It was "open" for anybody with a handicap of two or better.

He told us they had the chance to watch the last seven or so holes of the opening round. Most had finished up, putted out and hit the practice range. Interviews were being set up with the first round leaders.

All through the broadcast, Max said, came interruptions and news flashes about what was happening in the Middle East. He said there were even rumors of terrorists on Mexican soil, plotting an actual assault on US cities. But despite the omens and impending doom, they were able to watch some fairly decent golf. You know, the important stuff.

The first round leader at minus three was, surprisingly, Tiger Woods, making a career comeback for the ages. Being older and without as much raw power, he was forced to reevaluate his game. What emerged was a little more forgiving, a lot more fun-loving and a little less serious golfer. Where he once seemed to fight the crowds, now he was one of the guys with an actual personality.

The telecast was interrupted again just before Gary McCord interviewed Tiger. The latest news was about escalating tension overseas, American troops on foreign soil, and European borders closed to all outsiders. It was brief and to the point. The Skirmishes had begun.

ABC Sports came back on as Tiger was answering an all too serious question from McCord about a chip-in on fifteen. Max said you could see a dozen or so pros behind them on the practice range, honing their games for Round Two.

Tiger flashed his dazzling smile and was about to answer when Max said the darndest thing happened. Through the TV he heard what sounded like calliope music, getting louder and louder, noisy enough to interrupt the usually verbose McCord. The melody filled the TV set with rhythm and cascading notes and drowned out their conversation. The camera stayed on Tiger.

Max said Tiger looked up in the sky… and smiled. Although the whistling music drowned out his words, Max could read Tiger's lips. *Wow, that's neat.* Those were Tiger Woods' last words.

Wow, that's neat.

The TV went to static. They tried other stations, but only snow was pouring from the old picture tube no matter where they looked.

An old PhilCo radio was kept in the back of the shop which only picked up AM stations. They pulled it out and fired it up. After five minutes or so, a grunt named Al was able to tune into a faint signal being broadcast from Nashville.

The bombs had come. First from Mexico, where they suspected there might be terrorists. But also from Canada, who, unbeknownst to the US, had secretly been seized by loyalists from the old Soviet Union. Nuclear warheads perched atop lightning fast missiles were upon NORAD before they even registered on their top-notch, multi-billion dollar radar units. The United States of America never stood a chance.

However, due to the unbridled brainpower without the burden of moral reasoning in Washington, we, the most powerful nation in the world, have fail-safe devices. These mechanisms are designed to launch a full arsenal of nuclear weapons at strategic targets half a world away in the event there were no longer any Americans alive to push the button. It worked to perfection.

In about an average workday, it was over. Not a single nation escaped bombings of one kind or another. *It was interesting*, I thought, *that none of the nations involved chose to use nukes - they all used standard non-radioactive bombs.* I guess, maybe at the final hour, reason won out over full tilt insanity. At least a little.

Oh, but it got better. I found out later what happened to the *rest* of humanity.

The use of non-nuclear weapons only prolonged the inevitable. Combined with conventional bombs were also some brilliant *unconventional* means by which humankind had devised to exterminate itself. Each nation thought themselves to be isolated, the last survivors. Each were mistaken.

Rumor had it the North Koreans had engineered a nasty little bug which mimicked the common cold. The slick little twist was that after two hours from exposure, the virus multiplied exponentially within minutes. In the time it would take to watch a sitcom, infected people died of a complete physiological shutdown. The Japanese, Chinese and Australian (who knows how the Australians got on the North Korean shit-list) populations were nearly exterminated.

Then there was the former Soviet Union, disguised as a loose conglomerate of Slavic nations. They engineered a way to transmit a wave through all cell phone satellites which disrupted signals sent from the brain to the heart muscles. You didn't even have to have your cell phone on. Once activated, anyone within 200 feet of a live cell phone was toast. As you know, everybody has one of those little electronic leashes. *Zap* - and pretty much everybody else dropped dead of a heart attack.

The Egyptians put the final icing on the cake. They had deployed a weapon programmed to zero in on certain races' DNA make-up. Needless to say, the Jews were Target Number One, including all Israeli allies, of whom the United States proudly counted themselves. With a flip of a switch, those targeted simply turned to ash, right out of the remake of *The War of the Worlds*, their own little death-ray. It was fired from a dozen satellites in low-earth orbit. That little ditty took out pretty much everyone else, alive or even already dead. *Poof.*

Human civilization as we knew it was, shall we say, history. Add all those 'preemptive strikes' together and, *boom* - within days the world population went from almost seven billion to just over half a million, a catastrophic reduction of the earth's poor souls. Still sounds like a ton of people remaining, I know. But it's a big old world filled with relatively few scared people.

Some were spared, however. Like me, Andy and Terri, and Max. Who knows why we aren't dead. I can guess all day, but ultimately I have no idea why we didn't get it like everybody else. Maybe because we were isolated in the mountains of Eastern Tennessee, without cellular signal. Maybe nobody thought the residents of Nowheresville, USA posed a threat. Maybe the powers that be took mercy on those of us foolish enough to be playing this damned game. But, in the end, does it really matter?

We didn't hear a thing while on the golf course. It snuck up on us like the shanks. One minute you're driving the ball two-fifty down the middle of the fairway, the next moment you've duck-hooked into the gallery with no hope of recovery.

"That's the bitch of it all," said Max. "No mulligans in war, huh?"

◉

Max had finished and fresh tears streaked his cheeks. The bottle of wine was now empty and at his feet. He looked embarrassed, having to recount the end of the world to total strangers.

How could we have missed all that? I thought. Sure, the last nine at Graysburg Hills was fairly deserted, but I just figured it was because it was late and these East Tennessee folk liked to get in before dark. It never occurred to me that the decent people of the world had taken the time to mourn the death of life. The mountains had evidently shielded the area from a majority of the damage and fallout.

I looked over at my golf partners. Andy was crying too, a sight I never thought I'd see. I didn't think that God had equipped country boys from Haywood County with tear ducts. I was wrong.

Max had shuffled off and was just about to step down from the porch. I felt like I needed to say something.

"Hey, Max," I called after him. "I'm sorry." It was lame I know, but at least it was an effort.

"Don't be, Mister," he said, a smile shadowing his face through the tears. "It was overdue, dontcha' think?"

"What are you going to do?" I asked.

"Sell my clubs," he replied. "I don't think golf's gonna be a priority for some time to come."

In a sane world, he would have been dead-on right. But, as you know, this world is far from sane.

◉

I turned my attention back to my friends. *God, what to say*, I thought. Words don't seem to matter when nobody's around to hear them. Terri looked like she was on the verge of being sick. Andy had regrouped.

"What do we do?" I asked.

"We go home," said Terri. "We go back to Asheville." She turned to her husband. "Andy, we have to find mom and dad, and your parents, and Mimi and Papaw. We have to make sure they're all right…"

"I know, baby," Andy said in that affectionate tone I'd heard many times after Terri had three-putted and was down on life. "Let's go."

They started to walk off together.

I didn't move.

Andy stopped and turned to me. "Pards? You coming?"

There are times in your life when it all hinges on a decision. Take the promotion or decline. Have the cheeseburger or the salad. Lay up or go for it. And it's when you make those choices, those resolutions… it is then that you know how it feels to relish the freedom of choice that God both blessed us and cursed us with. According to the wise golf sage Roy McAvoy, there were defining moments that made us or broke us. This was one. This was a *defining moment*.

The sun was up. There was no breeze. All was still.

Never had an empty tee box looked so inviting.

"I'm staying," I whispered, barely loud enough to be heard. In my head, it sounded like I shouted it at the top of my lungs. "I'm playing."

"You're loony," he said. *Loony* was what he called me when I played all the time with the illusion of getting better, of getting a jump on the field, of getting an edge on other players. "What's the point?"

"I–"

"It's *over*," Andy said, incredulous to the last. "It's all over, Dave! Golf doesn't matter anymore! Didn't you hear Max?

People are *dead*, nations have fallen and the country is in ruins! In case you hadn't noticed, golf's not exactly at its height of popularity right now, not exactly a priority."

"No, not now, Pards," I replied calmly, not thinking, just talking from my gut. "But it will be again, mark my words. As long as there are people who understand what the game is really about, they'll play." Andy hated it when I got all philosophical on him.

Terri had enough. "What are you trying to prove? That you're better than the rest of the world? That you can come through this unscathed? That golf is higher than all this?" Anger had replaced her tears, patience had been ousted. She buried her face in Andy's chest. I couldn't blame her for being upset.

"I love you guys," I told them. "You know that. You go do what you gotta do. I have to do what I have to do. You know I don't have any family, that you two are the closest friends I have in this world. Everything important to me is in the back of the Cherokee."

"But–," Andy started.

"You guys go to your family," I interrupted. "They need you. I'll be all right. Somehow, I know I'll be all right."

"You sure?" Andy asked.

"I'm sure," I said.

"You know where to find us, right?"

"I know."

"Anything we can do? Anybody we can call?"

"Take in my dogs, will you? They wouldn't understand."

"Like *we* do?"

"Like *I* do?"

"How will you live?"

"Day to day." I stole that line from *Rambo II*. I never thought I'd get a chance to use it.

"Where will you go? What will you do?" Andy asked.

"Well, right now, I'm gonna get the speed down on the greens and go play thirty-six or so. With nobody in front of me, I can probably be finished by mid-afternoon."

"And after?" Terri peeked out from Andy's tear-soaked shirt.

"Lots of golf left. I figure it's not going to be too hard to get on some pretty decent courses, now that... Well, let's just say that *somebody* has to play this damned game." I tried to smile.

They tried to smile back.

We shook hands, hugged, made promises we knew we had no intentions of keeping, and parted ways.

Andy and Terri headed for their car through the empty parking lot. They didn't even bother to take their clubs with them. They just left them in the rack next to the clubhouse.

I walked toward the putting green, wondering if I had finally snapped and had gone stark raving mad. Well, I did play golf, you know; I was probably halfway there to begin with.

I suddenly had an important thought. I stopped and turned. Andy and Terri were just getting to their car.

"Pards!" I shouted.

He turned back toward me. Even at this distance I was reminded of how big Andy really was. It was a shame that his knees never cooperated and gave him a chance at some major college football. Terri seemed small and childlike at his side.

"Yeah?"

"When this is all over, when the country gets back on its feet and people start rebuilding..."

"Yeah?"

"You know what they're gonna want to do, don't you?" He could see my smile from across the parking lot.

"I know," Andy replied. "But I want to hear you say it."

"They're gonna want to play golf. And I'm going to see to it that they still have a game to play."

"How?"

"By keeping the game alive. The sign's wrong. Golf's not dead. Wars come and go, nations rise and fall. Look at history. Golf survives." I felt as though I was babbling uncontrollably.

"If I know you, Pards, you'll find a way." He smiled back.

"Think so, huh?"

"Yeah. I've got a feeling that your name is going to be right there in the same breath with Old Tom Morris, Henry Vardon, Donald Ross."

"Why do you say that?" I asked, sincerely.

"Because you're just crazy enough, just passionate enough about golf to pull it off. I can't imagine anybody else in your shoes, tackling what lies ahead of you." He wasn't smiling anymore. He was sincere.

I needed that. I really did. "Thanks."

"Either that," Andy said, "Or you're as crazy as a shithouse rat."

He was still serious.

But… so was I.

◎

I posted an eighty-one and a seventy-nine. Not bad for post-apocalyptic golf I suppose. I kept my scorecards. I wasn't sure if handicaps were needed now, but I wasn't about to be unprepared.

I sat on the clubhouse porch, silent now that Max had gone too. I was able to get a Coke and a sandwich from the refrigerator inside. Max had evidently unlocked all the doors before leaving. I guess he would rather folk be able to get in and help themselves than kick the doors down to loot the inventory.

I sat there and watched the sun dip toward the horizon. I couldn't remember the last time I'd just paused and enjoyed a sunset. Odd, greenish clouds had begun to rise near the skyline. I supposed I had to prepare myself for radiation, fallout, mutants; everything I'd seen in bad science fiction movies.

Later, I thought.

I grabbed my putter and went to the putting green. I was rolling the ball too well to stop now.

I'll deal with the end of the world later.

◎

I made my way to Knoxville the next day. While all this golf in the aftermath of the world's last war was certainly unique, I figured I needed to peek in on common sense just once.

The highways were deserted on the trip west. I think I passed exactly five cars headed the opposite way as I drove the two hundred or so miles into Big Orange country. I encountered only one car headed my way: a 1969 vintage Mustang in showroom condition blasted by me doing well over a hundred. Even going that fast, I thought I could still make out the familiar chord of Hank, Jr. singing about country boys surviving anything.

Ah... the classics.

I drove the streets of downtown Knoxville in awe. Deserted cities I'd seen in disaster movies like *Night of the Comet* and *I Am Legend* always fascinated me. But actually standing in the middle of what should have been one of the busiest intersections in the south with not so much as a pizza delivery car running you off the road... Well, to say the least, it was spooky. Haunted. Unnatural.

The sooner I could get out of the city and back to where I could see grass growing, the better.

I passed a Dodge dealership and thought about trading in my ten year old Jeep for a new one. I bet they could make me a great deal. Probably even-stevens. Especially since there was no one working the lot. Probably never would be again. But I had just replaced the engine the summer before and the Cherokee was running well. Besides, I knew all the idiosyncrasies of the old rust bucket. I knew how to work on it and how to tweak it to run even better. Why tempt fate? There was a time in my past when I would have been coaxed into helping myself. Not anymore. It's funny how the end of the world instills values in a person.

I drove through what was left of the University of Tennessee's main campus. Evidently, the students had taken this war thing pretty badly. Most of the buildings, dorms and labs alike, had been gutted with fire. Windows were gone, there were no longer doors to the outside; just empty, open holes into abandoned hallways.

The immense football stadium, the pride and joy of the Vols, was laid flat. How when and why, I'll never know. It was like the student body, knowing things would never, *could* never be the same, had banded together with all the bulldozers and dynamite they could muster. The rows and rows of seats which used to tower above the campus like a modern day Roman cathedral were now mountains of rubble and twisted steel. If I didn't know better, I would have sworn this stadium was one of the targets for a hostile guided missile. I should have figured radical ISIS cells didn't particularly appreciate Tennessee football.

I held onto that thought. It comforted me more than the truth.

Continuing my tour through campus, I found the baseball complex in nearly the same condition. It was as if someone was consciously trying to obliterate all memory of organized sports. The only thing that reminded me this used to be one of the south's premier diamonds was what was left of the outfield foul lines: smatterings of iconic Tennessee Orange dotted the burnt green of the grass.

◎

I stopped at a nearby strip mall on the way out of Knoxville. Myself and an older lady were the only two patrons at a connected Food Lion. We purposely avoided one another and never made eye contact. Most of the items in the store had not been touched. It looked as though only a handful of people had been in there since things escalated. If there had been many people in and out, including some sort of management to run the store, I would have gladly paid for the privilege of shopping. As it was, it looked as though there were no more than a score of people alive in the entire city of Knoxville.

I was able to stock my Cherokee to the brim with food and supplies. I noticed a Nevada Bob's next door and went in, more to satisfy my curiosity than anything else. It appeared as though I was the first person to grace the store since the owner had abandoned the place. Everything was orderly, albeit a little dusty. There were plenty of clubs, shoes and supplies available for the taking.

As I saw it, all I needed was balls. I cleaned them out of every case of Precept Extra Spin they had and grabbed a half dozen or so Precept hats. I left all the high-priced Titleist balls. Precepts were far more durable with just as much spin. I was a pretty good walking endorsement now that everybody was dead.

On a hunch, I went into the back room where new equipment was stored until the manufacturers decide it's time to place the latest innovations into the general golfing public hands. After looking through several boxes which had evidently just been delivered prior to the *ultimate delivery*, I found what I was looking for: the most recent Mizuno driver, designed by the now permanently retired Mr. Faldo and scheduled for a truly terminal release date. I was rather abruptly reminded of my status in the golfing world. There were zero left-handed drivers of this particular model. *Figures*, I thought. *Even post-apocalypse, there is still a stigma attached to being a southpaw.* I settled for a Cobra driver, from one of the few companies which catered to my minority.

I got to my Jeep, loaded up, and drove over to the nearest grass island in the middle of the parking lot. I grabbed half dozen shag balls and teed them up, hitting balls towards a McDonalds a block down the street. The club was pure. The ball flight consistent. I could work the ball at will. And it was *long*. I felt as though I had one up on the field. Whatever field there may ever be. Right now, the field consisted of one: me.

Nevertheless, I felt good heading out of Knoxville. At least as good as one *can* feel, what with the end of the world and all.

Where to go, what to do.

Tiiiiime is on myyy side... That one was from *Fallen* with Denzel Washington and John Goodman. *Damn*, I thought. *Hollywood's gonna be hard pressed for new material for some time to come.* I had watched way too many movies in my time.

A plan was forming in what sometimes passes for a brain on top of my neck. I didn't have the details at the time; I didn't have the specifics or even the generalities. I just had some vague idea festering in the corner of my mind, attracting flies.

No, I didn't know how or why. I didn't know who or what or when. I didn't even know the if's, and's or but's of it all. But I did know one thing.

I knew the *where*. I knew *exactly* the where.

Augusta.

It's about a three hour drive from Knoxville to Atlanta on normal travel days. But, since humanity was kind've, well... *dead*, there wasn't really any traffic to get in my way. You've seen, no doubt, all the apocalyptic movies, where cars are strewn all over the highways, roads clogged and virtually impassable. I was surprised to find none of that. The highways were surprisingly clear of automobile carcasses. I literally had the road to myself. It was the North Georgia Autobahn. *'Bout damned time*, I thought.

I'd kept my Cherokee in top running shape, and now it was time to put it to the test. Hitting triple digits on southbound I75 was my idea of heaven. I'd always been pretty good behind the wheel, with unfilled dreams and lost aspirations of becoming a racecar driver. And now, with all the idiots out of the way, it was time to prove it. The Cherokee seemed to respond, too, handling beautifully. Eventually I knew I would need to get something with a little more *oomph* under the hood. But for now, I was content to run the wheels off my baby.

I made it from Knoxville to the outskirts of Atlanta in just under two and a half hours. I'm sure *somebody* would've been impressed, had there been a soul around.

Miles before I reached it, I could see smoke rising from

where Atlanta had been. Evidently, it had taken one on the chin, so to speak. I would later find out the city had taken a direct hit from one of those initial smart bombs.

Non-nuclear, non-radioactive, true. But still bad enough to ruin your day. Or level a city.

I steered clear, going around the beltway until I met up with I20. From there it was a direct shot to Augusta. Once again, I stretched out my Cherokee's legs, so to speak.

I think I'd only seen a couple dozen people at the most, either roaming around listlessly, scurrying along the highway, or, like myself, driving to beat the band. I wondered where all the bodies were, but I never saw a one. It was like the Rapture had come and gone, leaving me behind.

While speeding across Georgia, I tried to come up with a game plan of sorts. I had absolutely no idea of what I was going to do or how I was going to do it. All I had was the one obsessive destination in mind. I was assuming the golf gods would smack me across the forehead with some sort of divine inspiration when I got there.

Along the way I stopped at Reynolds Plantation just outside Lake Oconee and took in a quick round. I'd always heard about this place, but never thought I could afford it. Well, it appears they've cut their greens fees quite a bit. I guess post-apocalyptic golf is a rare breed. Just about as rare, I'd say, as the almost-extinct human race.

The course was deserted, of course. And it was apparent that, even after just a couple of days, the greens were getting a little furry. I was used to much slicker putting surfaces, but considering that humanity had just about destroyed itself, I supposed I could give the greens keeper a little slack. Poor fellow was either toast or had run off when the bombs started falling. Most sane people would've.

I posted an eighty-four without a birdie. Not bad, I'd say, having never seen the layout and playing every hole pretty much blind. I made a mental note to get back over here some day and give it another go.

It was late in the afternoon when I came upon the outskirts of Augusta. It snuck up on me and I almost drove right into a barricade which had been constructed at an overpass just outside the city.

Sitting at the city limits sign on the highway was a vintage yellow school bus. In it were the first people I'd seen that I could get close enough to tell if they were friend or foe.

They were foe.

I stopped the Cherokee about twenty yards from the bus which was positioned so as to completely block all traffic from coming through. Obviously its occupants intended for no one to go by without an altercation of some sort.

I sat in the car for a full five minutes, but it seemed much longer. I could make out the silhouettes of the occupants milling about inside the bus, no doubt coming up with a plan of what to do with (or to) this intruder in the olive green four-wheel drive vehicle.

The door of the bus folded back on itself and a black giant stepped out. The guy stood over seven feet tall if he was an inch, but he moved smoothly and with an athletic grace so few have. He also looked vaguely familiar.

"Stop right there," he said, a slight Boston inflection in his words. *There* came out more as *they-uh*; the accent seemed incongruous coming from a black guy. His familiarity was bugging the hell outta me. "Far enough, Amigo."

I had the window rolled down. "Is it OK for me to get out?" I yelled. "I don't want any trouble."

"Fine by me, Cochise," the tall man said. "As long as you don't mind staring down the business end of my shotgun while you do."

I opened the door as slowly as I could, watching him intently. I managed to get out of the Jeep and keep my hands in plain sight at the same time. I looked down at the pavement and saw blackish-red stains blotted all over the place. I'm no expert, but I have seen my share of cop shows. I was pretty certain it was dried blood.

"And just so you know," he said, before I could utter a word, "You also have half a dozen other weapons trained on you." I looked down and counted five red laser dots grouped center-mass on my chest. I could only assume the sixth was in the middle of my forehead.

"Not taking any chances are you, my friend?" I said this as calmly as I could. "I'm not here to cause anybody any trouble."

"Damn straight, you aren't. And don't call me 'friend', friend. There are no 'friends' these days. Or ain't you noticed, the world's gone to shit." He spat tobacco juice on the pavement at his feet.

If the situation weren't already strange enough, Armageddon come and gone, I was now dealing with a giant black man who had a Yankee accent, was chewing tobacco, using Southern slang and calling me Mexican nicknames. And to beat it all, he had a small army with him. Judging by the looks of the blood stains on the road, his troop meant business. I imagined a band of Mad Max type tattooed bikers, dressed in all leather, with spiked collars and skull caps, ready to blast me a new one if I so much as blinked wrong.

"Listen," I started, staying put beside my open door. "I've just driven down from Knoxville and all I want to do is get past you and go on my way. Peacefully."

"Yeah, you and every other scrag that's come along. And it's the ones like you, the skinny, little ones, which can cause the most trouble. What's your business here, anyway? Family? Drug dealings? What?" The shotgun never wavered.

"No," I said. "No family. In fact, I don't know... *didn't* know anybody in this town."

"What then? What are you looking for?"

"You wouldn't believe me if I told you."

"No 'if' about it, Poncho. You *will* tell me and *I'll* be the judge of the truth."

Only at that point did I realize this could actually be the end of the line for me. It would really suck to have survived all the bombings, all the terminal technology, just to be shot down on I20 by an overzealous black Goliath. Then it hit me. I finally recognized the guy.

"Hey," I said. "Aren't you the center for the Atlanta–"

"No sirree, Bob. I ain't nobody, same as you." I could tell he was diverting me from the truth. I was certain I knew where I'd seen him before.

"But–," I started.

"Everybody's nobody now," he cut me off. "Don't matter who we were *before*, it's who we are *now* that matters." A touch of regret flickered across his features. How it must feel for someone who was relatively famous to now be reduced to the land of commoners like the rest of us. And, insult upon injury, it had to come when the world finally ended and nobody really cared.

"OK," I said, leaving him his anonymity. "No problem. I'm just in town to play golf." There, I said it.

He looked at me. I looked at him.

I knew his mind was going through its paces, wondering if I was either off my rocker or had gotten bit by a zombie. Either way, he had a decision to make: Put me down or let me pass.

"Golf, huh?" His eyes locked with mine.

"Yep. Golf."

"Figures," he said. "First person we see come through here and he's batshit crazy."

"*First* person?" I said, not understanding. "But the stains on the pavement...?"

He grinned, straight, stark white teeth in contrast to his dark skin. I realized the barrel of the shotgun was now pointed at the ground.

"Worked, didn't it? Hell, I know the world's all spent, but I wouldn't hurt anyone. I didn't push the button to start it all and I sure as hell ain't gonna end it with nobody." I could see he was enjoying this.

"Karo syrup and food coloring." He pointed to the pavement at my feet. "Looks convincing, don't it?"

"Um, yeah," I said, relieved, finally realizing this guy and his group was all show. Good to know there were still some decent people in this recently de-populated world.

"C'mon out!" he hollered. From out of the bus and behind the parked cars flanking it several people emerged: Two young women, three kids no older than twelve, one senior citizen and a couple of middle-aged men. All of them looked like school teachers. None of them looked like body-pierced, leather-clad Hell's Angels. Only two of them wielded weapons; the other four had laser pointers.

I finally started breathing again.

I stepped away from the Cherokee and took a tentative step toward the large black man. "What is all this?"

"It's a front. A show. A put-on, just in case there are some people coming through here that are out for no-good."

"Have you seriously not had anybody come through here?" I was having trouble with that concept.

"Nope. Not a damn soul. Not until you." His face showed his confusion. "You'd think there would be more people around after Judgment Day, ya know?"

"Yeah, that's what I was thinking too. Not that I'm complaining. I've seen enough movies to be scared of what's supposed to be happening at the end of the world." I walked over to the giant man and extended my hand. "David Parr."

"Alfie Ray. Pleased to meet you." My small hand disappeared into his enormous handshake.

"I knew it, dammit. I watched you play in the NBA Finals last season. You had two double-doubles in that series, didn't you?" I asked.

"*Three* triple-doubles, but who's counting? I'd settle for just a pick-up game with some of my old teammates these days." His grin was contagious.

"Yeah," I said, "I'm sure the competition is kinda scarce."

"So, seriously David. What *are* you doing here?" I think I

piqued his interest more than anything.

"Seriously, Alfie. Here to play golf, big guy. No shit." His face betrayed the reaction I figured I'd get when I started telling people why I was doing what I was doing. "Augusta."

"Shoulda known, with a name like Parr. It may be your destiny. Or your curse."

Alfie roared with laughter. Some of the others in the group started laughing also. I wasn't sure if it was nervousness or if they were genuinely amused. I joined them, too. *Heck, why not?*

○

Finding Augusta National was easy enough. In Augusta, Georgia, all signs literally pointed to the nation's most famous private golf club.

Driving down the magnolia-lined entrance, I was reminded how often I had seen these images on TV, hoping beyond hope of ever being able to come here and watch The Masters in person. I have a few friends, rather *had* a few friends who were somehow able to get practice round tickets, mostly through work or relatives.

Looks like I was going to get a one-up on them; where they were only able to watch, I was going to play this course.

However, on the drive in, I could see this was going to be an uphill battle. The usually manicured trees and shrubbery were now unkempt and sprawling. Tufts of grass were coming up through the cracks in the driveway and Bermuda had started encroaching onto the blacktop.

Not a good sign for what I was likely to find on the course.

I stopped in the clubhouse to see what kind of shape it was in. Surprisingly, there was very little damage to the building or contents themselves. As was the situation at Graysberg Hills and Reynolds Plantation, the typical, end of the world surviving public evidently didn't put much thought into raiding the local golf clubs. I guess the general thought was there were many better targets to put their efforts into. Like gas and food and water.

Suckers. They simply didn't have their priorities in the right places.

I was impatient to get to the golf course itself. Brother, was I ever disappointed. I guess I had forgotten that it had been almost a week since the Skirmishes began. I was shocked at how tall the grass had gotten on the number one tee box. It was up over my ankles. I could have cried.

I was determined to at least hit one drive. This was the same launching pad I had watched Jack and Arnie and Gary take their customary and symbolic tee shots to herald in many a Masters.

Taking a wedge from my bag, I swung and hacked and flailed about like an old farmer with a scythe. Eventually, I was able to clear off an area big enough to tee it up and have a little room ahead to get the ball upward without getting entangled in the weeds.

I pulled the new Cobra driver from my bag and a brand new Precept EV from its sleeve. Inserting the four inch tee into the ground, and placing the ball in the cradle, I took a few practice swings to loosen up. This was it; my first tee shot at Augusta National.

Waggle. Waggle.

Slowly taking the driver back, I loaded my weight onto my left side (I'm left-handed, remember), paused at the top and brought the club down into the perfect slot, on its way to a drive struck pure.

And topped the hell out of it.

It didn't travel more than ten yards. It was hard to tell because the long grass gobbled it up almost immediately.

Now, what's the first thing a golfer does when he duffs a shot? Look around to see who is looking. Never mind the Day of Reckoning had come and gone, never mind almost all of humanity had been obliterated. I fueled that habit, quickly looking around, making sure no one was snickering at this fool trying to play golf.

I laughed. I mean, what do you do? Curse the golf gods?

Immediately I walked forward to the last place I'd seen the ball disappear, and looked in vain for a good five minutes to no avail. I stomped and dragged my feet and hacked into the thick Bermuda with my club, not uncovering so much as a shag ball.

Looking back on it now, what did I really expect? To launch a perfectly stuck tee shot down the center of the number one fairway, with a slight draw, garnering 'oohs' and 'ahs' from the imaginary crowd?

I really did need to get a grip on reality. As if it wasn't bad enough I was on this impossible quest to keep golf alive in the waning days of civilization, I was expecting my quality of play to be better than ever.

The magnitude of the moment, the events of the past week and the enormity of the task ahead and had finally caught up with me. Slowly going to my knees in front of Augusta National's Number One tee box, I finally shed a tear for what *really* mattered.

Humanity? Our country? Civilization?

No.

All golfers hate losing golf balls. But all serious golfers hate losing *new* golf balls.

At least that's what I told myself as the tears flowed. Here I was: one lonely man with the proverbial quest of trying to make a difference in this post-apocalyptic world.

Talk about *defining moments*.

◙

Over the next two months, I was able to elicit the help of Alfie and his gang. Interestingly enough, there wasn't a big influx of people into town. I suppose the typical doomsday survivor had better things to do. Alfie left a couple of guards on lookout, but for the most part, time was split between scavenging for supplies and helping me get Augusta National back into playing shape.

It was a challenge at first, learning how to use the equipment and the grounds keeping machinery. I had to do a little convincing to persuade some of the townsfolk to give up their gas and diesel, but the solid reasoning of 'what-better-use-for-fuel?' combined with 'where-else-you-gonna-go?' soon convinced them to see it my way. And, if it all worked out like I envisioned it would, there'd be plenty of opportunity to eventually recoup everything and more.

We managed to round up a crew of forty-five men and women ranging in age from sixteen to retirement. As compensation, other than a purpose for which to work, I gave them all golf lessons. At least golf as I saw it. Which, at times, can be pretty humorous. The good thing is most of them didn't know any better. I could have been teaching them all the worst habits imaginable and they would have taken it in greedily. But by the time the course was ready, most were hitting the ball pretty consistently.

I don't want to downplay the amount of time and effort which went into getting the nation's most famous golf course back into playing shape. It would never be what it once was, but considering the events around the destruction of the civilized world, I thing we did a pretty good job. I wondered if this was how Bobby Jones felt when he and Clifford Roberts first had the idea of Augusta National back in the early 1930's.

As weeks passed, word spread that some fool in the south had reopened August National to public play. And slowly, ever so slowly, people began to show up.

If you build it, they will come. Remember that line from the classic movie?

Well, did they ever.

◉

At first, curiosity seekers arrived to see how one town was putting its efforts into revitalizing golf instead of rebuilding the country or finding ways of reconstituting the infrastructure. There was plenty of derision and questions of sanity. We quickly convinced the naysayers there were plenty of communities devoted to those types of tasks. We were sticking with what we knew.

The good news was that, whenever someone came and went, so did word about our project. Everyone wanted to know the name of the crazy son-of-a-bitch who managed to pull this off. Now, I'm not one to brag or toot my own horn, but I am rather proud of what WE had been able to accomplish. I would tell them that my name was David Parr, but the Augusta Project was bigger than just one person. It was a way to retain a sense of humanity.

Soon we were receiving people from two and three states away, all coming in to play the famed course. Some even stayed to help us maintain the property and within six months, Augusta National was once again THE stop along the way for golfers of all types. We had professionals and hackers alike come in and play, right alongside one another.

It was how golf was meant to be.

◉

A year has passed since the fateful day which brought the world as we know it to an end. Some say that mankind as a whole is better off, starting again basically from scratch. We have been able to hold onto the things that matter, discard the frivolities and build solid basics to enable future generations the means to keep going.

I am proud to say that golf is one of those foundations.

The country still isn't back. That will take decades or longer. I know there are a hundred more important things to be done than to play golf. But if there isn't something like this great game to sidetrack us once in a while, then what has it all been worth?

The nation is rebuilding a little at a time. I heard there is a new government up and running, an administration intent on not making the same mistakes as the last. A new army has been formed from volunteers all across the land, but this army builds instead of destroys. It brings food, shelter and aid to those who need it. I suppose there will be a time in the future when it will have to change its priorities, but hopefully the rest of the world has learned a lesson too. I briefly wondered if there was some Scottish fool in Europe sitting on the veranda at the Old Course, one he had personally brought back from the brink, having this same internal conversation.

One could only hope.

In two weeks we will be hosting the first annual new masters, with a little 'm'. It will not be the big 'M' elitist tournament of the past century. Instead, it will be a celebration of everything that makes golf the game it was meant to be: integrity, honesty, perseverance, attitude (and altitude on some of those tough approach shots), mental toughness, imagination, clarity… and a hundred other adjectives I don't have time to list.

◎

I was sitting on the porch this morning, watching the crowd on the practice green rolling putts, getting the speed down. At Augusta, speed is everything when it comes to putting. We made sure to keep that aspect with our greens. The late Gary McCord would have still been able to talk about body bags being piled up next to most greens.

"Old Tom Morris, Henry Vardon, Donald Ross… and David Parr." The Haywood county drawl was unmistakable.

I laughed to myself, knowing what I would see when I located the source of those words. I looked over and saw Andrew Smith standing at the end of the porch, bigger than ever, with his wife Terri at his side.

"If I remember correctly," I said, "I believe I have two bucks of yours from the last time we teed it up, Pards," I smiled. "Come to collect?"

"That. And to see for myself the crazy dreamer who managed to pull off the biggest golfing miracle since Larry Mize sank that chip back in '87."

"It's no big deal," I said, trying to stay humble. "It's just a little get together to give people hope."

"No big deal? Really?" Andy looked at me, a bit awed at the surreal nature of the conversation. "Did you know the new president of the freakin' country is on his way here to play in your 'little' tournament?"

I hadn't heard that. I bet Alfie was keeping it a surprise. Leave it to my four ball partner to spill the beans.

I stood up from the rocking chair, knees aching a little more than usual, back a little stiffer than the day before. Even in the world beyond its end, age will eventually take its toll.

"C'mon, guys," I said, wrapping my arms around each of my two best friends in the world. We started down the magnolia-lined driveway to the course. "Let me show you around this old goat track."

We all three laughed at the irony.

Bobby Jones would have been proud.

INSIDE

IT SURE IS LONELY in here.

Not lonely enough.

Oh, yeah. I forgot. You like it all
by yourself, don't you?

It's better than putting up
with your shit.

My crap? You're one to talk. My
crap is every bit your crap as well.

You're pitiful. You aren't
even man enough to curse.

How does cursing prove I'm a man?

Well, if you had a pair, you'd
know what I was talking about.

Balls or brains.
What's mine is yours.

Don't confuse me with facts.

Facts? Let's go over those 'facts'.

Your version of them, at least.

Fact One: You're stuck in here
with me, like it or not.

That would be *not*.

Fact Two: You're insane.

I'm insane? If I'm insane
then you are too.

Fact Three: Whatever happens to
one of us happens to the other.

Unless I get to you first.

And what would you do?

Shut you up for starters.

You can't shut me up. You know
it and that drives you crazy.
Well... crazier, that is.

You think you're funny, don't you?

Of course I am. Just ask me.

I don't know which of us is more
screwed in the head. You, Mr. Goodie
Two-Shoes. Or me, the one who
sees it like it really is.

Like it really is, huh? Oh, do tell.

If it weren't for me, we'd still
be stuck lobbying for whatever
bullshit cause that needed us.

A political gun for hire. A necessary
cog in the wheel even here in the
'enlightened' 21st century. We were
an integral part of the plan.

More like an *insignificant*
part of the plan.

Well, it's better than the alternative.

Than *my* alternative? One where
our name will be famous forever?

Don't you mean *infamous*?

What's the difference? Either way,
we will be remembered.

Yes, we would be. But for all the
wrong reasons.

Wrong reasons? By giving hope to
the hopeless?

You mean lying to the masses.

By showing how to live
by example?

More like putting up a front to
fool everyone into thinking
we are someone we aren't?

People look up to us.
They admire me.

Every bit as much as I am
ashamed of you.

You're just making it worse.

How?

By fighting me.
By constantly talking in my head.

I'm the voice of reason.

I don't need reason. I have intellect. I
have knowledge. And knowledge, as
we all know, is power.

Yes, that's you: a mental giant
and a moral midget.

That's not politically correct.

Maybe not, but it's reality.

A lie.

The truth.

This discussion is wearing thin.

Do you think everyone has
these types of conversations
with themselves?

Probably so. Mankind is a plurality.
Each person is a duality.
We all have inner conflict.

Maybe. But your everyday Joe Schmo
doesn't have his finger on the button.

My finger isn't on the button.

No. But it's within arm's reach.

Meaning what?

Meaning that if the masses knew
how screwed in the head you were,
they wouldn't be sleeping very well.

Hey, they voted me into office.
They knew I was the right man at
the right time for this country.
They trusted me with their salvation.

We're the President, not God.

May as well be. I'm the only one
in whom I trust.

You're a real piece of work,
you know that?

And you're a chickenshit coward.
Here. Watch.

What are you doing?

Putting my finger on the button.

Why?

Why not? What better way to secure
a place in history?

Think about what you're doing.

Oh, I *have* been thinking about
it, all right. Thinking about it for
a long time.

I know. I'm in here, too.
Remember?

Yeah. Don't remind me.

Do you really want to die?

May as well go out in a blaze of glory.

Back to that infamous place in
history, are we?

My name will be remembered with
all those who stood for their causes and
weren't afraid to risk everything.

Such as?

Leonidas.

More like Xerxes.

Caesar.

I'd say Caligula.

Lincoln.

No. Mussolini.

Reagan.

Hitler.

I'm not going to win this battle,
am I?

Not as long as I'm around.

I was afraid you'd say that.

I was afraid you were going to
push the button.

Not this time, pussy.

Name calling? Really?

There. It's back at arm's length again.
Satisfied?

Not far enough away.

Never close enough.

This is going nowhere.

I told you that from the start.

Well, back to safe subjects.

About damned time.

Sure is dark in here.

Darker than you can imagine.

THE GIRL WHO KEPT A BOOK IN HER PURSE

ALL THROUGH HER LIFE, Valerie constantly had a book with her. It was simply her thing, a part of who she was.

Just like her first boyfriend, Kenny Roberts, had dark hair, and her BFF from grade school, Renee Johnson, had freckles, and her current boss, Dwayne Worley, had a moustache. Having a book at the ready and wait was just who Valerie Robinson was.

Everybody knew it.

She was known as the girl who kept a book in her purse. And she was cool with that.

A famous author once opined on why more people didn't carry a book with them all the time. In his opinion, it was the perfect entertainment: no batteries needed, no advertisements, hours of enjoyment or moments of needed escape, perfectly adaptable to one's personality and interests, deep and meaningful or light and insubstantial. Books were the perfect diversion. Of course, he *was* an author and, therefore motivated to convince people to buy his books. Nevertheless, in Valerie's opinion, he had a valid point.

Even when she was in kindergarten, Valerie remembered always having a picture book with her. As she progressed in school, her level of reading was continually a step ahead. By the eighth grade she was already reading Jane Austen and Victor Hugo. In high school and through college, she went through a myriad of stages: soft porn romance novels, biographies, science fiction and science fact, horror and suspense, fables and fairy tales, detective novels, spy thrillers, modern day vampire romances, apocalyptic zombie books, from poetry to textbooks. Her tastes ran from King and Koontz, to Asimov, Bradbury and Clark. She sampled authors like a smorgasbord, from Graham, Sparks and Steele to Grisham, Flynn and Meltzer. Her list of novels read like a buffet of off-topic literary volumes.

After she graduated with a degree in Publishing, she soon became a proofreader, editor and eventually a publisher for one of the big New York distribution houses. She had always wanted to make her living in books and the written word.

Even out of school, Valerie still kept to her obsessive reading ways. She was always in the middle of at least one book. It was as if she were her own best customer.

In fact, so immersed in the belief that she always had to have a book (or two or three) in progress, in her mind, she became convinced that if she were to completely finish whatever books she were reading, and she was truly between books, she would most certainly die.

Hence, the need, however irrational, was viable.

Therefore, whenever she went on a trip, she always had her current book plus a couple packed away, just in case. It didn't matter there were bookstores in the airports and Barnes and Nobles in every major city.

Whenever she slept over at her boyfriend's apartment, she always had the book she was working on, plus a back-up. Never mind the fact that her apartment was just the next building over. In the little time it would take to run to her place for a replacement, she could be hit by a car, murdered in the stairwell, or fall down an empty elevator shaft.

To Valerie Robinson, not reading was certain death.

And the fact that she preferred *actual* books to Kindle or e-readers just made it more problematic at times. She knew from a rational point of view that she could fit hundreds and hundreds of books onto an electronic hand-held device. *But it just wasn't the same,* she thought. There was nothing as visceral as holding an honest to God, flesh and blood book in her hands.

She had also tried her hand at writing, but soon found she didn't have the talent or creativity to become successful. She was OK with that. She did the next best thing: provide readers with what she loved most.

Books to read.

By her fourth year at the publishing house, Valerie had moved up the chain of command and was now the Senior VP in charge of new authors. It was a role she took most seriously and one she valued immensely. Introducing fledgling authors to the world was, she imagined, like watching your child walk across the stage at graduation, full of hope and promise, confidence and trepidation, their future laid out in front of them.

She was good at what she did. A few of her discoveries had become successful, landing on the bestseller list more than once. One of her star authors introduced the world to the latest vampire craze, agreeing to a multi-year book deal and signing over the rights to a movie series which was rumored to be on Steven Spielberg's short list.

Not bad for a little girl who always had a book in her hands.

○

Her latest find was a recluse who lived in the mountains of Virginia. Word had it there were a couple of other publishing houses who had an eye on him as well. It was imperative that she get to him immediately if she wanted her recent string of successes to continue. Even though it was early February and the weather was a factor, Valerie was determined to get to this guy first. She had a reputation for tenacity.

After spending most of the night on a red-eye to Dulles, Valerie braved the winter roads and headed into the Appalachians to a forgotten town in Virginia's northwest corner. She managed to rent a small cabin reachable only by way of a winding dirt road which led into some of the most beautiful scenery she had ever laid her eyes on. Heavy snow on evergreen braches formed a canopy of white and ice which made her feel like she was driving through some winter fantasy land.

Between the flight and the drive from the airport, most of the day was gone. By the time she got to the cabin, dusk had already started to turn the white snow into ash. Fat, wet snowflakes drifted lazily from the sky.

After unloading her one suitcase from the rental car, she surveyed the small one room cottage: fireplace, a little table with a lamp next to a twin bed, recliner, dresser, mirror, sink, small glass fronted cabinets, a mini-fridge and an area partitioned off which she could only assume was the toilet and shower.

No TV.

No radio.

And for sure, no internet.

She checked her phone. No cell reception either.

For others, these accommodations might have been something of a nightmare. To Valerie, it was a dream.

She was halfway through the latest Steven King, a sequel to a previous book. A Blake Crouch novel was next on her list, followed by an older James Patterson that she'd never read. All of them were unpacked and waiting on the nightstand between the bed and the recliner.

She heated up some beans on the stove. Within a couple of hours she had finished the horror master's most recent book. As good a stopping point as any, she took a quick shower and got ready for bed.

Going to the door, she wanted to take one last look at the winter scene outside the cabin. When she opened the door, she was shocked. Snow was coming down so thickly she couldn't see the car which she had parked not twenty feet from the door. Snow had drifted halfway up the door and spilled into the room. She had heard of white outs before, but never thought she'd ever see one personally. It was simultaneously beautiful and frightening, wrapped up together in the same emotion.

Surprised more than anything, she was able to sweep most of the snow out before it melted and got the door shut. Hopefully the storm would let up and she would be able to make her appointment in the morning.

Getting into bed, Valerie began the Crouch novel. Banking on the success he'd had with the Wayward Pines series, he was venturing into the science part of fiction with his latest book. Her intent was to read herself to sleep, like she always did. She made a good-sized fifty page dent into the book before the peaceful silence and heavy eyelids took her to sleep.

◉

Diffused morning light through the windows woke her. It took her a few minutes to realize where she was and orient herself.

Then she remembered the snow from last night. She got out of bed and went to the door, opened it, and laughed.

The snow had drifted up all the way to the top. She took her hands and managed to carve out a hole into the snow and through to the other side. It was still falling, as hard as ever. Her rental car was a nondescript white mound, completely covered.

Closing the door, she resigned herself to the fact that she wasn't going to make it to her appointment, at least not this morning. Maybe it would melt off by the afternoon and she could try then.

The good thing was if Valerie was snowed in then nobody else would be paying a visit to *her* newfound author. The bad thing was she couldn't even call him and let him know she wouldn't be making it this morning.

Resigned to the situation, she made herself some breakfast and coffee. Taking the quilt from the bed, she camped herself on the recliner with her book. It was an easy read and within a few hours, she was flipping over the last page.

She took another look outside and the scene hadn't changed: it was still snowing at the same pace. She was officially stranded.

She fixed herself a tuna sandwich for lunch and curled back up in the chair. Always the reader, she started in on the Patterson book, his first Alex Cross novel that Valerie had meant to read a long time ago.

◉

It wasn't until she hit the last of his short chapters that Valerie realized how quickly his books were consumed. She'd read the entire book in one sitting.

She hadn't planned on going through *all* the books she'd brought on this trip, originally planned for just overnight. Normally, having three books on hand was more than enough. She stared at the stack of books on the table, every word in each which she had already consumed, and then looked at her suitcase, leaning against the dresser.

Her *bookless* suitcase.

Then, panic set in.

What if it were true? What if, without a book being read, without being in the middle of one, without starting a new one, that she would really die?

Rationally, being a grown woman, she knew this was one of the most outlandish thoughts she could have. But it was a thought she'd had with her for, literally, her whole life. Thinking back, she couldn't remember a time, ever, when she wasn't reading a book.

Until now.

Valerie literally had never faced this reality before. And, irrational or not, it scared her.

What if I worry myself so badly that I have a heart attack? Was this a self-fulfilling prophecy?

Trying to compose herself, she was determined to not give in to these crazy thoughts.

I am not going to die, she told herself. *I am not going to die. I'm just between books, that's all. Get a grip.*

Nevertheless, she got up and went to the sparse bathroom area. Below the sink she found a bottle of Rid-Ex and a container of Clorox. She read both labels thoroughly.

She looked around the room. Under the kitchen sink, she found a bottle of dishwashing liquid, two roach motels and a box of Brillo Pads. She read those labels, too.

In the fridge were only milk and fruit juice. It didn't take long to read the labels on those bottles.

In the cupboard she found four cans of beans, one jar of peanut butter, two cans of tuna, an opened bag of Doritos and a loaf of stale bread. Those labels were at least more interesting than the others. But they too read rather fast.

She went back to her chair and sat down heavily. She tried starting one of the books again, but in her mind, she already knew what was going to happen. It just wasn't the same. She quickly gave up on that notion.

Valerie laid her now fully completed final book on her lap and wondered if there was going to be a conflict of some sort. She half expected the book to disappear.

There was no conflict, no divergence. There was not a paradox, no inconsistency or any contradiction. In fact, the universe could not have cared less.

The book remained.

Everything else, however, Valerie, the chair, the rug, the cabin, the snow, the woods, the world and everything in it...

Everything.

It all... just... disappeared.

EPILOGUE: THE THIRTEENTH SIDE

DAYLIGHT, FAINT AS IT was, forced its way into my eyes.

Almost afraid to open them, I allowed my eyelids to part a bit, just enough to see the light was coming from above, not from the box.

The box.

It sat in my lap, as lifeless as boxes were meant to be. No glow shone from within its walls. It was dark and dull and everything a plastic container should be. I felt its sides with my fingers, ran my nails across its surface. It was unremarkable.

But there was *everything* remarkable about the journey from which I had returned. What I had just experienced was as alien to me as anything I had ever experienced.

Alien.

Odd I chose that particular word to describe it. And yet, alien it was.

If I tried to rationalize what happened to me overnight, I know I'd keep coming back to the logical conclusion that I had been dreaming. An extremely *vivid* dream, but a hallucination nonetheless. Yet I knew this was much more than a product of my subconscious mind. It could be even turn out to be much more than a life.

My life.

Regaining my senses, raw after what they had been through during the night, I took in the room. Light was spilling through the cracks in the door above the stairs where I had originally come in. The morning glow was enough to illuminate the room without the expired firelight. The empty space looked like it did when I first entered. Nothing had changed during my brief stay just like nothing had changed in the years it lay abandoned.

I grabbed my backpack for the water jug. My thirst was severe and the water was the sweetest I'd ever tasted. I finished the bottle in seconds.

As I was putting it back into the backpack, my hand brushed against the cardboard cover of my composition book.

Or what was left of it; I had torn out several pages to get the fire going last night. There was still a hundred or so crisp, white, virgin pages almost glowing back at me. I guess better words would be *beckoning to me.*

Suddenly I saw, with a clarity I hadn't felt in years, the meaning of what had happened to me.

Purpose. Something I hadn't known in years.

I now had purpose in my thoughts, my reasoning, my *soul.* I knew what I had to do. I knew now why my life had gone so awry, why I was forced to live on the streets and why, ultimately, I found myself at the very place I was: a forgotten shell of a man, merely seeking shelter from a winter's evening down in an abandoned depot who had somehow stumbled upon something otherworldly.

Stories. Those visions I had just experienced. They needed to be told. They needed someone to breathe life into them. They needed me as much as I needed them.

Across the room I noticed the aged, faded sign above the booths. *Tickets.* In this decrepit, abandoned station, twenty feet under the city streets, I may have found my ticket back to the real world.

I slid the old, chewed up No. 2 pencil out of the spirals, and, with a shaky hand, started to write:

I live on the streets, but I don't come from them.

AFTERWORD

AMONG A HUNDRED REASONS for why I needed to put virtual pen to cybernetic paper, here are the two which stand out above the others:

Author Vince Flynn was asked by his newlywed wife: *On your deathbed, what would be the one regret in your life that, if given the chance, you had never done?* His answer was simple, immediate and life-changing: *Write a novel.* Upon returning from their honeymoon, his wife encouraged him to set up a regular writing schedule and gave him the means and support to forestall any remorse he might have in his life.

Flynn died a few years ago, but not without having more than a dozen successful novels to his credit. He found a way of not letting his life become that unfulfilled regret he didn't even know he had until someone asked him a simple question. That hit a chord with me.

Steve Irwin, the late Australian crocodile hunter, was killed in a freak accident while on a routine swim with stingrays, something he'd done dozens of times before. Many agreed that at least he died doing what he loved. That stuck with me. *Going out of this life while doing something you love.*

I suddenly realized I had no idea what that would be like. In the life I was living, I couldn't imagine the meaning of such a concept. Aside from my wife and kids, I had nothing *die-worthy.*

These two instances helped me realize that I needed a purpose other than what the status quo said it should be. I recognized that I would never be at peace with myself or anyone else until I found my purpose. I needed to make a difference, not only in my life, but in others' as well.

With renewed commitment, I dove headfirst back into this collection of stories; one I had started years before but never quite had the guts to complete.

I can only suppose it turned out all right.

◙

Now for what really matters:

My dad taught me the value of the written word. By the time he passed, he had volumes upon volumes of notebooks in which he had handwritten quotes which were of importance to him. I'd love to know what he'd think, seeing me sitting in one of the local stores, signing books. I think he'd be proud.

My family & friends, mom & brother helped me see the cost of displaced words. I regret you've seen me, year after year, working at jobs my heart just wasn't into but stayed with them anyway because That's The Way It's Supposed To Be Done. Well, I've got news for you… I truly believe THIS is what I was born to do.

My wife helped me realize that words have meanings. Thanks for trusting in this crazy preemptive deathbed notion and listening to my incoherent ramblings about story ideas. Whether it's successful or not, I appreciate in advance you *not* taking my stories literally and having me committed.

My girls have shown me that sometimes words aren't enough. Some concepts, ideas, feelings are so inexpressible that they defy description. That's how it is when I think of you two in my life. Hopefully one day you can look back on your crazy old man and think, wow, he really was an OK guy.

And, of course, thanks to the Big Guy upstairs; *the Creator of all words.*

◉

With any luck, by finishing this book, hopefully the first of many to come, I will finally be pursuing that elusive die-worthy passion.

Wish me luck!

But if you've read this far, you already have.

M. K. Bagwell
April, 2017
Asheville, NC, US